OF FLAMES AND CURSES

CURSED REALMS

BOOK ONE

WHITNEY L. SPRADLING

Midnight Tide
PUBLISHING

Praise for Of Flames and Curses

"For someone who grew up on the 10th Kingdom (a Hallmark miniseries from the early 2000's), Of Flames and Curses was nostalgic in all the right ways. From a faerie gate in Central Park, to the idea that all fortune tellers are elves, I loved all the little details. They painted a vivid picture of a world where magic lives alongside us, if we just look hard enough."

-Lou Wilham
Author of The Hex Next Door

"A thrilling Fae adventure with a cast of characters that will capture your heart. This is a book you won't want to put down." (#TeamAsh)

-Devon Thiele
Author of Burnout

CONTENT WARNING

This book contains adult themes that may not be appropriate for all audiences. These themes include: graphic on page sex and sexual content, language, the mention and discussion of suicide, mental health issues, torture, blood, death, and violence.

If you or someone you know needs help, please call the Suicide and Crisis Lifeline at 988.
You are not alone. Help is available.

To my Midnight Tide Publishing family. Thank you for taking a chance on me and this story.

Chapter One

What is it they say about death? That it's God's will? That time heals all things? Fuck. That. Then again, when something not of this world brutally murders your sister, the traditional mourning process is bound to look a little different.

As Lainey watched her sister's casket get lowered into the freshly dug grave, she didn't feel the soft rain slowly soaking through her black dress or the chill wind blowing her hair around her face. Thoughts swirled through her head like the autumn leaves blowing from the trees, and she had no way to control them. She had to be cursed somehow. There was no other reason for all the heartbreak she had experienced in her twenty-six years of living.

Her life had been a trail of loss and death. Her father had been MIA since she was three. When she was ten, her mother was admitted to a psych ward, then took her own life five years later. Even before her mom was admitted, it had been just her and Emma.

Now Emma was gone too, and Lainey was completely alone.

She had spent her entire life trying to do good. She had helped with her mom as much as she could. When it was just her and Emma, Lainey always listened to her sister and did everything she could to make Emma's job of caring for her as easy as possible. What good had all that done? In the end, she still ended up alone. She was done following the rules and trying to be the good girl. It hadn't gotten her anywhere in life except here, at her sister's funeral.

Staring into her sister's freshly dug grave, Lainey wished she could go back in time, back before her sister walked out the door that fateful night. Instead of watching Emma leave, she would have done something, said something, to make her sister stay and talk to her. Instead, the next person to walk through that door had been a New York City police officer with the news that Emma's body had been found in Central Park.

Lainey remembered the numbness that settled over her body like a thick cloak—she was still wearing it days later—as the officer's condolences did nothing to ease her pain. She answered his questions on autopilot. The white fog of grief and disbelief taking up residence in her brain prevented her from feeling anything.

The following days were a blur of numbness as she prepared for her sister's burial. There were only two things that stood out from the fog: Emma's diary, and a strange persistent feeling Lainey couldn't shake—something was about to happen.

A heavy hand on her shoulder dragged her back from the thoughts she had lost herself in. Thoughts of her miserable life, thoughts of her purpose in life, thoughts of being alone.

"How're you holding up, Lainey?" The voice and the hand belonged to her boyfriend, Alex. Although, "boyfriend" was a generous term. His main purpose in her life was to entertain her when she was bored.

Lainey shrugged his hand off her shoulder and didn't respond. How the fuck did he think she was doing? She'd just lost the last member of her family.

"Listen, my mom wants you to come over for dinner tonight. She even offered you a place to stay, if you don't want to be alone."

"No thanks," she mumbled. Tearing her gaze from the casket now being covered with dirt, Lainey turned on her heel and walked away. The last place she wanted to be was surrounded by a loving family who hadn't suffered the losses she had. She couldn't deal with their "I'm so sorry" and "We're here if you need anything" platitudes. She wasn't up to sitting around a table watching from the sidelines as people went on with their lives, as if her world hadn't just come crumbling down around her.

Lainey ignored Alex as he followed her and attempted to engage her in conversation. His voice buzzed in the background like an annoying gnat she couldn't get rid of. Eventually, he caught on to her silent treatment. He stopped trying to talk and let her walk away. It would only be a matter of time before she had to deal with him, though.

The rain became a steady downpour, soaking through her clothes and chilling her to the bone, as she walked home to the apartment she had shared with Emma. She didn't feel any of it. The noises of the city and the sights she ambled past didn't register. She was utterly and completely numb.

The first feeling that penetrated her cloak of numbness was exhaustion. As she walked through her front door, she realized she couldn't keep living here alone. Rent for a two-bedroom apartment in the city was astronomical. Her waitress income would barely be enough to cover one bedroom, let alone two. When she thought about having to move, the little energy she had remaining seeped away.

Lainey looked around the small apartment she had shared with Emma for most of their lives. The living room and kitchen were basically one large room. There was no table for eating, no chairs for sitting. The lone couch was the separation between the two rooms, and it had definitely seen better days. No television, no coffee table, no end tables. The bare minimum. A short hallway led to two bedrooms and one bathroom. It wasn't much, but it had been home. With Emma, it was home.

As the exhaustion spread into her bones and muscles, her

wet clothes weighed her down. She trudged to the bathroom and turned on the shower. The sound of her clothes slapping wetly against the cheap linoleum as she let them fall to the floor was loud in the quiet of the apartment. The quiet got to her, pressed in on her, and made her twitchy. She imagined her life being permanently quiet—no noise around her, no people to keep her company, no one to love her. No place for her to belong. An itch started between her shoulder blades, the uncomfortable feeling spurring her to grab her cell off the counter.

Loud music was just what she needed. As the first notes of Coheed and Cambria filtered through the air, she turned the volume up as loud as it would go and stepped into the shower. The chaotic notes of the music washed over and through her, and she let them drive away the quiet loneliness that had been her constant companion for three days.

She stood under the spray, letting the water warm her chilled skin. With her head hanging down, the water dripped over her face and down her chin. If only it could wash away her anguish. She closed her eyes and replayed the last conversation she'd had with her sister.

"Where are you going?" Lainey asked as Emma lined her eyes with black liner.

"Out."

Lainey raised one brow and crossed her arms over her chest. "Out where?"

"None of your business," Emma snapped as she stepped back to admire her reflection.

Taken aback by her sister's harsh tone, Lainey searched Emma's face in the mirror, trying to find the sister she had known her whole life. She couldn't seem to find her. Despite the familiar blond curls and bright blue eyes, her sister had become a stranger. The past two months, Emma had been growing more and more distant. They had never been super close despite being only three years apart —their relationship had always been more of a big sister caring for a little sister type of thing—but they had never been hostile toward each other.

"What's going on, Emma? You've been a complete bitch lately."

Emma turned from the mirror to meet her sister's stare. Her blue eyes—the same as Lainey's—were like chips of ice that showed no feeling whatsoever. "Has it ever occurred to you that I'm sick and tired of being the big sister? Of always having to take care of you?"

"I'm twenty-six years old. You hardly have to take care of me anymore."

"I have been dealing with you for the past twenty years. For once, I want to live my own life. Without you."

Reeling from the verbal lashing and at a loss for words, Lainey watched her sister put on her high heels and walk out the front door.

Little did she know, that would be the last time she saw her sister, the last conversation they would ever have. Regret left a bitter taste in her mouth. She hated that those had been the last words between them. Lainey completely understood her sister's frustration at having to raise her. Emma never got to have a childhood. She was always cooking, cleaning, and working. She did everything for Lainey when their parents were gone, including dropping out of school. Emma supported the two of them until Lainey was old enough to get a job.

Lainey never quite realized how much it affected her sister. She always took for granted that Emma would be there for her. Now, she wished she could tell her how much she appreciated everything that had been done for her. She wished she could tell Emma she understood the resentment she felt toward the end. Lainey knew Emma loved her—she'd proved it every day that she cared for her—and those words spoken on her last night alive didn't change that fact. But it jaded the memories a bit.

Lainey sighed and turned the water off. The threadbare towel she wrapped around her shoulders was scratchy and rough as she dried off. She kept the music playing as she dressed and wrapped her black hair in the towel. After a second of hesitation, she slowly walked down the hall to Emma's room.

The urge to knock was strong, but Lainey pushed it aside as she slowly opened the door. Everything was exactly as it had been when Emma left that night. Her makeup lay scattered on the table in front of her mirror. Various items of clothing were strewn about the bed and floor, as if she had tried on multiple pieces before settling on the outfit she had walked out the door wearing. The lingering smell of Emma's perfume still scented the air. It felt as though Lainey could just wait for a couple more minutes and Emma would walk into her room, pissed off that Lainey was in there without permission.

This was the third time she had been in Emma's room since her death. The second had been to borrow the black dress she had worn to the funeral. *Borrow*. Like she could give it back to Emma now. Shaking her head, she walked to the rickety bedside table and opened the drawer. The notebook, covered in matted purple fur, stared back at her.

Lainey pulled out the little journal and sat on the edge of Emma's bed. Emma had always kept a diary. Lainey had tried to keep one when she was younger, but she always forgot to write in it. When she did remember, she never quite knew what to write. Who would ever want to read about her boring life, anyway?

The matted fur was rough as she ran her hands over it. She knew what she would find if she flipped it open. Her sister's scrawling handwriting, all loops and flowing lines. Emma had had perfect penmanship, unlike Lainey's illegible chicken scratch. Lainey also knew what she would read if she turned to the most recent entries in the diary. She had, after all, already read through the entire thing the night she found out Emma was gone for good.

She hesitated, her hand hovering over the cover, before opening and flipping through to the second to last entry. She held her breath as she reread her sister's words, hoping they had changed. Hoping she had imagined the whole thing. Hoping for something, anything, other than what was actually written on the pages. As her eyes scanned the words, she knew she hadn't imagined it.

Her sister had been hiding something, and it had cost her her life.

September 17

I met with Beck tonight for dinner. He was acting really strange. I accused him of cheating on me, and he swore up and down he wasn't. We ended up leaving the restaurant before our food was brought out. We sat on a bench in Central Park, and he eventually told me what was going on. I have to admit, I thought he was lying at first, but the more he talked and the more he showed me, the more I believed him. I'm not sure what it means or how to go on from here. But I guess I'll have to decide soon.

He told me he wasn't human. He told me he was a faerie. Fae is what he called himself. Like a legit creature from a fairytale. He showed me his teeth, and they were pointy, like a vampire's. When I asked how I hadn't noticed that before, he said he glamoured himself. He showed me how that works. I saw with my own eyes as his teeth went from pointy to normal in a heartbeat. He also showed me how his eyes glow when his glamor is off. They really fucking glowed.

I seriously wonder if I'm going crazy. Maybe I have whatever mom had. I remember her saying weird things, like how dad's eyes glowed when he was angry. Maybe this craziness is genetic. Although, for some reason, something is telling me Beck wasn't lying and that this is completely true. Then again, crazy people don't know they're crazy, right?

I think I'm going to call Beck. I need to talk about this. I need to make sure I'm not going insane. I need to know if this is real.

Lainey slammed the diary shut. As she had read the entry for the second time, goosebumps broke out over her skin. Throwing the diary back in the drawer, she stood and rubbed her arms, looking around the room. There had to be a reasonable explanation for Emma's last two entries. Maybe she really had been going crazy? Or maybe she had been doing drugs? Drugs made more sense, especially with the gruesome way she had been murdered and the distance that had grown between them.

Lainey narrowed her eyes and swung her gaze from the nightstand to the bed. In a rush, she threw off the covers and lifted the mattress. Nothing. She laid on her belly and used her phone as a flashlight to sweep under the bed. Nothing. She jumped up and went to Emma's makeup table. She opened drawers and pawed through the tubes and containers and brushes. Nothing. Cursing, Lainey went to the closet. She swept aside hangers and looked in shoe boxes. She patted the length of the shelf that ran along the top. She even went so far as to prod the floorboards, looking for a hidey hole. Again, nothing.

"What the fuck was going on, Emma?" she asked in the silence that followed her war path through the room.

Lainey took a last glance at the nightstand and debated rereading the final entry, but she couldn't handle it right now. Her nerves were shot, and she had no idea what to think anymore. She closed the bedroom door behind her and made a pit stop in the kitchen. The bottle of Absolut was cold in her hands as she grabbed it from the freezer. The healthy swig she took made her eyes water as the liquid burned its way down her throat and into her stomach. She welcomed the burn. Finally, a feeling in the emptiness.

She took her bottle of vodka and headed for her bed. Collapsing against the headboard, Lainey stared at the wall in front of her with the white chipping paint and the hole in the drywall. She tipped the bottle back, again and again, until the room was spinning. Lost in oblivion, Lainey closed her eyes and tried to sleep for the night.

Chapter Two

"Fu-uck," Lainey groaned as soon her brain came back online the next morning. She grabbed her head between her hands, begging it to quit pounding. Maybe drinking a third of a bottle of vodka was not such a great idea. Then again, her thoughts were solely focused on not throwing up instead of her sister's death for once. Silver lining, she supposed.

Her hand slapped the bedside table until her fingers felt her phone. Gingerly opening her eyes, she ignored the missed calls and numerous texts from Alex and peeked at the time. She had one hour until she had to leave for work. Her boss had given her some time off, but she couldn't stand the thought of sitting alone in the apartment's silence. Planning Emma's funeral had kept her occupied, but with that over, she needed something else to do. Work would get the job done.

"Okay, Lainey. You can do this. Just stand up. Stand up and walk to the bathroom. A hot shower will make you feel like a new fucking person. Just stand up. Now. Right now. Do it." Apparently, her pep talk to herself worked because the next thing she knew, she was vertical and weaving out of her room to the bathroom. She had to pause once to take some breaths to avoid puking in the hallway, but once that passed, she was off to the races.

After a hot shower and steaming cup of coffee with a generous splash of vodka, Lainey dressed and packed her backpack with extra clothes, laptop, and charging cables. As a last-minute decision, she grabbed her sister's diary from the bedside table and shoved it into the backpack as well.

Outside, the rain had stopped, but the wind was chilly, so Lainey pulled her jacket closer and lifted the hood into place, tucking her black braid inside. She double checked the time and decided to walk to work. However, halfway through her trek through the urban jungle of New York City, she regretted that decision. Too much time for her to think and not enough for her mind to focus on besides Emma's death.

As she waited at a crosswalk for the little white man to appear, the hair on Lainey's neck stood on end. A creeping sensation followed, spreading from her shoulder blades to her arms and legs. She rolled her shoulders and peered around. The intersection was busy with cars bumper to bumper on the street, people rushing on the sidewalks hurrying to their destinations, and the occasional homeless person begging for some cash. Everything seemed as it should.

The sensation didn't go away, even after she crossed the street. She kept walking, eyes scanning her surroundings. The pepper spray she always carried with her was a comforting weight in her pocket as the feeling followed her. She paused and leaned against a brick wall, bending forward, pretending to adjust her black chucks. A glance behind showed nothing out of the ordinary.

As she straightened and looked around again, her eyes snagged on a shadowy doorway across the street. Someone was watching her from the shadows. She didn't know why she felt so sure about that, but she was convinced someone was there. Lainey squinted and leaned forward, trying to get a better view through the darkness. There was nothing to see, but a strange feeling of warmth passed through her, almost as if she had walked up to a bonfire and the heat from the flames was warming her skin.

Shaking herself, Lainey tightened her grip on the pepper spray and continued on her way to work, trying to ignore the sensation of eyes on her. She hurried, and by the time she walked through the back door of Carly's, she was completely unnerved. Her hands shook so badly that, as she hung her bag in her locker, she dropped the damn thing twice. Her laptop hitting the metal of the locker was loud in the silence of the staff room.

"Are you okay, Lainey?"

"Fuck!" Lainey jumped and whirled around. She placed her hand on her chest to keep her heart from beating right out. "You scared the shit out of me, Greg."

Her boss just looked her up and down with a critical eye. "You look horrible."

"I bet you get all the women with that line." Lainey rolled her eyes as she calmed her breathing and turned back to her locker. Her hands were still shaking from the walk through the city, and she couldn't shake the feeling of eyes between her shoulder blades.

"You don't have to be here tonight," Greg said. His gentle tone grated on her nerves. "Take some time off, Lainey."

"Thanks for the offer, but I'm good." Lainey closed her locker and turned to face her boss, plastering a fake smile on her face. "What section am I working tonight?"

After tying her apron around her waist and making sure she had plenty of pens, Lainey headed out to the main dining area to man her section for the night. She studiously ignored the looks of sympathy her coworkers gave her and dove headfirst into the work.

⁓ ⁕ ⁓

Her shift passed in a blessed blur. The restaurant was busy, and Lainey was constantly moving between tables. She barely had time to rest, let alone think. As the last patrons for the night left, Lainey sighed and began counting her tips. Good haul tonight.

Unfortunately, as soon as her body slowed down, her mind sped up. To not think about her sister, Lainey let her thoughts wander to her apartment and making rent. She really didn't want to move, but she didn't think she was going to have a choice.

Sighing, Lainey headed to the staff room and grabbed a change of clothes from her bag. After changing, she checked her phone. More missed calls and texts from Alex. She quickly deleted them and headed toward the back door in the kitchen. She didn't make it to the door. Cook stopped her.

"Here, Lainey." Cook's eyes were sad, but he thankfully said nothing else, just handed her a takeout bag.

Lainey thanked him and rushed through the door. Cook always gave the servers food to take home at the end of the night. It was one perk of working at Carly's: delicious, free food every night. Cut back on the grocery bill.

Instead of going home to the silent apartment, Lainey headed toward her favorite twenty-four-hour coffee shop. She hurried through the still bustling streets. Despite the colder weather and the late hour, the city was still hopping. It really was true what they said about the city. It never slept.

Lainey made it to the coffee shop without feeling like she was being watched, although the pepper spray remained in her hand regardless. She was kicking herself for not bringing her gun. Five years ago, she'd bought a .38, learned to shoot, and got her license to carry. Being a single female in the city was always a risk, however, lately, she had been slacking on carrying the weapon out of the apartment. A mistake she wouldn't make again.

Lainey ordered a latte, settled into a booth in the corner of the coffee shop, and pulled out her laptop. A quick check on her finances showed that if she skimped, she could afford the apartment for another three months. Drumming her fingers on the tabletop, Lainey stared at the numbers until her eyes crossed. She didn't want to have to ration her money. Morning coffee shop visits were a must, and she enjoyed trying new restaurants around the city.

As much as she dreaded everything that went into moving, she really didn't have a lot of belongings, so it wouldn't be too hard. Going through Emma's things would suck, but it was for the best. Getting out of the place that reminded her of Emma would be better for her in the long run. Releasing a breath, she pulled up another internet tab and began apartment hunting.

An hour later, her phone ringing drew her out of her meandering thoughts. Alex again. Still not wanting to deal with him, she turned off her phone and dropped it into her bag. A quick scan of her computer made Lainey realize she had been staring at the screen for the past forty-five minutes. She focused on the page to find she hadn't even looked at a single apartment. Her browser window was still open to Google, her search only halfway typed in. She slammed the laptop closed and pressed the heels of her hands into her eyes.

"Don't do it, Lainey," she whispered to herself. "Do not open that can of worms." Her gaze moved from her closed laptop to the bookbag on the floor at her feet. "Fuck."

She popped the laptop back open, and her fingers hovered over the keyboard. Taking a deep breath, Lainey typed three words she never thought she'd type together:

Are faeries real?

She hit enter and mentally kicked herself for googling if faeries existed. For the next thirty minutes, Lainey read articles on the little winged creatures of myth and folklore. She read articles that stated there was no evidence they existed but also no evidence that proved they didn't. She searched websites that went into detail on how to summon faeries and how to work with them. She scanned pictures of photoshopped landscapes with little Tinker Bells sitting on mushrooms.

"This is insane," she muttered. Crazy must run in the family. There was no way she actually believed her sister had been dating a faerie. There had to be a reasonable explanation for Emma's journal entries.

Her gaze once again moved to the bag at her feet. With a grimace, Lainey snatched the bag off the floor and rooted around inside until she felt the diary. She pulled out the little book and narrowed her eyes at it as if the diary alone was the reason for her current situation. Pushing the laptop back, Lainey set the diary in front of her. She distantly noted her fingers shaking as they reached out to flip the pages. The last entry, the one that, if real, would change everything. But it couldn't be real. Could it?

September 20

I'm not sure what to say. I think I actually believe Beck. He showed me things tonight that couldn't possibly happen in real life. He claimed he was an Earth Elemental, a member of the Seelie Court. He said faeries have been locked out of the faerie realm for years. That there was a curse, and he was trying to break it. Beck showed me more of his magic, and it was amazing. He did things that no human could ever do.

He also said that he had been searching for me, that I would help him break the curse. Beck told me I had faerie blood in me, but he couldn't tell how much or where it came from. He freaked me out a bit when he told me that. There is no way that can be true. I mean, I barely believe faeries exist, and now he wants me to believe I am part faerie?

He begged me to help him. I told him I would, only because, why not? What do I have to lose by helping him? Maybe I'll learn something in the process.

By the end of the entry, Lainey's hands were shaking so badly she had to set the diary down or risk dropping it. The nausea churning in her stomach had her swallowing repeatedly. Wiping her palms on her pants, Lainey shoved the diary back into the bag.

"Bad idea, Lainey," she chided herself.

She pulled the laptop back in front of her and pulled up Google again. This time, she typed her mom's name into the search bar. She scrolled through all the pages but found nothing that related to her mom.

She wished she knew her dad's name. Neither she nor Emma could ever remember it. Their mom never spoke his name after he left, and when she died, they couldn't find anything in their house with his name on it. Even their birth certificates just had their mom's name. It was as if he didn't exist.

Lainey rubbed her eyes as she realized the genealogy route was a dead end. She had no way of ever determining if Emma was part faerie—which would mean she was part faerie too. That was a rabbithole she was not prepared to go down.

"What are you even thinking, Lainey? Part faerie? You are just as crazy as mom."

And she was talking to herself. Yep, crazy.

Just as she was about to go back to researching faeries, a warmth washed over her. Her skin flushed, and a fine sweat broke out on her neck and chest. Her head snapped up, gaze landing directly on the mouth of the alley across from the coffee shop.

In the flickering light of a streetlight, she noticed a shape that stepped back into the shadows as soon as her gaze landed on it. A shape like a human man. A very large human man.

The flush across her skin quickly morphed into a chill. Goosebumps rose on her arms, causing the hair to stand on end. Maybe she had spent too much time thinking about that damn diary and what it meant. She must have fallen down the rabbit hole, because her instincts shouted at her that the man was not normal. She couldn't shake the feeling he wasn't human.

Lainey pulled out her phone from her bag, turned it on, and ordered an Uber. No way was she walking home with whatever that was across the street watching her.

She tried to act normal as she slowly packed her bag. The shaking in her limbs was hopefully not noticeable from far away. She pretended to play on her phone for a bit until she got the notification that her Uber was waiting. Quickly grabbing her bag and her coffee, she walked out the front door of the coffee shop.

She resolutely kept her eyes off the alley, despite the constant sensation of being watched shivering over her skin.

She hopped in the Uber and was relieved to hear the doors lock as she settled into the seat. The farther she got from the coffee shop, the more the sensation faded. Her anxiety and fear did not fade, however. Someone was stalking her. Could it be the person who murdered her sister? Were they coming after her next?

When the Uber dropped her off at the apartment, Lainey practically ran to the front door. Her heart skipped a beat each time the key scraped against the lock and bounced over the keyhole. Just as the key slid in, she straightened. Someone was behind her. She turned quickly but saw nothing. Her eyes nervously scanned her surroundings. They landed on a darker area of the street where no lights shone. She could just make out the outline of a person.

Turning the key, she rushed into the apartment lobby and made sure the door closed behind her. She ran up the three flights of stairs to her apartment and quickly let herself in. After making sure the door was locked, she grabbed her gun from the drawer in the kitchen and loaded it. Then she went through every room of the apartment and made sure all the blinds were closed. She hesitated at the window in her bedroom.

Lainey peeked between the blinds. Standing at the steps to the apartment was a man, illuminated by the lights of the building. He was wearing all black, and his shoulders were massive—all muscle under the leather he wore. His chin-length hair was dark brown, and the building lights brought out touches of red in the strands.

His head turned, and his gaze landed directly on Lainey. She couldn't make out the color of his eyes, but they almost looked like they were ... glowing. When her eyes met his, she could do nothing but stare. She was held in a trance as his gaze penetrated her, warmth washing through her body once more.

Lainey was breathing heavily by the time she was able to break the strange connection, falling backward and landing on her bed. She scooted herself back until she was sitting against the headboard, gun resting in her lap, facing the door. She strained her ears, sifting through all the sounds of the old apartment building—the neighbors above and below her, the creaking of floors and slamming of doors, the heat kicking on with a whoosh. Nothing out of the ordinary.

Nevertheless, she didn't get much sleep that night.

Chapter Three

The next day, Lainey found herself standing on the steps in front of the massive stone facade of the New York Public Library. The autumn wind blew her hair around her face, and she tucked it behind her ears for the hundredth time. She glanced at Fortitude, standing proud across from Patience. She quietly asked the lion to give her the fortitude she needed to walk through those wooden doors.

Releasing a breath, she walked forward. The longer she stood outside, the more likely it was that her stalker was going to find her, and because the library had a rule of no weapons, she'd had to leave her gun at home. Pushing through the doors, Lainey walked through the metal detector and let the guard search her bag. She made her way to the stairs and up to the third floor.

In the Rose Room, she claimed a spot where she had a good view of all the exits and quickly determined where to go to begin her search. She couldn't believe she was trying to find factual information at the library regarding faeries. The more she thought about her sister's murder and the diary, the crazier she thought she was. But for some reason, she couldn't let it go. Her sister had sacrificed everything for her. The least Lainey could do was get to the bottom of her sister's murder.

Letting her fingers trail over the spines of books, Lainey took a deep breath, inhaling the scents of leather and paper and dust. She absolutely loved libraries. There was something magical about them. They were full of truth, ideas, and dreams. In a library, you were never alone; rather, you were surrounded by the voices and words of those who had come before you. She came here whenever she could. Escaping into a book was the only way she survived.

She reached her destination and began scanning the titles, occasionally pulling a book down to skim the inside. She wasn't quite sure what it was she was expecting to find. It was more of a feeling than anything, and it annoyed her that she couldn't explain where the feeling was coming from.

"You won't find what you're looking for in the library."

Lainey whirled around at the deep voice directly behind her, and she immediately stepped back until her shoulders pressed against the bookshelf. She clutched a book to her chest like it could protect her from what was standing before her.

It was the man who had been stalking her. He was almost a foot taller than her, with shoulders that were so broad they blocked out the sight of the aisle behind him. He had enough muscles on him that Lainey had no doubt he could hurt her without a second thought.

All thought fled her mind as she stared at him, her fight-or-flight response apparently fleeing itself, leaving her frozen and at the mercy of this person. Nothing but a squeak escaped when she tried to open her mouth to speak.

His gaze traveled over her body, light brown eyes appearing to shimmer as he returned his gaze to her face. He said nothing, but his menacing stance said more than any words ever could. His arms were crossed over a massive chest, tattoos peeking out from under the black T-shirt he wore.

Lainey swallowed and managed to get one word out of her mouth before stalling out again. "What ..."

The man raised one brow in question, like he was asking her to continue.

She closed her eyes to block out his image, ignoring her inner voice screaming at her to not take her eyes off him. She couldn't see him, but holy shit, she could feel his presence. Warmth radiated off him, enveloping her in that fireside feeling she had been experiencing recently.

She forced her body to obey her commands and snapped her eyes open. "What are you?" She was proud when her voice only trembled slightly.

His grin evoked the image of things that go bump in the night—evil and horrifying. And, what the fuck ... his top canines were slightly pointed.

Lainey tried to take another step back, and a wave of terror washed through her when the bookshelf refused to move. She couldn't take her gaze off of his face and those teeth.

His nostrils flared as if he was scenting her—or maybe her fear—and his eyes shimmered again, almost glowing from within.

"Curious you ask *what* I am instead of *who* I am." His voice was deep, and Lainey felt it vibrate through her whole body. "I have a feeling you already know what I am."

"Did you kill my sister?" Lainey was surprised at the strength of her voice and the sudden resolve flowing through her blood. If this ... thing ... had killed Emma, she was going to do whatever she could to take him out.

His glowing eyes dimmed a bit, and he shook his head. His dark brown hair caught the light, illuminating the reddish tint within the strands. The sides and back of his chin-length hair was shaved. The rest was pulled back into a man bun, and Lainey was loath to admit he actually pulled the style off really well.

"I didn't kill your sister, but I know who did. I also have the answers to the questions you are currently asking yourself."

"If you even think about saying 'come with me,' I'm going to laugh." The quick burst of courage quickly faded, leaving her staring at the man with wide eyes. Shit, did she really just say that to someone who could kill her with his pinky?

The guy rolled his shoulders like he was trying to ease his frustration with her. "You don't have to come, but then you'll probably be joining your sister in the ground next." He turned on his heel and started walking.

As the sense of his power faded with each step he took, Lainey's courage—or maybe idiocy—returned, along with her curiosity and determination to find out what happened to Emma.

"Wait!" She winced at the volume of her own voice as it echoed in the quiet library.

The man stopped but didn't turn around.

"How do I know I can trust you?" she asked more quietly. "You can't honestly expect me to walk out of here with a complete stranger who has been following me around the city for the past few days. Especially after my sister was murdered."

He hesitated for a second before turning to face her. "Meet me at that coffee shop in one hour."

Before she could respond, he turned around and walked away, disappearing into the maze of bookshelves.

Lainey made her way back to the Rose Room on shaky legs. She sunk into the chair with no finesse, her legs giving out and gravity pulling her down. Without a doubt, he had been the one following her. She also knew without a doubt he wasn't human. Normal people didn't have glowing eyes or pointy teeth.

There was no way she was going to meet up with him, was there? She would be crazy to do that. She had no clue who he was, and she was a lone female in a very large city. It would be incredibly irresponsible to meet with him. This guy could be Emma's murderer, despite what he said. She couldn't trust him. She could trust no one but herself.

But he said he knew who killed Emma. He said he had answers to questions that had been in her head since she read her sister's diary. Could she trust what he had to say? Could he really be a faerie?

Lainey groaned and laid her forehead on the desk. She wasn't sure she had much of a choice. She had a feeling this man ... faerie ... whatever ... could find her anywhere if he really wanted. And her thirst for answers about Emma was overwhelming. The coffee shop was a public place. There would be people around. She would be perfectly safe, right?

Determination steeling her spine, Lainey stood and grabbed her bag. She was going to do this. She would deal with whatever consequences arose from her decision, but she was going to find the answers to the questions that had been plaguing her since Emma's death.

Lainey tried not to think as she opened the door to the coffee shop. If she thought too much about what she was about to do, she knew she would change her mind. She had debated calling the cops on her way to the coffee shop, but what the hell would she tell them? That she'd found a suspect in her sister's murder? What evidence would she provide them? Telling them his eyes glowed like Emma mentioned in her journal would provide her with a one-way ticket to the psych ward. Just like her mom.

No. She couldn't tell the cops, and she couldn't change her mind. Emma deserved to be honored better than that. Ignoring this possibility seemed like ignoring what Emma had gone through. Lainey desperately needed answers, and this was her only lead. She swallowed thickly and held her chin up as she searched the tables for the ... faerie.

He was sitting near the emergency exit. His large body took up most of the bench he occupied. He had put on a black leather jacket over his T-shirt, and he was currently lounging with one arm across the back of the bench. His eyes met hers when he looked up, flaring bright copper, before he blinked, and they returned to his normal light brown.

Lainey slid onto the bench across from him and looked him

in the eyes with a courage she didn't really feel. She clutched her bag tightly in one hand; the other grasped her pepper spray in a white-knuckled grip.

"You came." He sounded slightly surprised. The look he gave her was one of grudging respect.

"I need to know what happened to my sister."

He said nothing, just stared at her with an unnerving gaze that had her shifting in her seat.

"Dude, come on." She was getting impatient, despite her fear of him. "Just give me something, anything."

"Dude?" He quirked one brow, but he was not amused. His eyes positively burned with irritation.

"Well, you haven't told me your name."

"Dude" leaned forward and placed his cell phone on the table face down. He then rested his elbows on the table and rubbed his face. When he lowered his hands, he looked resigned. He leveled a stare at Lainey that had her swallowing again.

"My name is Phoenix, and yes, I'm fae." He paused, as if waiting for her to freak out.

When Lainey just stared at him with slightly widened eyes, he continued. "I'm a fire elemental, meaning I control fire and heat."

As he spoke, a wave of warmth washed over Lainey, smelling faintly of a bonfire. She jerked back in her seat. It was one thing to hear faeries existed; it was another thing entirely to experience something magical and not of this world. While she felt like screaming and running away, she didn't. Her sister hadn't been crazy or on drugs. Unless Lainey herself was going crazy. Shit, faeries existed?

"What does this have to do with my sister?" she asked hoarsely.

"It's a long and complicated story, but the gist of it is, someone was trying to break a curse with her as the sacrifice."

"How do I know it wasn't you?"

Phoenix shrugged his massive shoulders. "Fae can't lie."

Like she was going to believe that. Right. "Why have you been following me?"

At this question, Phoenix looked around, refusing to meet her eyes while he rubbed the back of his neck.

"I'm actually not sure why. For some reason, I'm drawn to you. Something about you calls to me." His gaze returned to her, and he appeared to look so deeply inside her, Lainey had to look away and hide her blush with her hair.

Phoenix's phone rang on the table, but he silenced it.

Lainey took a cleansing breath and focused her attention on the reason she'd agreed to meet with him. "So, you said you know who killed my sister. Who was it?"

"My half-brother, Beck. And before you ask, no, I was not part of it, nor would I have been if I had known he was going to do it."

Lainey looked at Phoenix. Really looked at him. His face was open, and his eyes were guileless. He honestly appeared to be telling the truth, and once again, Lainey found herself believing him against all her rational thoughts.

"You said he sacrificed her to break a curse. What curse?"

Phoenix opened his mouth to respond but quickly shut it and straightened. He looked out the window, body tensing as he went on high alert.

"Fuck. We have to go. Now." He stood in one powerful movement and reached his hand out to Lainey.

"Are you crazy? I'm not going anywhere with you. This is a public place, and I'm not leaving it."

"That's not going to matter, in like, two minutes." He looked out the window again, and a muscle ticked in his jaw. "I really need you to come with me." When she didn't move, he grudgingly ground out, "Please."

Apparently, please was the magic word. Lainey watched her hand reach out to grab Phoenix's, as if it had a mind of its own. As soon as her hand touched his, Phoenix tightened his grip and pulled her off the bench. She felt callouses rub against her smooth skin, and her mind balked at where they possibly could have come from. They were through the emergency door and out in the chilly air of the city before Lainey could blink.

She didn't have time to comprehend what was happening. All her focus was on keeping up with Phoenix as he rushed them down the street. He weaved in and out of pedestrians on the sidewalk, all the while turning to look over his shoulder. He swerved suddenly, pulling Lainey into an alley and almost tearing her arm from her body in the process.

"Ow! What the hell is wrong with you?" She yanked her hand, trying to get free of his grip, but he held too tightly.

Phoenix didn't answer, just kept dragging her down the alley. Fear took root inside her. This could be it. He could be leading her to her death. What the hell was she thinking, letting him drag her out of the coffee shop? She dug her heels into the ground, pulling her arm and fighting with everything she had. It made no difference. It was like a fly fighting an elephant. He completely overpowered her.

The alley opened up onto another busy street, and Phoenix led them into the throng of people crowding the sidewalk. He slouched down, curving his shoulders inward, and threw his arm over her shoulder. He checked over his own shoulder once more.

"Follow my lead," he said in her ear. "Relax a little."

"Relax? You want me to relax?" she shrieked. She ignored his hushing motions and continued, "You just dragged me out of the coffee shop and led me on a merry little chase through the city. What the hell was that about?"

Instead of answering her, he pulled out his phone, which was ringing again. "Yeah? Look, I'm a little busy right now, can your gloating wait? Fuck you. Thanks." He hung up, looked down at Lainey, and rolled his eyes at her expression. "You need to trust me on this. I promise I will tell you everything you need to know once we're safe."

"Safe from what? You haven't told me anything since I met you at the coffee shop except your name and that your brother

murdered my sister. You have gained no points in my book yet."
With a frustrated shriek, she threw his arm off her shoulder. "And
don't touch me."

Phoenix grunted. "I'm trying to keep you safe from my
brother. So unless you want to wait and say hi to him before he
kills you, you should shut up and follow me."

Lainey did just that. While she certainly didn't trust this guy,
she really didn't want to meet her sister's murderer armed only
with pepper spray. Fuck, why didn't she think to grab her gun
from the apartment before meeting with a stranger?

Her desire to continue living was apparently stronger than she
had thought. She let Phoenix lead her through the city until they
came to a parking garage. She reluctantly followed him through
the darkness to a shiny black motorcycle.

"Oh, hell no. I am not getting on that with you."

Phoenix's shoulders lifted as he took a deep breath before
turning to face her. "You will get on and you will do so without
arguing with me."

"Excuse me?"

Phoenix pulled out his phone and showed her the screen.
"You see that little blue dot? That is my brother. He is about a
block away from us and closing in quickly. Get on the fucking
bike and shut up." He swung his leg over the seat and flipped the
kickstand up with his foot, balancing the heavy machine with
ease.

Lainey wanted to argue. Her hackles raised at the way he was
speaking to her, and every instinct she had was screaming at her to
give him a piece of her mind. Unfortunately, her brain was in
survival mode and talked her into shutting her mouth and
agreeing.

Lainey swung her leg over the seat behind Phoenix. "You
know helmets keep your head from splattering like an egg on the
pavement when you crash," she muttered under her breath.

She heard him chuckle. "We'll be fine."

Phoenix revved the engine, and Lainey felt it rumble

underneath her as he eased the bike out of the parking garage and onto the busy streets of the city.

She leaned forward to speak in his ear. "Wouldn't it have been faster to walk? Traffic is horrible." His back was broad, and Lainey felt the muscles shifting as he steered the bike. She quickly sat back, putting as much space between them as the seat would allow.

To answer her question, Phoenix revved the engine again and shot off between the cars stopped in the lanes. He swerved in and out of stationary cars, going faster and faster, taking corners so fast the bike was almost parallel to the ground.

Lainey reflexively wrapped her arms around his waist and buried her face in his back. The wind tore at her hair, whipping it around in every direction and pulling strands loose from her braid. With her eyes closed, all she could hear was the sound of horns that quickly faded as they passed and the rumble of the engine underneath her. The wind chilled her face and numbed her lips. She wasn't dressed for this shit.

She didn't know how long they rode, but eventually she felt the bike slow, then come to a stop. Cautiously, she lifted her head and looked around. They were in another parking garage. This one was filled with a lot of expensive cars.

Phoenix turned off the engine and put the kickstand down. "You gonna let go of me?"

Lainey had to pry her stiff arms away from his waist. "I am never doing that again." Her heart was pounding in her chest and the adrenaline coursing through her veins penetrated her haze of nothingness, awakening her mind and body more than she was willing to admit.

Phoenix chuckled again and set off toward the elevator.

With no other choice, she followed him. "Where are we?" She adjusted her bag on her back but put the pepper spray in her pocket. Her brain still wasn't quite on board with trusting this man, despite her instincts telling her she could.

"My place."

Seeing as he didn't appear to want to say anymore, Lainey forced herself to close her mouth. It would do her no good to piss this guy off.

Tense silence filled the elevator on the ride from the garage to the lobby. A muscle in Phoenix's jaw ticked as consistently as a clock, and Lainey's foot tapped the pretty marble floor in time with it. Twice she opened her mouth to say something, but one scathing look from Phoenix had her shutting it quickly. Man, that guy had mastered the whole "resting bitch face" thing.

The elevator opened into an extravagant lobby. Marble walls and floors with gold trim and expensive leather furniture greeted her, and her eyes about popped out of her head. The ceiling had to have been at least three stories tall, with massive crystal and gold chandeliers casting warm light on the floor below. The place dripped money, and Lainey found her eyes traveling to Phoenix. What the hell did he do for a living to afford an apartment in a place like this?

Another tense elevator ride, this one to the very top floor, and Lainey was following Phoenix down another marble and gold hallway. He stopped at one of two doors and entered a code on the keypad to the right. A beep and click, and they were inside his apartment.

Maybe penthouse was more like it.

Lainey whistled as she looked around the open floor plan apartment. Floor-to-ceiling windows displayed a spectacular view of the city that would be beautiful at night. Plush white furniture around a gas fireplace filled the living area. The kitchen was—surprise—marble, with stainless steel appliances. A pool table filled the space to the left of the living area, along with a small hallway that presumably led to the bed and bathrooms.

"Glad you made it home in one piece."

Lainey jumped at the voice. She had been so distracted by the opulence of the apartment, she didn't see the occupant sprawled in a chair in front of the fireplace.

The man pointed a remote at a TV that hung above the

fireplace, and the screen turned off. He stood smoothly, and Lainey swallowed—he was as big as Phoenix. He was wearing jeans and an old-school Green Day T-shirt. His blond hair fell to his shoulders in loose waves. His bright green eyes bore into Lainey and appeared to glow from within.

Fae. He was also fae.

Lainey took a step back but bumped into Phoenix, who was blocking her only escape route. Unless she wanted to go out the window. Didn't seem like such a bad idea at the moment. Surrounded by two huge men who were not human, Lainey had no idea what to do.

Chapter Four

"Cool it, Ash. You're freaking her out." Phoenix led Lainey to the couch opposite the second fae male.

Her legs gave out, and she plopped onto the cushion with a bounce. She stared at the second fae. He was beautiful, but there was something slightly cruel about his features. Duh—the glowing, green eyes. Those were totally not normal. Between one blink and the next, his eyes turned to a normal green, still bright but no longer glowing.

His now normal green eyes narrowed, and his nostrils flared as he studied her. A pulse of energy hit Lainey in the chest, like a static shock but stronger, and she had the distinct impression of fresh cut fields and wildflowers.

She turned to Phoenix with wide eyes. He seemed safer to her somehow, although her instincts still told her to shy away from him.

He sighed as he sat in the other chair across from her. "This is Ash. He is an earth elemental. He is also a man whore, so stay away from him."

"Excuse me?" Ash placed a hand on his chest, mock outrage flooding his features. "I can't help that the women flock to me." He brushed his blond hair away from his face in a dramatic gesture. "Besides, why don't you let Beautiful here decide for herself," he added with a wink in Lainey's direction.

Mouth hanging open, Lainey just stared at him. She could see why women would throw themselves at him. She had a sudden urge to run her hands through those gloriously thick waves.

Phoenix snorted and crossed his arms over his chest, stretching his black T-shirt tight over his shoulders. The sight drew Lainey's eyes away from Ash.

"Okay, so, what now?" she asked tentatively, refocusing on the important task at hand. "Are we safe from your brother?"

The levity in the room dropped away in an instant, both males quickly turning serious. The change had Lainey sitting back in her seat. She would not want to meet one of these guys alone in an alley.

Oh wait. She had already done that. Sort of.

"We are safe here," Phoenix answered. "Ash has managed to do something techy to track Beck's phone. We're able to keep track of him now. But any time you leave this apartment, you will be at risk of him finding you."

"So you just want me to hole myself up in here? I don't even know you guys. And I have a job, you know. A life." Well, that last bit was a stretch. She wasn't sure quite what her life was at the moment.

"We'll figure something out, but for right now, yeah. You should stay here."

Lainey geared up for an argument, but Phoenix cut her off.

"Why don't we start by answering your questions? I'm sure you have some."

She tried to organize her thoughts into something less chaotic. She definitely had questions—she had millions of them, it felt like. But she had no idea where to start.

Seeming to understand, Phoenix spoke up. "How about we start with the basics? What we are and why we're here."

"That sounds good."

Phoenix rubbed his face and took a deep breath, collecting his own thoughts.

"Fae have existed since the beginning of time. We live in the faerie realm, or as we call it, Faerie. There are doors between Faerie and Earth, places where the veil is thinnest. We have always been able to travel back and forth between the worlds. That is, until twenty-three years ago, when a curse locked the doors to Faerie. Fae were trapped on whichever side they happened to be on when the curse was created."

"You said your brother was using my sister as a sacrifice to break a curse. It was this curse he was trying to break?"

"My half-brother, but yeah. He learned somewhere of a way to break the curse, and he believed your sister was the key."

"Why my sister?"

"I'm not positive about his exact reasons. I know part of it was because she was half fae."

Lainey stared at Phoenix, wishing she hadn't heard him right. Even though she'd read that in Emma's diary, it was something else to hear it spoken out loud.

"That makes you half fae as well," Phoenix continued.

Still staring, Lainey had no clue what to say, or do, or think. Was she even breathing? She stared at him so long that her eyes burned, but she still couldn't make herself blink. Was this what shock felt like? She wasn't cold or trembling. Maybe it affected everyone differently? Now she was just rambling inside her own head.

Phoenix got up and walked to the kitchen. He returned a second later with a bottle of water. After handing it to her, he returned to the chair and waited.

Lainey gratefully chugged half the bottle. "Have anything stronger?"

Ash raised one brow and grinned at her. "That's my kind of woman," he muttered under his breath.

Phoenix shot him another glare before answering. "Probably

not a good idea to get drunk right now. Besides, there is a lot more you need to know."

She replaced the cap and took a bracing breath. "What else? Tell me everything."

"You are half Sylph," Phoenix continued. "An air elemental."

"How do you know? I have no powers."

"More powerful fae can sense other fae's powers. I could sense you as soon as I laid eyes on you."

"How has no one ever noticed this before?" Lainey asked.

"Less powerful fae may be able to tell you have some fae blood, but with your blood diluted, it's unlikely. It's probably how you've gone so long without being discovered."

"Sylphs feel like a fresh breeze when you tune into them," Ash explained. "The stronger the emotions, the stronger the breeze. Right now, you feel like a hurricane."

"Is that why I could sense Phoenix when he was stalking me?"

Both males looked taken aback.

"What do you mean?" Phoenix asked.

"When I first sensed you hiding in the alley on my way to work. It felt like I stepped up to a bonfire."

Phoenix's eyes went wide. "As a half-breed, you shouldn't be able to tune into someone." He looked at his friend, who appeared equally surprised. "Can you feel Ash?"

Lainey focused on the blond fae. "I can't really feel him, but I get a sense of fresh cut grass when I look at him."

The males looked at each other, a silent conversation passing between them. Uncomfortable, Lainey began picking at the label on the bottle of water.

Eventually, Phoenix returned his gaze to her. "Do you know which of your parents would have been fae?"

"It would have been my dad. He disappeared when I was three. Ten years later, my mom ended up in a psych ward before she killed herself. There was nothing special about her, besides that."

Holy shit. So much made sense now. Their mom was always rambling about their dad. She always said things about air and wind and glowing eyes. When he disappeared, she had to have wondered if he ever really existed. And if not, who fathered her children? No wonder she went crazy. A sudden pang of sadness rang through her at the thought of what her mom had gone through, quickly followed by anger at her dad for being the cause of it.

"Okay," Lainey said, forcing her thoughts to focus. "I'm half fae. Emma was half fae. What does that have to do with the curse and why Emma was used as a sacrifice?"

"That is something I intend to find out." Phoenix turned to Ash. "I need you to do whatever it is you do to find out where Beck has been since coming to Earth. All the places he visited and people he talked to."

"I can do that." Ash immediately went to a desk in the corner Lainey had missed. He sat in the chair behind two monitors and began typing.

"Wait." Lainey held her hand up. Something Phoenix said caught her attention. "You said 'since coming to Earth.' He hasn't been here the entire time, since the curse started? I thought the curse locked everyone in or out?"

"It does," Phoenix sighed. "There have been rumors about ways to cross, but they always involved things that are best left alone. Dark magic, so to speak."

Lainey settled back on the couch, tucking her legs under her. So many things had happened in the past few weeks, she was surprised she wasn't feeling more ... something. She didn't quite understand why she wasn't in a corner somewhere in the fetal position, rocking back and forth.

Instead, she felt calm in a way. Relieved, almost. She now knew what caused her sister's death, at least for the most part. She knew why her mom had taken her own life. For the longest time, she had blamed her mom for everything bad that had happened in her life. Now, she couldn't help but feel empathy for the woman who had suffered her own traumatizing experiences.

Retreating into her thoughts, Lainey didn't even notice when her eyes grew heavy and her head started bobbing on her neck. She didn't know how long she had sat on the couch, but she eventually became aware of a blanket being draped over her and a pillow placed under her head, which had somehow found its way to the couch cushion.

She didn't even try to fight as sleep crept in. She hadn't had a good night's sleep since Emma's death. Despite the fact that two strange men who were not human surrounded her, she felt safe, and that feeling pulled her under before she could even think of fighting it.

The smell intruded upon her sleep first, quickly followed by the sound of a percolating coffee machine. Lainey sat up and oriented herself to her surroundings. Marble floors, glass windows letting in the early morning light, expensive leather furniture. The penthouse. Phoenix and Ash. Memory rushed back to consciousness, and Lainey mentally prepared herself for another day of new discoveries.

The smell of coffee fortified her further. She turned her head toward the kitchen and was rewarded with quite the sight. Phoenix was making breakfast, wearing nothing but a pair of black sweatpants clinging low on his hips. Lainey's eyes widened as she took in his muscled back, the deep grooves and shifting planes. His shoulders were wide, and she traced the line of his back as it tapered to his trim waist.

What really caught her eye was the tattoo. A beautiful, black-inked phoenix on the left half of his back. Clouds of smoke rose from the long tail of the bird, which exploded up from his waist. The wings spread, one onto his shoulder, the other past his spine as they lifted the phoenix from the proverbial ashes. The bird itself was a fearsome creature with its beak open in a scream of defiance. A few feathers fell from the wings down Phoenix's spine.

The shifting muscles of his back made the tattoo look alive, the wings moving with him.

As if he felt her eyes on him, Phoenix turned around, a mug in his hand. "You're awake. Would you like some coffee?"

Lainey had to swallow to work moisture back into her mouth. "Yes, please." She stood from the couch and walked into the kitchen. She was acutely aware of the fact she was wearing yesterday's clothes and her hair was a tangled mess on top of her head.

Phoenix handed her a mug and let her pour the coffee and add the cream on her own. He returned to the breakfast he was making without further comment. Lainey settled onto a barstool at the counter and discretely watched Phoenix as he moved about the kitchen.

She really couldn't stand his arrogance or rough demeanor, but he was definitely enjoyable to look at. His hair was down, swept to one side, exposing the shaved side of his head. The dark strands fell to his chin, the red hidden in the brown catching the light and appearing to burn.

"Do you like bacon and eggs?" His deep voice took a moment to penetrate her thoughts.

"Yes," she said, her voice breathier than she had ever heard it.

He placed a plate in front of her, piled high with crispy bacon and scrambled eggs with gooey, melty cheese, and turned back to the counter. He stood with his back to her as he ate his breakfast.

"You better have saved some for me." Ash burst into the kitchen—shirtless, Lainey noted distantly—like a bolt of lightning. The air in the room immediately changed, charged with a kind of energy that matched his personality—energetic and playful.

Without a word, Phoenix slid a plate down the counter, heaped with food.

"Bacon." Ash drooled over the plate. "My favorite." He sat next to Lainey and dug in.

Silence ensued as they all finished their breakfast. Ash took her plate with his and dropped them into the sink once they had finished.

"So, what's the plan for today?" Ash asked as he leaned against the counter with his coffee.

Phoenix finally turned around. Lainey had to force her gaze away from him as it attempted to travel down his muscled and tattooed chest, to the V that disappeared into his pants. The guy looked like he was carved from stone.

"You're going to keep digging into Beck's records. I need to know what he's been up to, and quickly."

"I have to work today," Lainey offered tentatively.

Phoenix sighed and looked resigned. "Guess I'm babysitting."

Lainey sat up straighter at that. "Excuse me?"

Phoenix just rolled his eyes and walked away, heading toward the hallway Lainey hadn't explored yet.

"Asshole," she muttered as he disappeared.

Ash chuckled. "That he is, little halfling, that he is."

Lainey sat at the bar, twisting the mug of coffee in her hands. Her thoughts drifted to everything she'd learned last night. Half fae. What the hell did that mean?

"You look like you're thinking hard enough to hurt yourself," Ash stated as he hauled himself up to sit on the counter, his muscles rippling with the movement.

"Should I have powers? I have never noticed anything strange before."

Ash shrugged his heavily muscled shoulders. "That would depend on how much you got from your dad."

"I don't feel like I have any. How would I even know?"

"It's entirely possible you have some kind of block on your power. Your mind might have locked down on that part of you subconsciously, since it is so different from the human part. Only training would show if you have any abilities and if you will ever be able to access them."

Lainey bit her lip. Did she even want powers? What would she do with them? All her life, she had been an outsider. She never really got along with other classmates. She was known as the orphan and preferred to just be alone so she didn't have to see everyone else with their happy little families. Being half fae, having some kind of magical power, would only make her even more different. Where did she belong now?

"If you want, I'd be happy to help you train," Ash offered.

Lainey looked up at him. He sounded sincere, but the glint in his eyes and smirk on his lips made her narrow her eyes at him. "Train what?"

He chuckled. "You're a smart one. We could train whatever you wanted." He winked at her and blatantly ran his gaze over her body.

"You won't be doing any *training*, Ash." Phoenix entered the kitchen, his dark hair damp and gleaming.

Lainey noticed, with slight dejection, he had dressed. He wore jeans and a gray Henley, and he had a dagger and gun holstered to his chest. He carried his leather jacket in his hand.

"Party pooper," Ash muttered.

"So I don't get a say in if I want to learn how to use my powers, if I have any?" Lainey demanded. Every time Phoenix opened his mouth, she wanted to slap him.

"You'll train, don't worry," Phoenix answered, "but you'll be training with me, not Ash."

"Why you? What if I want to train with Ash?" She wasn't sure if she was talking about magic training or the kind of training Ash was hinting at. Maybe a little of both. Ash was quite good looking as well.

Phoenix gave her a hard stare. "You'll train with me because I said so."

Again, Lainey had to fight back the urge to smack him. "No need to be so bossy, Tinker Bell."

Ash choked on his coffee, the black liquid spraying out of his mouth as he coughed and spluttered. "Tinker Bell! That's great! I'm going to call you Tink from now on." He was laughing so hard he had to wipe tears from his eyes.

The look Phoenix directed toward Lainey actually sent a chill through her. He always gave off a dangerous vibe, but this was something else entirely. She swallowed and looked away, reminding herself she really didn't know these two fae, and they were far more powerful than she was.

"Let's go," Phoenix ordered, jerking his head toward the door.

Lainey reluctantly jumped off the stool and grabbed her bag. She hated obeying his commands, but she needed to get to work. She swallowed her sarcastic remark and followed Phoenix out the door.

Chapter Five

"Do you even know how to use that thing?" Phoenix dubiously watched Lainey place her gun in the holster at the small of her back.

They had returned to her apartment, where she showered and packed a few bags for her mini vacation at Phoenix's place.

She didn't bother looking at him as she replied, "Yes. I can show you by using you as target practice if you'd like."

Phoenix snorted. "Regular bullets can't kill fae."

She paused and looked up. "Then why the hell am I bothering with this?"

"It will slow us down, but regular bullets won't do any major damage. I have some bullets at my place you can use."

"What kind of bullets?"

"The only metal that can kill a fae is silver."

"So you're like werewolves?"

Phoenix looked her straight in the eye as he said, "That is an urban legend. Any bullet can kill a werewolf."

Lainey blinked. "Are you saying werewolves exist?"

"Among other things," he replied offhandedly. "Are you ready?"

"Yes," Lainey answered faintly.

She followed Phoenix out into the cold in a daze. Werewolves existed. What else existed? Did she even want to know?

Realizing Phoenix was ahead of her and walking swiftly, Lainey took a deep breath to focus her mind and caught up to him.

"So," she began. "You're a fire elemental. What does that mean? What exactly can you do?"

He did not look happy about answering her question, but to his credit, he did so reluctantly. "I can control fire—make it, get rid of it, direct it. I can also control heat to an extent, although so can earth elementals. Some powers overlap a bit."

"What other kind of fae are there? I know about fire, earth, and air. I'm assuming there are more?"

"There are more than I could ever teach you. There is a hierarchy among fae—greater fae and lesser fae. Basically, any fae that look human are greater. Among the greater fae, there are the elementals who stand higher in society than any other fae." Phoenix stopped at a crosswalk and waited to continue until there were no other people around them. "The four elementals are Pygmies, Undines, Salamanders, and Sylphs. Or earth, water, fire, and air, respectively."

"You said 'society.' So what type of society is it?"

"There are two courts in Faerie. The Seelie and Unseelie. In a very basic explanation of the two courts, the Seelie are good and the Unseelie are evil. Although that is not always an appropriate description of the courts. The two courts were once both considered good, but sometime along the way, they started following different paths."

"What court do you belong to?"

Phoenix hesitated before he said, "That is a complicated answer."

Uncertainty settled in her gut at his non-answer. "How is it complicated? You are either Seelie or Unseelie, right?"

A muscle ticked in his jaw. "Technically, I would be considered Unseelie, although that is no fault of my own."

Was he saying he was part of the evil court? His brother *had* murdered her sister. That was certainly evil. If Beck had murdered Emma because she was half fae ... Lainey's thoughts sped up as she fully thought through everything she had learned last night. She was half fae, Phoenix could use her the same way Beck used Emma.

Lainey stopped in the middle of the sidewalk, suspicion swirling deep in her gut.

Phoenix noticed she had stopped and turned to face her. "What now?"

Best to just ask him. He said fae couldn't lie. Unless that was a lie. Her head hurt from all this thinking.

"What are your plans for me? Are you going to use me like your brother used Emma?"

"Half-brother, and no."

"Then what are you going to do with me?"

"Nothing." Phoenix turned and started walking again, not caring if she followed.

Lainey growled under her breath and marched along after him.

"Nothing? Then why are you babysitting me?"

"Unless you have forgotten, which I somehow don't think you did, my half-brother is still out there trying to find you so he can attempt to break the curse again. I'm trying to keep you alive long enough for me to find some other way, so another innocent person doesn't die."

"What if you can't find another way? Are you going to off me, then?"

"Who the hell says 'off me?' You're not in the mafia."

Lainey attempted to grab his arm to drag him to a stop. It didn't work. Instead, Phoenix kept walking, dragging her along with him until she let go.

"Arh! Why are you so difficult?" she shouted, throwing her arms up in the air. She ignored the surrounding people who gave them funny looks.

"Why do you ask so many questions?"

"Why do you avoid answering all my questions? *Are* you going to kill me if you can't find another way?"

Phoenix stopped and turned to face her again. "No. I will not kill you. I'm not into that type of thing."

The fire drained out of her. Her shoulders slumped, and she felt as if her head weighed a hundred pounds—she let it drop forward for a moment before lifting it again. "I am so overwhelmed," she whispered. "I just lost my sister, my only family. I find out fae exist, and not only exist, but that I am half fae. A crazy fae killer is trying to murder me. And an asshole of a fae is leading me around the city like a dog, avoiding all my questions." She blinked rapidly to avoid crying. "I just feel like giving up. Letting Beck find me and ending all of this."

It would be easier. She wouldn't have to worry about what to do with her life now that she was utterly and completely alone. The constant fight with herself to keep going was getting exhausting. She had avoided the question just beneath the surface that had been poking and prodding her since Emma died. What purpose did she have in life now? Why bother going on when there was no one else to live for?

"Fuck," Phoenix cursed quietly. He grabbed her arm and walked her to the closest alley. He came to a stop and looked at her, his eyes uncharacteristically soft. "You don't want to give up. You're stronger than that."

"How do you know? You don't know me at all."

"I think you'd be surprised how much I do know you. Besides, it doesn't take much to learn you're a fighter. You have shown me that every second we have been together."

Lainey backed up against the wall of the alley. She closed her eyes and pressed her fingers into the cold, rough brick, grounding herself. She inhaled the cool autumn air and let it settle her. When she opened her eyes, Phoenix was staring at her, a strange look in his eyes she couldn't define.

"I'm sorry about your sister," he said. "I'm sorry I haven't been the most forthcoming or the easiest person to get along with. It's just who I am. I'll try to do better at making this easier for you."

Lainey nodded, not sure what else to say. She pushed off the wall and continued the walk to Carly's.

Before she entered the back door, Phoenix stopped her with a hand on her arm.

"I'll be outside circling the building, looking for any signs of Beck. When you're off, we'll head back to the apartment. Hopefully, Ash will have found something by then."

Lainey nodded again and pushed the door open, leaving Phoenix outside in the cold to keep watch.

"Are you sure this is the right place?" Lainey squinted through the darkness at the dilapidated structure before them.

Her shift at Carly's passed without incident, and upon their return to the apartment, Ash had informed them he found something interesting in his search.

"Beck's phone records indicated he visited this place three times. Seems really suspicious to me." Ash double checked the address with the list he'd made on his phone.

The little sign in front of the building showed a hand, palm facing them, with an eye in the center and rays of light behind it.

"'Madam Elvie, Spiritual Medium, Master Spell Caster'," Lainey read from the website she'd pulled up on her phone after a quick Google search. "'I can make your deepest desires a reality.'" Lainey snorted. "Do people actually believe this crap?"

"Fifty bucks she's an elf," Ash said as he looked over Lainey's shoulder at her phone.

Phoenix grunted in what Lainey assumed was agreement.

"Wait, elves exist too?" Lainey looked between them with wide eyes.

"Elves are fae," Ash answered. "However, they aren't your

typical *Lord of the Rings* elves. Many elves will work in this ... uh ... industry. They are incredibly attuned to the spirit realm and nature—both past and present."

"And they are very educated in all things magic," Phoenix added.

"So you're telling me, if I were to visit a psychic who just so happened to be an elf, it would be like visiting a legit psychic?"

"Exactly." Ash smiled brightly and patted her on the shoulder before walking up to the front door.

The building was falling apart. Faded red brick crumbled from the walls, and the wooden steps to the front door were disintegrating. It didn't look like they could hold the weight of a house cat, let alone the guys standing next to her. Shutters hung at odd angles, some screeching noisily as they blew in the autumn breeze. Light shone through the panes of glass, dimmed by dark curtains.

The steps creaked alarmingly as they climbed to the top but miraculously held. Phoenix lifted his fist to knock, but there was no need. The door opened of its own accord on a soft groan. The two men straightened their shoulders and pushed their way inside, Lainey following cautiously behind them.

She was relieved to see the inside of the building was nicer than the outside. Brightly colored rugs and artwork covered dark paneled floors and walls. Green plants filled the space with their earthy scent, mixing with the incense that lay thick in the air. Swirling clouds of smoke eddied in their wake as they wandered from the front entrance to a sitting room. Cushions in every color imaginable were strewn about the floor, surrounding a round table that appeared to have been cleaved from some kind of stone.

The sound of soft clacking had the three turning toward the opposite side of the entryway. Emerging from the veil of beads could only have been Madam Elvie. She was tall and willowy, with smooth, dark skin. Her long hair was so black, it was almost blue and fell in loose waves past her waist. She wore voluminous robes of dark purple and a matching turban wound around her head. The jangle of gold jewelry followed in her wake.

Her pale blue eyes stood out in stark contrast to her dark skin, and they widened in surprise as she beheld who stood before her.

"So, I am graced by the Cursed Child." Her voice was melodious and held an air of magic, as if she wove the sound of many voices together behind her own.

Phoenix straightened further, his shoulders tensing to the point that it looked painful. "We have some questions for you. If you would be so kind as to answer them."

The elf smiled. "I know why you are here. You seek the same answers your brother sought." Her gaze drifted to Lainey, and the look that lit up her face had Lainey taking a step back. She looked as if she were ravenous and Lainey was the only source of food in the room. Her nostrils flared delicately, and Madam Elvie's smile turned dark. "You will not fail where your brother did. Although, I may not have given him all the necessary details."

Phoenix looked at Lainey quickly before facing the elf again. "What was my half-brother looking for when he visited you?"

"He wanted to know how to break the curse. Would you like to know what I told him?" She didn't wait for an answer before she continued, "To break the curse, a sacrifice must be made. As the curse was created because of the birth of an innocent half-breed"—her hard gaze returned to Phoenix briefly, before coming back to Lainey—"only the death of an innocent half-breed can break it."

Lainey stopped breathing. Both Ash and Phoenix were looking at her, and Lainey felt her heart speed up. This was it. They were going to murder her. This was the confirmation they needed. Her death would break the curse.

Phoenix narrowed his eyes before turning back to the elf. "But Beck already attempted that and failed. He killed Lainey's sister, who was also a half-breed."

"But she wasn't innocent, was she, Lainey?" The elf smiled knowingly at Lainey.

"What do you mean? Of course she was! She never did anything wrong!"

The elf's smile grew. "Oh, but I'm not talking about that kind of innocence. Your sister was not a virgin, was she?"

The blood drained from Lainey's face. No way. She couldn't mean that.

Phoenix was looking at her strangely, and Lainey let her hair fall forward to hide her burning cheeks.

"Like I said, you will not fail where your brother did." The glee in Madam Elvie's voice chilled the blood in Lainey's veins.

"There has to be another way to break the curse," Phoenix argued. "A way that doesn't end in the death of someone who doesn't deserve it."

"Well, of course there is another way." Madam Elvie clucked her tongue. "No true curse has only one way to break it."

"And?" Ash demanded.

"I don't know what it is." At the looks of her three visitors, Madam Elvie raised a finger before they could protest. "But my sister was the one who created the curse at the behest of the queens. She would know how to break it without involving Lainey's blood being spilled."

"Where is your sister?" Ash was practically vibrating with impatience.

"She is in Faerie, of course."

At this, Phoenix lost his temper. "What the fuck! Quit leading us around in pointless circles. You know we can't get to Faerie. Why tempt us with that option?"

"Who says you can't get to Faerie? Your brother made it across the divide."

"Half-brother. And I don't want to know what he did or who he killed to do it."

"There is a way that doesn't involve blood or death. I will require three objects. Bring me them, and I can get you to Faerie."

Phoenix looked at the elf suspiciously. "What objects?"

CHAPTER SIX

LAINEY PACED IN FRONT OF THE WINDOWS IN Phoenix's apartment. The beautiful view of the city lit up at night did not register with her. She kept one eye on the two fae occupying the other half of the room.

Phoenix was scowling at his phone as he texted furiously with his dad. The thought amused her. Logically, fae had to have parents, but for some reason, she pictured them being hatched from eggs. Ash was on his computer, brow drawn in thought. Lainey was on edge, waiting for the knife to drop. Literally.

Madam Elvie had asked them to bring her the tail feather of a white hawk, the Black Tourmaline Amulet of Azura—whatever that was—and the essence of a will-o'-the-wisp, because along with werewolves and elves, this glowing magical creature also existed.

"Okay, can someone please explain exactly what this curse is?" Lainey stopped her pacing and placed her hands on her hips. Through all of this, the curse was the one thing she didn't quite understand.

Phoenix put his phone down and pinched the bridge of his nose. "The curse is my fault," he said after a few beats of tense silence.

Ash looked up from his computer screens. "I swear to everything holy, Nix, if I hear you say that one more fucking time, I'm going to beat you within an inch of your life. It. Is. Not. Your fucking fault." For the first time since Lainey had laid eyes on Ash, he looked terrifying.

Phoenix ignored Ash and continued. "My dad was mated to an earth elemental. Beck was born of that woman. On a scouting mission twenty-four years ago, my father wandered into the cave of a banshee. In Faerie, banshees aren't what humans depict them as. They are more of a vampire fairy. They lure men into their caves and seduce them. The result is always the death of the male." Phoenix stood from his seat and took up Lainey's spot in front of the windows, pacing while lost in thought.

Lainey sat on the couch, feet tucked under her, eyes glued on Phoenix. She had a feeling this wasn't something he talked about regularly, and she knew this would be the only chance she had to learn about his history. She didn't want to miss anything.

"For some reason, this banshee didn't kill my dad. Instead, they fell in love. Nine months later, I was born. No one had ever heard of a banshee giving birth before. It's not known whether that is because it's extremely rare, or because they kill the male before anything can happen." Phoenix's face turned vulpine as he continued, "Either way, I am the product of my dad's adultery. The half-breed fire elemental and something else—not banshee because they are only female. I am another breed entirely."

"Why the curse, though?" Lainey asked tentatively.

"The banshee died giving birth to me. My dad brought me home and told his mate the truth. She was livid. They were members of the Seelie queen's court—my dad was one of her army generals. The Seelie queen was disgusted with my dad and myself. She banned us from the court and sent us to live the rest of our lives in the Unseelie Court." Phoenix paused and looked out the window. He ran a hand through his hair, the strands tangling in his fingers. "Despite banshees being part of the Unseelie Court, the Unseelie queen refused my dad entry. She blamed him for the death of one of her subjects. Desperate to find a place to raise me without either of the courts interfering, my dad brought us to the human realm. When the queens found out, they enacted the curse to keep us out of Faerie for good, and to use us as an example of what would happen if you did something wrong."

Something here didn't add up. Lainey could understand some discontent from the queens and his wife ... mate ... whatever. But banishing them from the realms and creating a curse seemed a little extreme. She didn't voice that opinion, instead asking, "Why is your half-brother trying to break the curse?"

"When the queens enacted the curse, they didn't warn anybody. Whichever side you were on was the side you were forced to live in. There are many fae who are unhappy about that. Some were separated from their families permanently." He looked at Ash briefly with a bitter smile. "My best guess? Beck has lived his life with threats and violence since his dad and half-brother were the cause of the curse. He probably thinks if he breaks the curse, it will win him some glory. Or at least take him off the hit list."

Okay, all that made sense, in a sick twisted way. Except why Lainey and Emma had been targeted. "Not that I wish death on anyone else, but why can't Beck find another half-breed to break the curse? Why me and Emma?"

Ash answered this question, but he kept a cautious eye on Phoenix, who had gone silent. "Half-breeds are extremely rare. The female's body, either fae or human, can sense there is something different about the fetus growing inside them. The body determines the pregnancy isn't viable. Most will end in miscarriage." His green eyes landed on Lainey. "It is actually pretty incredible your mom carried two half-breeds to term successfully."

Lainey shivered at his statement. As if it wasn't enough to be half fae and hunted, now she was an anomaly too. Her gaze drifted to Phoenix. He was still staring out the window, like the view held all the answers. He was obviously lost in his own thoughts, not even aware of Lainey or Ash behind him.

She thought of his story, how he was also a half-breed, and not just any half-breed but something unknown entirely. He had probably lived his whole life being ridiculed for what he was—both for being a half-breed as well as the cause of the curse. But Ash was right. Phoenix wasn't the cause. His dad was, in a way. Although, Lainey thought the queen's choice of punishment slightly harsh.

It kind of explained his gruff demeanor. He'd had to be hard his whole life to survive. That, of course, didn't excuse him for his actions, but it did explain them. Despite herself, Lainey felt her dislike of the guy crumble a bit, and she hated herself for that.

Shaking herself back to the present, Lainey asked Ash, "What about these three things Madam Elvie asked for?"

Ash groaned. "Well, the feather and will-o'-the-wisp essence will be easy enough to get. The amulet is another story."

"What is the amulet, exactly?"

"A myth," Ash answered, and he plopped onto the couch next to her, his weight practically throwing her off the cushions. "Drink?" he asked, holding up a bottle of vodka.

She glared at him and rearranged herself, but snatched the bottle from his hand.

"The Black Tourmaline Amulet was believed to have belonged to the Unseelie queen's sister, Princess Azura. Thousands of years ago, the princess imbued incredible magic into the amulet. You see, she saw her sister for what she truly was—evil. As the younger sister, Azura knew Esmeray would become queen, and her reign would be dark and dangerous."

"What did Azura do with the amulet?" Lainey asked, handing the vodka back to Ash.

"Nothing. She didn't get a chance to use it. She had planned to take her sister out of the picture and claim the throne for herself, but Queen Esmeray found out. She had her sister brutally murdered, and the amulet was sent to the human realm. That is all anyone knows."

"What power did the amulet have?" She accepted the bottle again and took another swallow. A pleasant tingling settled into Lainey's limbs.

"The story claims that when Azura infused her magic into the black tourmaline, it morphed. The wearer of the amulet would then be able to use that magic, combined with their own, to wipe out any wards or protection spells. It would have been the only way to kill Queen Esmeray. She has herself so wrapped in protection spells, nothing can get through them to harm her."

"And now Madam Elvie wants it? That sounds a little suspicious."

Ash shrugged and accepted the vodka from Lainey. "Elves are curious creatures. They typically don't have any ambitions beyond their own enjoyment. I don't know Madam Elvie, but in the little time we spent with her, she seems like she enjoys the showmanship of being a seer." He paused before taking another swig of vodka. "Besides, many elves are able to read the threads that compose the fabric of our world. I have a suspicion there is something she isn't telling us."

"It doesn't matter. The story of the amulet is just that: a story." Phoenix finally emerged from his thoughts and grabbed the bottle of vodka from Ash before sitting on the chair by the fireplace.

"How can you be so sure? If Madam Elvie wants it, there must be a reason."

"She wants to send us on a pointless quest before breaking the curse." Phoenix dismissed further comment by turning to Ash. "Can you find anything on the location of the amulet?"

"Wait, you said it was just a story!" Lainey exclaimed.

"The amulet is real enough, the bullshit about the magic is just a story." Phoenix growled, actually growled, when Lainey snatched the vodka from his hands.

"Whoa there, tiger," Ash placated, making calming motions

with his hands toward Phoenix. "I found some hits on the amulet. Some were a little far fetched, but two of them I believe could be legit."

"What have we got?" Phoenix stood from his chair and went to the kitchen. He returned with another bottle of vodka.

"There is a distant relation of Queen Esmeray and Princess Azura who chose to live in the human realm. Some believe the amulet was given to her for safekeeping." Ash handed his bottle to Lainey. "The second theory is that the amulet was found years and years ago and placed in the Met."

"Well that's easy enough to prove or disprove. Tomorrow, we will head to the Met and see if it's there." Phoenix settled back in the chair with his vodka. His eyes were haunted. Whatever memories and feelings he'd dragged up retelling his story were still very much front and center.

"If the amulet is in the Met, how do you propose we get it?" Lainey asked. Her limbs were now feeling pleasantly light, as if they could float up to the ceiling.

A wicked glint appeared in Ash's eyes, along with a grin that showcased his pointed canines. "A heist. Just like in the movies." He actually rubbed his hands together gleefully.

"That's what I was afraid of," Lainey sighed.

They all sat in silence for a few, drinking vodka and getting lost in their own thoughts. Eventually, Phoenix got up and went to his room, followed by Ash shortly after. Lainey had been given a room, but she didn't feel like heading there now. She was buzzing, only partially a result of drinking too much vodka, and she couldn't get her body to sit still—or her mind to shut up. Instead, she stood in front of the windows, watching the lights flicker across the city.

She wasn't sure how long she'd been standing there when she heard footsteps behind her. She turned slowly, not wanting to risk tipping over from a spinning room. Phoenix stood in the living room, shirtless, with low-slung pants showing an indecent amount of skin. His eyes widened in surprise at the sight of her.

"I'm sorry," she said quickly. "I couldn't sleep. I'll head to my room now."

Before she could move, Phoenix walked toward her. Well, *prowled* was more like it. His gaze burned as it drifted over her. His slow approach had her body tingling for a whole different reason. The closer he got, the warmer she felt. She wasn't sure if that was his magic or her body's reaction to him. She tried to shake the feelings that overcame her but failed. Miserably.

He stopped with just inches between them. This time, the flare of heat that washed over her was definitely his magic. The scent of bonfire wafted around them. Her body—her magic— responded. A gentle breeze swirled around them, lifting strands of their hair. His eyes glowed copper in response. Lainey was completely entranced by those eyes, drawn into their molten, swirling depths.

Every thought flew out of her mind as he lifted a hand and traced his finger over her collar bone. His skin was as warm as his magic. A callus from his frequent practice with various weapons scraped gently. Lainey's breath quickened, deep heaving breaths, as her body reacted to Phoenix without her permission.

She knew she should be pushing him away. He irritated her and drove her fucking crazy with his domineering bullshit, but for some reason, she couldn't bring those thoughts to the surface of her mind. She was so lonely, and she couldn't remember the last time she'd enjoyed the touch of another person. Alex didn't count. Lainey couldn't actually stand him. He was just a good way to pass the time.

It wasn't until Phoenix's gaze dipped to her mouth, and his lips parted slightly, a hint of fang peeking through, that Lainey snapped back to reality. She took a trembling step back, then another, until her shoulders bumped the window behind her. She was breathing heavily as she stared at him with wide eyes. Had he used his magic on her somehow? She shook her head to clear it and quickly stepped around him, putting as much distance between them as possible.

Phoenix remained facing the window. His shoulders were tense, and his hands were fisted at his sides. "Fuck," she heard him mumble under his breath.

Lainey turned around and walked to her room on shaking legs. She would never let herself drink around him again. She couldn't let her guard down near him. Her thoughts were so consumed by Phoenix as she settled down in bed for the night that she didn't even think about her magic and how it had finally manifested.

Chapter Seven

"Do you have everything you need?" Phoenix looked Ash over, ensuring the other fae had everything ready for his trip.

"Yes, Tink, I'm good." Ash was leaving for Texas to get the tail feather of a white hawk.

Apparently, one perk of being an earth elemental was that he could communicate with animals. Getting the feather would be a piece of cake for him. Unfortunately, white hawks were only found in southern Texas. That also meant Lainey would be alone with Phoenix for a few days.

"You two can handle the essence without me, right?" Ash eyed them curiously.

Lainey was studiously avoiding looking at Phoenix, and he was doing likewise. Neither of them acknowledged the other.

Phoenix gave Ash a flat stare. "Of course I can handle that. We'll also check out the Met and see if the amulet is there."

"No breaking and entering without me!" Ash complained.

Phoenix snorted. "Of course not."

Satisfied, Ash walked over to Lainey and gave her a big smacking kiss on the cheek. "Be good while I'm gone, little half-breed."

She smacked his chest, but couldn't resist the smile that pulled at the corners of her mouth. Ash was like a big teddy bear, cute and loveable, but she knew there was danger lurking beneath the surface. She could see it in his eyes and the way he moved with a lethal grace. Okay, maybe he was more like a dangerous teddy bear.

As the door shut behind Ash, Phoenix turned to the hallway and headed toward his room. "We leave in an hour." Was all he said as he disappeared down the hallway.

"Lovely," Lainey muttered. "This is going to be fan-fucking-tastic."

The Metropolitan Museum of Art was, surprisingly, a place Lainey had never visited. She preferred the library and books to art and statues. She had to admit the building was beautiful, though. Standing with Phoenix on the steps leading up to the front entrance, she admired the facade. The soaring arches and stone pillars evoked a sense of times gone by.

They entered the Great Hall, where Lainey had to keep her chin from hitting the floor. She was always amazed when entering the library, but the Met surpassed the beauty of the library by miles, in her opinion. The cathedral-like ceiling took her breath away, and the open, airy feel brought a smile to her face. They traversed the marble floor, their shoes clicking quietly in the hushed bustle of the museum.

"Can you give me any idea what exactly we are looking for?" Laney asked, as they made their way deeper into the building.

"The amulet was attached to a gold chain, but the chain may or may not be missing. The amulet itself is set in gold. It is rumored to have been a fairly simple piece of jewelry—a large, raw black tourmaline, roughly oval shaped, encased in gold and set with black diamonds."

"Oh, simple, right," Lainey muttered. She knew little about

gemstones, but the words "raw" and "encased in diamonds" made her think it was anything but simple.

They made their way around the museum, looking closely at all the jewelry. Neither one of them mentioned what had happened, or almost happened, the night before. Lainey got the impression Phoenix didn't lose control of himself very often, and last night had been a definite loss of control. He was back to his normal self today, surrounded by his iron will and miles-tall stone wall.

They had been walking through the museum for thirty minutes when Lainey caught the glimmer of black stone from the corner of her eye. She held her breath and approached the pedestal.

The necklace, nestled in a bed of white velvet, was exactly as Phoenix described. The black tourmaline was the size of a robin's egg, with vertical striations showing it was, indeed, a raw stone. No shiny, reflective surface here—it actually appeared to swallow the light surrounding it. The black diamonds surrounding the tourmaline were the size of peas, and they did shimmer and shine in the light above the pedestal.

"Phoenix," Lainey breathed. She couldn't tear her eyes away from the amulet. She could feel it. The closer she got to it, the more its presence became known to her. "It's so cold. It's like silver fire. Like the cold of the moon." Lainey wasn't sure what any of that meant, but as she said it, it felt right.

Phoenix appeared next to her and sucked in a breath. His eyes darted to Lainey before returning to the amulet. "That's definitely it."

"Can you feel it? Please tell me it's not just me."

"I can feel it. And you're right. It's like the cold of the moon. Azura was the princess of the night sky, so that makes sense."

Though she was relieved she wasn't the only one who could feel it, she was still uncomfortable with the fact she could sense magic but not understand any of it.

"It's beautiful." She still couldn't look away from it. She wasn't sure she had blinked since her eyes beheld it.

Phoenix grabbed her arm and pulled her back. "Be careful," he hissed.

Lainey jerked when she realized her hand was pressed to the glass covering the amulet. She didn't even remember lifting her arm.

Phoenix studied her closely with a furrowed brow. "It's calling to you, isn't it?"

"What does that mean?" Her voice trembled as she looked at him. She didn't dare look at the amulet again.

"I'm not sure," he admitted. "Come on. We know it's here, now we have to find a way to get it."

They left the museum and headed back to the apartment to prepare for their trip to the Catskills. It was time to catch a will-o'-the-wisp.

Luckily for Lainey, they took a car. She wasn't sure she would have survived the three-hour drive on a motorcycle. For multiple reasons. One of which was the awkwardness of being so close to Phoenix.

Instead, she was sitting shotgun in his white Audi R8. That was about all she knew of the car, and only because he'd told her that's what it was. She had to admit, it was a slick-looking car.

The drive started awkwardly. Neither of them wanted to talk to the other, so tense silence filled the car. As Phoenix sped along the highway, Lainey loosened up a bit. Her curiosity had grown since the other night. She didn't look too closely at the reason behind why she wanted to know more about the fae in the driver's seat.

One question kept popping into her head that she just had to ask, even though she suspected he would blow her off. "Where do you guys get your money? You're too young to be as rich as you are." She paused, brow scrunched as another thought floated into her head. "Come to think of it, how old are you guys? Do fae age differently?"

"We start off aging the same way humans do. When we hit thirty, the aging process slows dramatically. The average lifespan of a fae is about five thousand years."

"Holy shit. Will I live that long?"

Phoenix shrugged. "We probably won't know that answer for a while. It depends on which parent you end up taking after the most. If your mom or dad's blood will be the strongest."

Lainey bit her lip. It was impossible to imagine living that long and aging slowly. Instead of dwelling on it, she asked again, "How old are you and Ash? And where do you get your money?"

"I'm twenty-four, Ash is twenty-five. And, when my dad fled Faerie, he grabbed as much as he could to sell in the human realm. Gems, gold, jewelry. He made a killing off of it."

"Do you remember anything about Faerie?" she asked him as the road and trees swept by in a blur.

"No. I was one when my dad brought me to the human realm. I don't remember anything of Faerie."

She didn't miss the longing in his voice, and damn if it didn't do something to her.

"So you were raised in NYC? Just like any normal human?"

"To an extent, yes." Phoenix must have been feeling particularly chatty to agree to answer her questions. He adjusted his grip on the wheel before continuing. "I went to school like every other human kid, but at home, my dad taught me fae history and culture. He trained me in weapons and magic as well."

"How did you meet Ash?"

"Believe it or not, we went to the same school. He was a grade above me. His dad was locked out of the human realm when the curse was created. His mom raised him and his older sister alone."

"That's terrible," Lainey said. She couldn't imagine what that must have been like, knowing their husband and father was alive but not able to get to him. She had so many questions for Ash now, but since he wasn't here, she turned her curiosity elsewhere. "Are fae common here? Like, can I expect to run into any?"

Phoenix bobbed his head from side to side. "Yes and no. There are more fae in and around New York City because there was a gate to Faerie in Central Park. Anywhere there was a gate, there is a higher concentration of fae." He paused before continuing. "Older fae are more common, but they are well trained in masking their identity. You probably wouldn't know you ran into one unless they wanted you to know. Younger fae are very uncommon. Most fae don't want to raise children in the human realm and are hoping for the curse to break so they can go back home."

"So it was crazy lucky you and Ash went to the same school."

"It was. We recognized each other immediately because neither of us knew how to mask our identities beyond our glamor."

"Do you know any other fae?"

"Yeah, but we don't interact much. We all try to keep a distance from each other. Too much risk of being discovered if we all congregate in one place. A single fae, or even two, can fairly easily blend in. Put more of us together, and you start to notice things that don't seem right. Our size, beauty, the essence of our power. It all becomes more noticeable in larger groups."

Lainey let the conversation lapse into silence as she pondered Phoenix's history. She tried to put herself in his shoes. A young fae forced to live in the human realm because of a mistake his dad made. A young fae living with the weight of the curse, and blaming himself for it, while dealing with the ridicule other fae would have shown him.

She couldn't help but notice the similarities between her life and his. While they were raised very differently and experienced vastly different things, they'd both lived a rather lonely and sometimes scary life. Both of them had a family torn apart by one thing or another. They were both ridiculed for something a parent had done—everyone made fun of Lainey for having a mom who was 'crazy,' and Phoenix's dad was the cause of the curse.

She was starting to view Phoenix in a different light. A light more similar to how she viewed herself. Lainey wasn't always easy to get along with. She was scared of letting people in and kept them at a distance because they always left her in some way. She tended to be more cynical. Living through the things she had made it difficult for her to remain positive all the time. Phoenix seemed to be very similar in that regard.

Lainey returned her focus to the world passing by outside the window as she cautiously gave voice to another question. "Do banshees have magic?" She saw Phoenix jerk from the corner of her eye.

"Why?"

"I'm only wondering ... I mean ... You're half banshee, or whatever ..." Shit, this wasn't going well. Lainey swallowed and plowed forward. "Do you have any other abilities besides fire magic?"

"Yes."

Phoenix's answer was so quiet, Lainey could barely hear it. She turned her head toward him and let her gaze rove over his profile. His jaw was tightly clenched, as were his hands on the steering wheel. His eyes were hooded, as if he were trying to hide his thoughts from escaping through them.

Without her permission, her gaze moved to his lips. They were bracketed by strain and pressed into a flat line. But she knew they were normally full, the bottom slightly fuller than the top. She jerked her gaze away quickly. Unfortunately, it landed on his chest. His very broad, muscled chest, that was clearly defined under the black Henley he wore.

Lainey made a noise in the back of her throat and forced herself to look forward. She settled back against the seat and dropped the conversation. Clearly, he wasn't going to further explain.

Phoenix surprised Lainey by shaking off his tension and asking, "What about you? What was your childhood like?"

It took all of her self-control to not whip her head in his direction with her mouth gaping open. "Well, like I said, my dad disappeared when I was one. My mom went crazy, which I'm thinking had something to do with my dad being fae. She lived in a psych ward for the majority of my childhood until she killed herself when I was fifteen years old. Emma raised me through all of it."

"I imagine that wasn't easy."

Lainey snorted. "Not in the slightest."

"You have no other family? Grandparents? Aunts or uncles?"

"I'm assuming my dad's family is in Faerie and could care less about me, if they even know I exist." That wasn't bitterness in her voice, not at all. "My mom never talked about her family. I know she grew up in Georgia before moving to New York City. I have never been able to find anything on her family, though."

"I was always grateful I at least had my dad. He fucked up, big time, but he always took care of me."

Lainey had to hold back her surge of jealousy. Even when her mom was living at home, she was never really present. The only mother figure she had in her life was Emma, and she wasn't really a mom.

Lainey was trying to figure out how to respond when Phoenix surprised her again.

"So, last night ..." He began before trailing off.

Lainey froze. She opened her mouth to respond, but closed it quickly. What was there to say about the other night? She had been drunk; her guard was down. She was still mourning the death of her sister and had been feeling lonely. It was a mistake. All perfectly valid reasons. All felt wrong to say for some reason.

"I felt your magic," Phoenix eventually said.

Oh, right. Her magic. Not the almost kiss. Why did her stomach sink at his statement?

"Um, yeah. I noticed that," she said stumbling over her words.

"Did you feel anything? Any indication your magic was at the surface?"

Did she feel anything? Assuming he didn't mean the raging desire, no she hadn't.

"What would it feel like? I don't even know how it works."

Phoenix hummed in the back of his throat. "I can always feel my magic. It's like an ember burning softly in my gut. If I want to use it, I stoke the flames, letting them rise to the surface. I can feel the heat and arid air flowing through my body." He glanced at Lainey quickly before returning his gaze to the road. "I don't know what your magic would feel like, but I'd imagine something akin to the wind."

"I didn't notice that," she breathed. She didn't add, *I only noticed the way your fire magic made me feel, and the burning low in my stomach at how close you stood to me.*

"Focus now," Phoenix suggested. "See if you notice any sensation in your body that isn't normal."

Lainey complied. She closed her eyes and focused on her body. She had to work hard to tune out the sound of the car flying down the highway and the feel of her body swaying in the seat. She had to work even harder to ignore the gentle heat of Phoenix in the seat next to her.

She focused on her stomach, deep inside of it, trying to feel anything like wind or air. She felt nothing as her focus quickly returned to Phoenix. She could smell him. He smelled like a fall night and a burning bonfire. It was entirely too enticing. She opened her eyes quickly, dimming her other senses.

"I don't feel anything," she lied. She felt only him.

"We'll keep working on it. It will be important for you to be competent in your magic. If something were to happen, if you get into a situation where your emotions run high, your magic might manifest, and you will need to be able to control it. It will also be good for you to be able to defend yourself if the need arises."

She knew what he was saying was true, but if training had her thoughts wandering the direction they just did—to him—she wasn't sure she wanted to try. She needed to get her body under control. Phoenix was a road she did not want to go down. At all.

They lapsed into silence for the rest of the ride. Eventually, Phoenix pulled off the highway and made his way down winding roads to a small cabin in the middle of nowhere.

Lainey eyed the wooden structure suspiciously. "That's an awfully small cabin. Are you sure we will both fit inside?"

"We will."

They didn't speak as they unloaded their bags and entered the cabin. Lainey stared in disbelief.

"There is no way we are going to survive this trip if we have to stay in this cabin together."

The wraparound porch was a nice touch, but deceiving. Inside, the cabin consisted of two rooms: a living room with a pull-out couch and a kitchen. There was also a small bathroom. It was nicely furnished and clean, at least. It was a place Lainey would have enjoyed staying in by herself, or even with a boyfriend for a romantic getaway. Phoenix was not that person.

In response, Phoenix just grunted and dropped his bag by the door. Lainey followed suit.

Phoenix checked his watch before heading back to the car. "We should head to the field now, before it gets dark," he called over his shoulder. "That way we can scout and find a good spot to wait for the will-o'-the-wisps to show up."

Lainey didn't say anything, just hopped back in the car and let Phoenix drive them to their destination. The drive wasn't far, only thirty minutes or so, but after a day of being in the car with him, she was ready to get out.

The landscape was beautiful. She had never been to the Catskills, and the rolling hills and mountains were beautiful in autumn, the reds, yellows, and oranges seeming to catch fire as the sun began its slow descent. It was strange, but as she looked out over the trees, she could imagine Phoenix walking through the landscape. She imagined the setting sun turning the red in his hair to glowing fire. Just like his personality.

Banishing thoughts of Phoenix from her head, Lainey tried to imagine what they would be doing tonight. She wasn't quite sure what will-o'-the-wisps were, but she pictured herself and Phoenix running through the trees catching large lightning bugs. The image caused a chuckle to rasp up her throat. She wasn't able to hold it back.

"Why are you laughing?" Phoenix asked suspiciously.

"Are we just going to be catching really large lightning bugs? Did you bring a massive jar to put them in?" She snorted again, unable to contain it.

She felt, more than saw, Phoenix roll his eyes. "No. It's nothing like catching lightning bugs."

"Can you explain what exactly we will be doing then?"

Phoenix pulled off the road and parked the car in a small parking lot. He didn't reply until he had grabbed some gear from his trunk and started walking down a narrow trail.

Lainey hurried to keep up.

"We have to trick them so we can get close to them. In order to do that, we have to drug them."

"Please don't tell me we're going to date rape a glowing mythical creature."

Phoenix shot a disgusted look in her direction. "That is wrong on so many levels." He shook his head before continuing, "No. We drug them, and it causes them to relax. They will slow down enough for us to catch them, so we can get the essence."

Phoenix slowed as he approached a clearing. The light was fading fast, but Lainey could see a lake in the distance, butted up against the base of a mountain. Tall grasses swayed in the chilly autumn breeze, and colorful leaves blew around them in swirling spirals. It was a magical place, Lainey could feel it in the air.

Phoenix walked along the edge of the clearing, searching for the right spot to sit and wait for the glowing faeries to appear. He finally settled on a spot with a fallen tree right at the edge of the forest. He jumped over the log and settled down on his haunches, leaving Lainey to scramble over on her own. Not that she would have accepted his help anyway.

Lainey peered into the bag Phoenix was rifling through, suspicion worming its way through her. She glanced at him through narrowed eyes.

"Did you really bring me here to kill me?" She subtly moved her hand to the small of her back where her gun was holstered. Luckily, Phoenix had provided her with the silver bullets to harm a fae.

He barely looked at her before pulling out rope, daggers, little bottles with pills clinking inside, and ... was that a mortar and pestle?

"I'm not going to kill you. Take your hand away from your gun before you shoot your own ass off."

She sheepishly removed her hand and thanked the stars the sun had set and her burning cheeks were hidden in the dark. She watched with intrigue, and a little caution, as Phoenix took a small flashlight out of the bag and held it between his teeth. He placed the mortar in front of him and dumped half a bottle of little white pills into it. He began to grind the pills into a fine dust.

Once the pills were nothing but a powdery white substance, he looked at Lainey quickly before ducking his head. He drew a dagger down his wrist, cutting his skin open. Lainey watched as blood welled from the cut. In the dark, it was almost black. Phoenix held his wrist over the mortar and let a few drops of his blood fall onto the powder.

He licked the bloody wound on his wrist before mixing the blood and powder together until a thick paste sat in the bottom of the mortar. The next ingredient he added was water from a water bottle. She expected bursts of light and smoke, but nothing happened. A little anticlimactic in Lainey's opinion. Once the mixture was runny, Phoenix cleaned up the supplies, leaving the mortar and dagger at his feet.

As he was packing the supplies, Lainey glanced at his wrist.

She gasped. It was completely healed. Not even a scratch marred the smooth surface. Her eyes flew to his, and Phoenix quickly pulled the sleeve of his leather jacket down, hiding the evidence.

She would have just assumed it had something to do with fae healing powers, not that she knew anything about that either, but Phoenix's response made her question that assumption.

"Now what?" she asked without looking at him.

"Now we wait."

Chapter Eight

Waiting sucked. Lainey was crouched next to Phoenix behind the log. Her legs had fallen asleep thirty minutes ago, and she was so cold her shivering was pissing off Phoenix.

He had taken his bowl of blood and crushed pills and dribbled it around the field before they settled in to wait. Now he kept glaring at Lainey whenever she shivered so hard she moved the log.

"If you keep making all that noise, we are going to be here all night," he quietly growled at her.

"Dude, I can't help it," she replied through chattering teeth. "It's freezing up here, and we're not moving, so I'm just getting colder."

Phoenix groaned before removing his leather jacket and practically throwing it at her. She didn't hesitate before shoving her arms through the sleeves. This time, it was Lainey who groaned as the body heat trapped in the jacket soaked through her skin to her bones.

She tried not to notice how the leather was warmer than it should have been, like his fire magic was helping to keep him warm. She also tried not to notice how his scent surrounded her in the jacket. Subtly, she buried her nose in the leather and inhaled. It was a surprisingly comforting smell.

She was just about to thank him when Phoenix stiffened next to her. Glancing out across the field, all words and thoughts flew from her mind.

On the edge of the clearing, small glowing orbs appeared. They grew in number until they covered the field in a soft yellow light. Lainey held her breath as the orbs enlarged. Within seconds, they were the size of softballs, with faintly sparkling tails trailing behind them like comets as they floated through the clearing.

Their movements were slow and flowing unless they came close to one another. Then they zoomed away, almost too fast for Lainey to track with her human eyes.

Together, Lainey and Phoenix watched in silence as the will-o'-the-wisps sank to the ground, drawn to Phoenix's blood. Lainey watched in awe as their speed and agility were noticeably affected after they came into contact with the substance. Almost immediately, their movements became less flowing and more jerky. They ran into each other rather than speeding away.

Phoenix waited a few more minutes before standing and grabbing a few small vials from the bag at his feet. He stepped over the log, and Lainey followed suit, avoiding the mixture on the ground. As they neared the center of the field, the drunken swirling of the wisps completely enamored her.

The clearing was aglow, the soft yellow light casting the area into a romantic picture. Lainey couldn't help but watch Phoenix as he prowled through the wisps, the planes and angles of his face lit in stark relief. He stopped, and Lainey stopped next to him. Phoenix waited until a wisp lazed by, then grabbed it with one hand, his movement so fast, it was just a blur.

In his hand, the wisp pulsed softly. It almost reminded her of a jellyfish without the tentacles or arms—like a soft, squishy, see-through ball. Phoenix handed a vial to Lainey and with his other hand, he gently squeezed the ball of light over the vial. A shimmery, oily substance dripped into the opening.

"Ew, it's like will-o'-the-wisp piss," Lainey whispered.

Phoenix laughed, a burst of surprise that shocked both of them. He quickly sobered and let the wisp go. Waiting for another to float by.

They worked like that in silence for, what, ten minutes? Thirty? Sixty? Lainey had no idea. Time was a concept she couldn't grasp in this magical field. Phoenix's hands were glittery and glowing where he grabbed the wisps, and a few drops of wisp piss coated Lainey's hands as well.

By the time the vial was almost full, the wisps were beginning to disappear, their light dimming and their size growing smaller until they were nothing, not even a speck. Their number slowly dwindled until the clearing was once again cast in darkness.

"That was amazing," Lainey whispered, afraid to break the spell that had been cast in the clearing.

Phoenix opened his mouth to reply, then spun around, hand going to the dagger at his waist. His nostrils flared and his eyes narrowed as his gaze moved around the field. The tense lines of his body set Lainey on edge.

Lainey took her gun out of the holster and looked around. She couldn't see anything, but she felt a chill run down her spine, spider-webbing out toward her limbs. She slowly turned around, and her breath left her in a rush.

"Phoenix," she whispered.

Standing at the edge of the forest was a creature she had never seen before. It stood about six feet tall, with curling horns that added another two feet to its height. It had four legs but used two of them to stand. The others hung almost to the ground, with wicked claws that were as long as Lainey's hand. Beady red eyes stared out of fur so black, it appeared to swallow any light coming from the moon. The growl that emanated from the mouth full of dagger-sharp teeth dried Lainey's mouth and froze her to the spot.

Phoenix turned around and cursed. "Don't move."

"Not planning on it. What the hell is that thing?"

"A mountain troll. They are vicious and bloodthirsty. You

can't outrun it, so don't even try, and your bullets will only piss it off."

The creature snorted, steam rising from its pig-like snout, and it pawed at the ground with one of its clawed legs. Before Lainey could do anything, it charged forward. She screamed and fell backward, landing hard on her ass. Instinct took over, and she raised her arms and fired off a round, her aim true despite her shaking limbs.

Phoenix was right, the bullets only served to piss the creature off. Furious, the troll set its eyes on Lainey and was upon her before she could blink. Pain like she had never felt lanced through her stomach as claws tore through skin and muscle. She distantly heard Phoenix cursing and muttering under his breath, but all her focus was on trying to crawl away from the beast.

Before another swipe of claws took her head off, fire enveloped the monster. Lainey shied away from the intensity of the flame, the heat hot enough to tighten the skin across her face. The bone chilling sound of the beast howling in pain echoed through the clearing, and the cold wind swirled the smell of burning hair around them.

Lainey collapsed onto the ground and attempted to keep her insides inside her body by wrapping one arm around her stomach while the other continued to pull her backward. Every gasp of breath sent lightning shooting through her abdomen. Tears streamed down her face at the intensity of the pain and were dried instantly in the heat from the fire.

She felt hands slide under her legs and around her back. Then she was lifted into the air, the movement making her groan. Her vision started to blur, the edges getting darker and darker. Phoenix laid her gently on the ground, a safe distance from the beastly campfire. He knelt next to her to assess her injury.

"I told you not to shoot it," he muttered as he pulled her arms away from her stomach.

Lainey whimpered and her vision checkerboarded. She caught

sight of Phoenix's hands, now smeared with her blood, and bile rose in her throat.

"Ow," was all she was able to get out. The slightest movements sent her to the edge of passing out.

"Yeah, I imagine that stings a bit." Phoenix rolled up the sleeve of his Henley and bit into his wrist using his sharpened canines. Blood welled once again, dark in the dimly lit clearing. He lifted his gaze to hers, pausing briefly with a look in his glowing eyes Lainey couldn't define. He gritted his teeth and placed his wrist over Lainey's stomach, making a fist. Drops of blood fell into her wound and fizzled.

Lightning shot through her veins, lighting up every part of body in agony. She arched her back and screamed until her voice went out and her vision went black. She welcomed the darkness greedily.

Lainey gradually rose to consciousness. First, she was aware of a dull throbbing in her belly. Then, she noticed the warmth soaking into her skin and the smell of embers and bonfire. The last thing she noticed was a gentle hand brushing her hair away from her face. That sensation she had to have imagined. There was no one left alive who would care for her like that.

Slowly, she opened her eyes and looked around. She was in the little cabin they had left their bags in before going wisp hunting. She was lying on the couch in front of the fireplace with a roaring fire burning inside, which explained the warmth and the smell. Except, she wasn't so sure. Sitting on the floor by her head was Phoenix, staring at her with wide, worried eyes.

As she looked at him, she could have sworn relief flooded his features before his mask of indifference fell back into place.

"You're awake." His voice couldn't have been more bored. However, as he stood from his spot on the floor, Lainey heard his bones popping, as if he had been sitting in the position for hours.

"How long have I been out?" She had to clear her throat, and the action made her wince. She placed her hand on her throat, expecting to find some kind of injury there. It burned like fire had been shoved down her gullet.

Phoenix went to the kitchen and brought back a glass of water. "You screamed pretty loud, your throat will probably be sore for a bit."

Lainey gratefully drank the entire glass, and when Phoenix went back to refill it, she searched her memory for what had happened. The monster, her guts falling out of her stomach, Phoenix setting the thing on fire with his magic. Her eyes popped open, and she stared at him in shock and disbelief.

"What did you do to me?" she rasped. She remembered him biting his wrist and letting his blood drip into her wound. The resulting pain was something she wasn't bound to forget anytime soon.

Phoenix handed her the glass and looked away. If she didn't know any better, she would've said he looked sheepish.

"It was the only way to save you." He rubbed the back of his neck, which was turning an alarming shade of red.

Was he actually embarrassed?

"What did you do? Do I have some weird blood disease now because of you?"

He snorted. "No. One of the ... perks ... of being born of a banshee is a type of healing magic. It's not common, and most fae frown upon it because it involves the use of blood."

"That is some serious vampire shit," Lainey muttered. She looked down at her stomach and gasped.

"Yeah, you almost died."

Lainey glanced at him again. The dry tone of his words didn't hide the shaking of his voice. She had scared him. Then again, looking at what was left of her shirt and his jacket, she was surprised she wasn't a pile of bloody ribbons.

"I'm sorry about your jacket," she offered.

He shrugged. "It's all right. I have more."

That didn't surprise her at all.

"What now?" she asked. She studiously avoided looking at him. The tension in the air had grown thicker.

"We'll wait another night for you to heal up, then we'll head back to the city and plan our museum heist."

Lainey nodded. She was feeling better, surprisingly better, but she still felt incredibly weak. Another night of rest would be a good idea. But the thought of being stuck in this little cabin with Phoenix had her feeling on edge.

She struggled to sit up. She hated feeling so weak in his presence. Lying flat on her back, incapacitated, was not a position she wanted to put herself in with him. Her arms shook embarrassingly, and her abdomen complained with every slight movement. She panted and gritted her teeth, but she was determined to sit up properly.

Phoenix jumped in immediately. He grabbed her shoulders and helped ease her to a sitting position. He then began arranging pillows behind her, fluffing and plumping them until she was sitting up comfortably. He went to grab the blanket to cover her, but stopped himself. He was acting very mother-henish, and it unnerved her.

Lainey covered herself instead and was ashamed to admit she had needed his help to sit up all the way. She never would have made it without him. And not just to the sitting position. Ugh, she absolutely hated how confused she felt about Phoenix.

She couldn't stand the way he talked to her and the way he bossed her around. She hated that she understood where he came from. She really hated that she seemed to be developing a little crush on him. She found her body's reaction to his presence annoying. The way he smelled so good and the occasional times he would look at her with something other than hostility. She wanted to smother the butterflies that took flight in her stomach when he touched her.

After a tense silence—Phoenix looking out the window and

Lainey folding and unfolding the edge of the blanket—Phoenix turned around and looked at her.

"Do you feel up for some training?" He was standing awkwardly, with his hands in the pockets of his black cargo pants. "Nothing too crazy, just trying to feel your magic, not trying to use it."

"I think so. It's worth a shot, at least." She tried to imagine what it would have been like to use magic against that beast. Things may have turned out very differently if she had.

Phoenix slowly sat at the other end of the couch. He stared at the fireplace instead of looking at her. "Try feeling for it again. Close your eyes and focus your thoughts inward. Try feeling every sensation inside your body."

She followed his directions. This time, she was able to keep her attention away from Phoenix. Maybe it was due to almost dying, but she felt the sudden need to understand her magic and how to use it.

She tuned out everything but the sensations of her body. Her breath, moving in and out of her lungs. Her heart, a steady thumping in her chest. Even the slight twinges in her abdomen with each subtle movement. She looked deeper into herself, past all of those sensations. She burrowed further and further until she felt something.

It was like the presence of something foreign in her body. An empty space that was meant to be filled. In her mind, she could imagine a small kernel of magic in her core, buried deep in that empty space and wrapped in cobwebs and dust. She imagined herself blowing the dust off and revealing her magic. She imagined reaching deep within her to the now exposed place filled with swirling magic. A sudden gust of wind blew through the cabin. She opened her eyes, and her mouth dropped open.

"Well, that's one way to do it," Phoenix said wryly as he brushed his hair back into order.

The wind had blown the fire out, and smoke curled lazily through the room in the aftermath of her magical tantrum.

Pillows and blankets were strewn about the room, and the curtains on the window had been blown aside.

"Oh, shit. I didn't mean to do that."

"It will take time to learn the control you need." Phoenix lifted a hand, and the fire burst to life in the fireplace once again. "Next time, instead of a hurricane, picture a gentle breeze."

Lainey nodded and swallowed. She rolled her shoulders and mentally prepared herself. This time, when she sunk into her own body, her magic was there, waiting. No longer a dusty seed waiting to be discovered. Now it flowed through her body, a current of air carrying her magic through her veins. It was an odd sensation, but not unwelcome. She felt more alive than she ever had.

She opened her eyes and looked at Phoenix as she imagined a gentle breeze blowing through the room. In her mind, she pictured herself cupping her hands in the magical pool in her core and drawing a tiny bit to the surface. Much to her surprise, and Phoenix's, that was exactly what happened. The flames in the fireplace flickered and bent to the wind but stayed lit. Strands of Phoenix's hair lifted and blew gently away from his face.

Phoenix gave her a strange look she couldn't interpret. "You're a quick learner."

"I have no clue how I did that. It feels natural, like an instinct I never knew I had. But I can feel my magic now."

"I can tell you've unlocked it. I can feel it too."

His eyes burned into her. They began to glow, the light brown turning to molten copper. Her breath caught in her throat.

"Do my eyes glow too?" She recalled Ash's eyes doing the same.

"Try again." His voice was lower, more intense.

Shivers worked their way down her spine at the sound. She cleared her throat and reached for her magic. She once again imagined a gentle breeze. When she looked at Phoenix again, the glow in his eyes intensified.

"Yes," he whispered. "Like swirling storm clouds." He didn't appear to notice he had leaned forward.

Come to think of it, Lainey was leaning forward too, ignoring the pain in her stomach. Her lips parted as she breathed in a shaky breath. Phoenix's eyes dropped to her mouth, and Lainey's core heated instantly. All thoughts of not liking the fae before her were wiped from her mind as Phoenix leaned in a little closer. The only thought she had was that she wanted his lips on hers.

Phoenix paused with less than an inch of space between them. His campfire scent surrounded her, and she could feel the warmth rolling off of him in waves. It relaxed her even further, and she found she wanted to bask in that warmth. He was so close, all she had to do was tip her head forward an inch and their lips would meet.

Phoenix closed the distance as if he could hear her thoughts. His mouth brushed hers gently, a whisper-soft caress that shot lightning through her veins once again. Only, this lightning didn't hurt. It ignited her blood. His lips were soft and firm against hers, and she wanted more.

Before they could go further, Phoenix's phone rang. He jumped up from the couch with a curse and shook himself violently before putting the phone to his ear.

"What? No, we'll be here until tomorrow, Lainey was gutted by a mountain troll. Yeah, she's fine. Yeah, we got the essence. No, I'm not being short with you. Uh-huh. Whatever." He put his phone in his pocket and walked out the front door, leaving Lainey panting and confused on the couch.

She touched her lips. She was still burning from the inside, desire warring with reality. Why was she surprised he had stormed out? And why did she care? As the fire in her veins cooled, a different fire began to burn in her, humiliation and determination. She wasn't sure why she felt that pull to him, but she was going to fight it. She wouldn't put herself in this position a third time. Never again.

CHAPTER NINE

THE RIDE HOME WAS EVEN MORE AWKWARD THAN THE ride to the mountains. They'd had plenty of awkward situations in their short time together, but this one was the cherry on top. Phoenix had stayed outside long into the night. When he finally came in, Lainey was already asleep on the couch. When she woke, he was packing their bags into the car. Neither brought up the kiss.

Lainey stared out the window the entire drive home. She kept repeating her new mantra to herself: Never again. Never again. Never again. Phoenix was content to sit in silence as well. The few times Lainey peeked at him from the corner of her eye, his jaw was so tight she thought it might snap.

When they reached the apartment, Ash was waiting for them with a grin.

"She lives!" He reached for her as if to pull her in for a hug but stopped at the last minute. He glanced at Phoenix and instantly pulled back. His eyes bounced between her and Phoenix, trying to assess what was different between them.

"You got the feather, I'm assuming?" Phoenix asked, interrupting Ash's pondering.

"Yep. Piece of cake." He grabbed a white feather off the

counter and twirled it between his fingers. "I take it that your escapade was not as easy?"

Phoenix grunted and plopped onto the couch. "That's an understatement. I didn't even think about how my blood would draw other creatures."

"You used your blood in the mixture instead of Lainey's?" The incredulity in Ash's voice peaked Lainey's interest.

"Yeah, a mistake I won't make again." Phoenix's words were barely audible as he rubbed his face with both hands.

"Lesson learned. Don't dwell on it."

Phoenix lifted his gaze to Ash. "Stop doing that."

"Doing what? Keeping you from falling off that ledge again? I'll do whatever the hell is needed to keep you out of that place, Nix."

Phoenix shrugged his shoulders uncomfortably, as if he was trying to shake off Ash's words. He stood in a rush and headed for the back rooms. "I'm going to shower. Tonight, we start planning our heist."

Lainey, who had remained standing in the kitchen, finally looked at Ash.

"What?" she asked when he just stared at her.

"What happened up there?"

"Nothing." Everything. "We got the essence. That thing attacked me. Phoenix saved me. Here we are." She shrugged and turned to the fridge. She wanted alcohol, but she would not make that mistake again either.

"How did he save you? Mountain trolls are brutal. Most people don't survive an attack."

Lainey ignored his question and continued her perusal of the fridge. She wasn't really looking for anything in particular, just trying to keep Ash off her back.

A large hand shot over her shoulder and slammed the fridge shut in her face. Lainey whirled around with a few choice words on the tip of her tongue that withered to dust as she saw his face.

Ash was always joking around, a glint in his eye and smirk on his lips. Now, he was deadly serious.

"Don't make me ask you again. How did Nix save you?" He leaned in, one hand still pressed to the fridge door.

Lainey averted her gaze and leaned back against the cool metal with her arms crossed over her chest. "He dribbled his blood in my wound," she mumbled, barely audible.

Ash pushed off the fridge violently, vile curses falling from his mouth as he walked away. He made it to the windows, then whirled around, piercing Lainey with his glare.

"Whoa, hold up!" She shouted, throwing her hands up. "You can't blame me for what he did. I didn't ask him to save me, he made that choice on his own! And last I checked, he is an adult and able to make his own decisions."

The growl that escaped from Ash took her aback. She opened her mouth to continue her tirade, pissed off that she was getting blamed for something she didn't really understand in the first place. Ash beat her to it.

"Do you understand what happened up there? Do you even know what any of that means?" He prowled toward her and didn't give her a chance to respond. "You know nothing about his life. I have been with him from the start. I watched him fall into hell, and it took me *years* to get him out. What happened up there? That pushed him to the edge. All it will take is a nudge to send him right back where he started." Ash lost steam, his words falling short, but his eyes still glowed their unearthly green. "What I told him is true. I will do anything to keep him from falling off that ledge again."

Lainey's anger cooled a little at his words. He was right. She knew nothing about Phoenix or his life. She knew nothing about what it meant to be fae or have magic. She was walking blindly through life, waiting for something to happen. Waiting to make a mistake that would ruin it all. But that wasn't her fault.

"You're right. I don't know him or what he has been through. But I stand by what I said. He made that choice. My getting injured was partly his fault. I'm fumbling my way through this. I know nothing. You guys have told me the bare minimum of what I need to know. Had I known his blood would have attracted other creatures, I could have said something. Maybe we could have prevented it." Lainey let her breath out in a rush, feeling suddenly exhausted. She slid to the floor and thumped her head back against the fridge.

Ash joined her on the floor, his sigh deflating his large body as the fight went out of him as well. "You're right," he admitted. "I'm sorry. I shouldn't have gotten mad at you. I'm just worried about him, and I took it out on you. That wasn't fair." He rubbed his hands over his face before he let his head fall back against the cabinet with a thunk. "We probably haven't been as open as we should have been. Part of that is because Nix doesn't trust people easily. That's no excuse, and we will do better at keeping you informed from here on out."

Lainey nodded absently. "Then how about you start with telling me what it means that Phoenix healed me with his blood." It wasn't a question. It was a test. Was he going to follow through with his promise of keeping her more informed?

Ash hesitated, his gaze drifting in the direction Phoenix had gone. They could still hear the shower going in Phoenix's room, so they had time.

Taking a deep breath, Ash began. "Because there haven't been any known children born of a banshee, Phoenix's abilities are his alone, and vastly different from other fae. Most fae have increased healing. Half-breeds sometimes do and sometimes don't. Nix, on the other hand, can use his blood to heal others. He can also heal himself at a quicker rate than normal fae."

Lainey thought back to how he had licked his wrist after making the drug for the wisps. It had completely healed his cut. She nodded for Ash to continue.

"Unfortunately, his blood also has properties similar to a banshee's magic."

"Which are?"

"Banshees use their magic to lure men into their cave. It's like a drug, or an aphrodisiac. It's almost impossible to fight off. Once in the caves, the banshee kills for sport, using the male's blood for sustenance."

A sinking feeling grew in her stomach. Suddenly glad she hadn't eaten anything recently, Lainey stared at Ash. "What are you saying?"

"Nix's blood is like that. One taste or one drop in your system, and it will work on you like a banshee's magic does on males."

Lainey's breath left her in a whoosh. "Are you saying I'm going to be forced to lust after Phoenix like a dog in heat? All because he used his blood to save me?"

"Well, that's one way to describe it." The wry tone to Ash's voice pissed Lainey off.

"This is funny to you, isn't it? You get to sit back and watch what happens like a bad soap opera." Lainey pushed off the floor and began pacing around the kitchen. "How do I fix it?"

"You don't."

She whirled on him, pointing a finger in his face. "What do you mean, 'I don't'?"

"There is nothing you can do. Try to fight it, I guess. If you want."

"If I want? What the hell does that mean? You think I want to lust after him like some simpering hussy?" Lainey realized she was screaming but she couldn't control herself.

This was too much. Too soon. She felt like she couldn't catch a break. All her life, she'd felt like she was running. Running toward something that didn't exist, running away from a life that, unfortunately, did exist. She felt like she could never stop running. Things moved around her too fast, and no matter how hard she ran, she couldn't keep up.

She was too young to remember her dad or the immediate impact his leaving had had on their lives. The long-term impact was felt years later. She had tried to outrun her mom's mental health issues, she had tried to keep up with everything she needed to do to help. She had failed at both. Her mom had still taken her own life, leaving her daughters to fend for themselves.

Then Emma. God, she had done everything she could to make life easier on Emma, and she had failed her too. Her sister had resented her at the end, and that thought had been plaguing her since their fight. Now she was also gone, leaving Lainey alone in the world.

Everyone who had ever mattered to her left her. Willingly or not. By their own hand or someone else's. It was too much for her to even comprehend. What had she done to deserve that? What could she have done differently to keep the people she loved with her?

And now? She had been thrown into a whole new world. A world where fairytales existed, and she had to navigate it alone. Sure, she had Ash and Phoenix, but the other night proved just how much she couldn't rely on them. She had been attacked and almost died. The only way to save her had been to tie her to her savior in a way she didn't want.

Had she ever had any control over her life? Everyone else's decisions had impacted her and prevented her from being able to make her own. She didn't want to lust after Phoenix like a hussy. She wasn't sure she would be able to fight it. She had had no control in that cabin. She wouldn't have been able to stop that kiss if her life depended on it.

She didn't realize she had been crying until a sob worked its way up her throat. She covered her mouth to muffle the sound, but it was pointless. She fell to the floor, the tile cool on her knees. She curled around herself, making herself as small as possible. Maybe if they couldn't see her, whoever controlled her fate would forget about her for a moment.

Her body was wracked with sobs, and tears fell relentlessly down her cheeks, staining her shirt. She barely registered the strong arms around her. The comforting scent of earth surrounded her and helped to ground her. Ash ran his big palm up and down her back, gently rocking her back and forth on the kitchen floor.

"I'm so sorry," he murmured. "I keep forgetting this is all so new to you. I can't imagine how overwhelming it all is."

He kept up his gentle tirade, speaking nonsense words. The bass of his voice vibrated against her and helped to calm her further. After a last sniffle, she looked up. Her eyes met with Phoenix's, who was standing just outside the hallway, a look on his face she couldn't decipher. Before anyone could say anything, he turned on his heel and returned to his room.

"You okay now?" Ash asked.

"Yeah." She wiped at her face, attempting to dry the stream of tears on her cheeks. "Thanks."

Ash stood and gave her his hand, helping her to her feet. "Sit down. I'll get you something to eat and drink."

She nodded and sat on the couch, fiddling with a pillow in her lap. She was so embarrassed. She never broke down like that. The stress of everything must have been getting to her.

"I'm sorry about the waterworks," she muttered.

"Don't apologize." Ash handed her a plate with a candy bar, donut, and muffin.

She raised an eyebrow in question at the spread.

"Don't judge. I don't cook."

"Clearly," she snorted. She glanced at the hallway before lowering her voice and asking, "What can I do to help him? I don't want to do something that pushes him over the edge. What does that even mean?"

Ash glanced down the hall as well and cleared his throat, clearly uncomfortable talking about this with her. "With everything he has dealt with in life, he struggles a bit with depression. Something happened last time, and he ... I don't know how to describe it ... lost himself. He stopped eating, he drank too much, he slept around. He was like a shell of himself."

Ash sighed and glanced down the hall again. His face was drawn, and shadows haunted his eyes. "I know it will be hard, with the whole blood bond thing, but try to respect his wishes. I don't think he really wants the blood bond, but I can't be sure. Just try to not push him on it. And don't ask why, it's not my place, and I won't tell you. And don't ask him, that will definitely be more than the nudge needed to send him over."

Apparently, that was where Ash drew the line on his promise of keeping Lainey informed. She nodded and took a bite of donut. Don't push the bond on him? She would do everything she could to not do that. She definitely didn't want to be chasing him around, begging him for attention she didn't want and that he didn't want to give her. What a mess.

It was another thirty minutes of silence, with Ash staring out the windows and Lainey eating her dinner of champions, before Phoenix returned. He didn't look at her or Ash, just sat in a chair and folded his arms across his chest.

"We need to figure out how to get the amulet."

Chapter Ten

They spent the night planning for their museum heist. Ash's gaze kept bouncing between Lainey and Phoenix. She had no idea what Phoenix was doing because she refused to look at him. Instead, she fiddled with her phone, using it to distract her from the fae sitting across from her. She sent Alex a message, breaking things off with him. Not very mature, but she really didn't care at the moment.

So far, she was doing good with not lusting after Phoenix. She felt no pull toward him besides her eyes, which she found fairly easy to combat. It got harder when they were closer in proximity to each other. She fought that by keeping a healthy distance from him. He did the same.

By the end of the night, her eyes were grainy and blurry, and her mind was exhausted. Ash was true to his word. As they planned, he kept her fully informed of all the magical aspects of their plan and what they meant. She provided ideas and feedback accordingly. It gave her a sense of satisfaction that she was part of something and able to contribute.

Their plan was simple in all actuality. Phoenix would get the necklace out of the display with his fire magic. While he did that, Lainey would have to stay away from him to avoid the distraction of wanting him. Instead, she would break into the security office and monitor the cameras, making sure Phoenix had a clear shot at the amulet. Ash's job was to create a diversion for the night guards, to get them out of the security office and keep them out.

The hard part was getting into the museum in the first place. This was also where Ash came in handy. He would use his magic to get a rat to chew the cable to the cameras outside and leading to the office, leaving them a clear path to get in.

Lainey fought with her eyeballs, trying to keep them open. She was losing the battle quickly.

"Why don't you go to bed, Lainey," Ash offered. "We've pretty much got this figured out. I'm going to hack into some databases to get the floor plan and layout of the camera and security systems, but I don't need you for that."

"I am exhausted."

"You're still healing, it's to be expected."

"Okay. Well. Goodnight, then." She let her gaze wander to Phoenix.

Their eyes met, and a shock of electricity passed between them. It was like the first time she'd seen his eyes when he was standing outside her apartment. She couldn't have torn her eyes away from his even if she had wanted to. And she didn't want to, not this time.

As they stared at each other, his eyes flashed molten copper, as if his whole body was heating and his magic was stirring inside him. She felt the temperature rising between them, then suddenly, a cool breeze cut through the room, lifting her hair from her shoulders. Her magic, mixing with his.

Nothing else existed. The tension crackled and snapped between them. Phoenix took one step toward her, and her body instantly reacted. Her heart thundered in her chest, and her breath came in quick bursts. Butterflies took flight in her stomach at the thought of Phoenix coming nearer. She craved the feel of his heat and magic surrounding her. She began to ache, and her core heated, wanting him desperately.

A throat cleared, penetrating the tension building around them. Awareness snapped so hard into Lainey, she stumbled backward. She gasped and placed a hand on her chest. Phoenix's eyes were wide, and his mouth was slightly parted. She quickly averted her gaze to prevent that from happening again.

She swallowed thickly. "Shit. I'm sorry. I'm going now." She stumbled out of the living room and into her appointed room. "Fuuuck," she whispered to herself in the darkness that welcomed her.

She had been doing so well at keeping her body under control. But one glance at Phoenix's eyes, and it was as if her body wasn't hers to control anymore. She began trembling. Her body fluttered like a leaf in the aftermath.

As the fog of lust began to dissipate, her anger rose. She felt profoundly violated by something she had no control over. It pissed her off that her body, the one thing that belonged solely to her, was not hers to command when Phoenix was around. She would have to make sure she and Phoenix were never alone together.

Gathering her strength, Lainey walked to the attached bathroom and turned on the shower. As soon as the temperature was as hot as the sun, she shed her clothes and stepped inside. The first thought she had was of the way the heat swirling through the shower felt different than Phoenix's.

This was humid and sticky. Phoenix's heat was dry and comforting. A fire on a cold, snowy night. She shook her head, trying to clear her thoughts. It didn't work. Her breathing increased and her mind began to wander.

What would have happened if Ash hadn't been there? She played out a possible scene in her head. She imagined Phoenix approaching her, his gait a slow, predatory prowl. With each step, the temperature around her would rise, his magic simmering the air around them. She imagined his hands encircling her waist and pulling her against him. She could practically feel the hard planes of his body against hers.

And his lips, when they met hers, would be soft yet unyielding. She imagined his kiss would be demanding. A claiming. She gasped suddenly as she realized where her hand had traveled. Her core was wet and waiting for Phoenix.

Lainey shouted in frustration and banged her hand on the shower wall. She had no idea how to stop this. She didn't want it. How was this fair?

Fighting back the tears that were once again threatening to fall, Lainey turned the shower off and wrapped a towel around herself. She climbed into bed, wet hair and all, and tried to find sleep. It was a long time coming, but eventually her eyes closed, and her mind turned off.

Lainey woke groggy and irritated, having not slept well. Dreams of Phoenix plagued her sleep, and even after taking care of business herself, she was still left feeling unfulfilled and needy.

She checked the clock and was shocked to see she had slept almost all day. They would be leaving for the Met soon. Luckily, the clothes she had grabbed from her place a few days ago were all black. She dressed in a pair of leggings, tunic, leather jacket, and her favorite ankle booties.

In desperate need of coffee, she headed for the kitchen. Unfortunately, the kitchen wasn't empty. Ash sat at the bar, nursing his own cup of coffee. He smirked at her as she entered, and Lainey's irritation grew even further. She said nothing, just headed for the coffee pot and poured herself a cup, adding cream and one sugar—just how she liked it. She debated adding some whiskey but decided against it. Of course, as she made to sit next to Ash, he just had to taunt her.

"You're looking a little worse for the wear."

Better yet, whiskey was a splendid idea. She turned back to the counter and pulled the bottle out of the cabinet, adding a healthy dose. Ash's chuckle made her want to punch him. She growled and spun around, propping a hip on the counter. Lainey leveled a look at him, daring him to say more. He wisely kept his mouth shut.

Just then, Phoenix entered the kitchen. Lainey groaned inwardly. Why couldn't he stay in his room just a little longer? Phoenix's gaze traveled down her body and back up, eyes briefly flaring copper before he looked away. Deciding that banging her head against the wall was a bad idea, she spun back to the alcohol and added even more whiskey to her coffee. Ash muttered something behind her she chose not to hear.

Phoenix cleared his throat. "Does everyone remember the plan?"

Ash nodded, and Lainey grunted. Phoenix raised a brow at her response but said nothing, luckily. She stared into her coffee, now more alcohol than caffeine, and listened to Phoenix go over the plan again anyway.

God, his voice was sexy. It penetrated her bones, making her shiver as she let the deep baritone notes float around her. Her magic surged in her veins, a gale of wind rising fast. She squeezed her eyes shut and forced it back, determined to not throw another magical tantrum. She was so focused on keeping her magic under wraps, she didn't notice when Phoenix asked her a question.

"Lainey?" Her name on his lips was almost too much for her to handle.

She swallowed thickly before responding, keeping her eyes squeezed shut. "Yeah?"

There was pause before he continued. "Are you sure you're ready to do this? If you're not, don't feel like you have to."

"I'm good," she gasped. "I can do it." She kept repeating that to herself, focusing on the words in her head rather than on Phoenix standing across the room.

She brought her cup to her nose and inhaled, flooding herself with the scents of whiskey and coffee, washing away the scents of smoke and fire. It helped. Her heart calmed, and her muscles relaxed. Her mind slowly cleared, and she was able to open her eyes. She avoided Phoenix like the plague and instead eyed Ash.

"When do we leave?" she asked.

Ash checked his watch. "Ten minutes. By the time we get there, the guards should be posted in the security office, ready to be distracted by moi."

Ten minutes. Nerves fluttered to life in her stomach. She had never done something like this before. If they were caught, they would be in major trouble. Breaking and entering into a major New York City museum, not to mention stealing priceless jewelry. She had to let herself trust these two guys. She knew they were more than capable of pulling this off, she just hoped she wasn't the reason they ended up getting caught.

The night was dark. Thick clouds had moved in, hiding any illumination the moon might have offered. The wind had picked up too, and Lainey huddled in her jacket and rubbed her hands together. She fiddled with the earpiece in her ear again, making sure it was secure.

"Can everyone hear me?" Phoenix's voice came through the earpiece, and her blood heated at the sound, despite the tinny quality to it.

"Good here," Ash muttered into the microphone clipped to his jacket.

"Yes," Lainey answered quietly into hers.

"Okay. Ash, you're on."

Lainey watched as Ash closed his eyes. She felt a pulse of energy from him and caught the scent of green grass and earthy dirt. She barely avoided screeching in fear as two enormous rats appeared in front of them.

They stood in front of Ash, looking up expectantly like they were listening to instructions. She supposed they were. Then they took off toward the building, naked tails swishing behind them.

Lainey shuddered at the sight, lip curling in disgust. Phoenix chuckled, and her gaze shot to him.

"Not a fan of rats?" he whispered.

Big mistake. She shouldn't have looked at him. Once her eyes landed on him, she couldn't look away. Locked in the moment again, all she could do was stare. He had pulled his hair into a man bun, the shaved sides displayed. His eyes glowed in the darkness as he watched her. He looked amazing in his black leather jacket, his broad shoulders looking even wider in the darkness somehow.

"We're good," Ash said as he opened his eyes.

The spell between her and Phoenix broke. They refocused on the mission before them. Phoenix took a deep breath, then pushed open the door. Lainey waited, holding her own breath, for the screech of the alarm. Nothing but silence. All three of them exhaled and swiftly entered the building.

They slunk down the narrow hall and stopped before another door.

"This will lead to the Great Hall. Lainey and I will go first. When we get to the security office, we'll let you know if it's clear for you to enter," Ash said to Phoenix.

Lainey followed Ash back the way they had come to a door they'd passed in the narrow hallway. They found a small set of stairs and took them to the basement. At the landing, Ash stopped and motioned for Lainey to wait. She pressed herself against the wall and tried to calm her beating heart. Focusing on her breathing, she inhaled and exhaled slowly until she felt slightly calmer.

She tensed when she heard shouting, followed closely by pounding footsteps. A few minutes later, Ash's voice crackled in her ear.

"Clear for Lainey."

Taking one more calming breath, she rounded the corner and headed to the office. The door was open, the soft glow of multiple screens spilling into the hallway. She slipped inside and closed the door, locking it behind her.

"I'm in." She sat in the chair and scanned the monitors. A few were dark, the cords having been chewed by the rats, although what the guards thought about the cameras going dark she had no idea. They obviously hadn't been too concerned until Ash made himself known.

She found the screens she was looking for and confirmed all was clear. "You're good to go, Phoenix."

Lainey watched as Phoenix appeared on one of the monitors and quickly made his way to the amulet. She kept her eyes scanning all the screens, ensuring no one snuck up on them. She had no clue where Ash had led the guards, but she didn't see him on any of the cameras. A sudden thought popped into her head, something they hadn't talked about.

"Do they record everything on the cameras? Won't they look back at the videos when they notice the amulet is gone?"

"Fuck," Phoenix cursed after a beat of silence. "Why didn't we think of that? I'll have to take care of that too."

Phoenix approached the amulet and tugged off his gloves. He raised his hands and they began to glow. No, not glow. Lainey squinted at the screen. They were wreathed in flame, but not the typical fire she associated with him. It was like the flame was tightly compressed against his hands, making them burn an unearthly red.

He slowly pressed his hands to the glass case surrounding the amulet, and Lainey watched in awe as the glass melted under his palms. It dripped down the marble plinth and puddled on the floor. Phoenix grabbed the amulet and shoved it into his pocket before slipping his gloves back on.

"Still clear?" He looked directly at the camera, and even through the monitor, she felt the buzz of electricity pass between them.

She quickly scanned the other screens before replying. "Yeah, still good."

"I'm going to make my way to you. I'll take care of the video, and then we head out. Ash, you still good?"

Ash's voice came through, slightly breathless, but the deranged joy couldn't be denied. "Doing great."

Lainey unlocked the door to the security office to let Phoenix in. He took her seat, wheeled it over to the computer, and began clicking, moving through screens so fast, Lainey could barely keep up.

"Where did you guys learn to do all of this?"

"Life gets a little boring when you're not human living in the human world," Phoenix answered distractedly. "Instead of video games and bars, we learned how to be deviants." He turned around and gave Lainey a wicked grin.

Her breath caught in her throat, and she had to force her gaze away. Motion on one of the monitors caught her eye. She leaned in and cursed.

"The guards are coming back."

"Shit, I lost them!" Ash said at the same time.

"Done." Phoenix stood and grabbed Lainey's arm, dragging her out of the office.

They reached the stairwell just as the sound of feet pounding on the stairs echoed through the space. Phoenix stopped so fast, she bumped into his back. He cursed and turned around, pulling her back down the hallway.

"There has to be another set of stairs somewhere," he muttered as his head swiveled around, searching the cramped space. "Ash, we need a backup stairwell. Now!"

Thank god for Ash. He'd studied all the blueprints of the Met he'd been able to get his hands on, and he did not let them down. "End of the hallway, door on the left. It will lead you to an exit behind the building. I'll meet you guys outside."

Phoenix pulled Lainey in front of him and pushed her forward. "Go!" He stopped briefly and turned around. She didn't know what he was doing, but she felt his magic rise to the surface. The air crackled like embers, and the scent of smoke permeated the hallway.

"That won't last long. Move." He prodded her faster.

"I am moving, stop pushing me!"

"You really want to argue right now?"

"I'll argue whenever I feel like it. Now, shut up." She reached the door and shoved through it. She pushed her legs faster as she ran up the steps, her breath sawing in and out of her chest. At the top of the stairs was a heavy metal door. She shouldered it open and ran out into the cold autumn air, Phoenix close on her heels.

"Where are we going?" she gasped, trying to get enough air into her lungs.

He pushed past her and started running down a side street. She followed, her lungs almost bursting from the need to breathe. A stitch had formed in her side, and she grabbed it in an attempt to ease the pain. Phoenix rounded another corner ahead of her. She made to pick up her pace, but searing pain exploded in her back.

A scream tore from her throat as she collapsed to the ground. She tried to push herself up, but her arms buckled. Her body suddenly felt as if it weighed a thousand pounds and was made of sand. More pain, this time the back of her head. A hand fisted in her hair and dragged her to her feet. She managed to lift her arms, to grab the hands holding her up, but that was all she could do.

Phoenix skidded back around the corner, a dagger in his hand. As his eyes widened, Lainey realized she had never seen Phoenix scared before. He was now. He panted and adjusted his grip on the dagger, widening his stance.

"Let her go." His words were barely understandable through the growl vibrating out of his chest.

Dark laughter from behind her gave Lainey an idea of who was holding her captive.

"Hello, brother. It is a pleasure to see you."

Chapter Eleven

Beck's voice was low and menacing.

He tightened his grip on her hair, and the pain almost eclipsed the burning she felt in her shoulder. Wetness slid down her back, and Lainey knew she was bleeding quite a bit. She couldn't manage anything more than small gasps. Every breath she took sent fire racing through her upper back.

Phoenix's eyes glowed copper as he took in the scene before him. Lainey could almost see his fury coming off of him in waves. She could feel his magic as it swirled around him, a violent tempest of fire and brimstone, ready to be released at her captor.

"Let her go," he growled.

Beck chuckled. "If only it were that easy." He angled her head using her hair, and she whimpered at the pain prickling her scalp. His gaze roved over her face. "She is lovely, isn't she?"

Another growl from Phoenix.

"I may be interested in a trade," Beck continued. His free hand began roaming around Lainey's body, sliding up and down her stomach, her breasts, her thighs. "You give me the amulet, and I'll return your half-breed."

Phoenix took a step closer, body tense and prepared to strike. Sharp pain in her shoulder made Lainey buck and thrash in Beck's grip. He pressed a finger into the wound on her back, twisting it back and forth. Lightning lashed out from the wound, searing through her body. Her vision turned white, and she screamed so loud she thought her throat would bleed.

"Uh-uh-uh," Beck crooned. "I wouldn't come any closer.

The air around them heated dangerously, Phoenix's anger coming to life as he reluctantly stopped. His gaze was focused intensely on Lainey, never wavering. He slowly reached into his pocket, pulling out the amulet.

"No!" she tried to shout, but her voice was hoarse. It came out more like a croak. He couldn't give up the amulet. It was their only way of breaking the curse without her death. Of course, that wouldn't matter if Beck didn't release her.

Phoenix's gaze never left hers as he tossed the amulet to Beck. Her captor caught the chain, the pendant swinging wildly back and forth. Lainey choked back a gasp as the hold on her hair tightened further.

Beck walked backward, dragging her with him. She had no choice but to follow or else risk her scalp ripping free from her head.

"Release her!" Phoenix shouted, stepping forward again. "You said you would let her go if I gave you the amulet."

Beck laughed again, the sound snaking its way down her spine and chilling her to the bone. He was deranged.

"I never said I would return her alive."

His arm banded around her middle, squeezing tightly as he continued walking backward. The fist holding her hair released but then reappeared at her throat, a knife's edge digging sharply into her skin.

"No closer, brother. I mean it. I'm taking her and the amulet. If you follow me, it will only be a slower, more painful death for her." At his words, the knife bit deeper into her neck, splitting the skin. The wet warmth of her blood flowed down her neck and under the collar of her shirt.

Phoenix froze again, eyes glued to the dagger at her neck. A muscle ticked in his jaw as he lifted his gaze to his brother. His eyes were positively glowing. The molten swirl of copper stunned her in its intensity. A pulse of his power flicked over her skin, his wrath releasing the leash he usually held on his magic. The warmth of his flames was a comfort to her, despite the knife at her throat.

"This will be the last mistake you ever make," Phoenix spoke quietly, all the more powerful in the hushed silence around them.

"Doubtful." Beck began walking backward again.

Lainey pleaded with Phoenix with her eyes. She begged him to do something, anything, to save her, to not let Beck take her. She didn't want to end up like her sister. A single tear dropped from one eye and slid down her cheek. Phoenix watched the tear with pure fury burning in his molten eyes.

"Don't do this, Beck," Phoenix growled. He risked one more step, and the air heated even more.

Phoenix stumbled to a stop as vines shot from the concrete under him, wrapping around his legs and snaring him to the spot, Beck's magic effectively stopping Phoenix's approach.

Beck used Phoenix's moment of disorientation to throw Lainey over his shoulder. The movement caused her back to scream in agony. The pain was so sharp, blackness swirled on the edges of her vision. She fought the urge to let the darkness claim her. A small part of her mind was yelling to keep fighting, to try to get away. Her limbs wouldn't obey, though. They felt like lead weights, dangling uselessly as Beck ran, farther from Phoenix and safety.

A small voice in the back of her head reminded her she had magic. Lainey reached for it, just like she had when practicing with Phoenix, but it slipped through her fingers. She could feel it flowing through her veins, but she couldn't get ahold of it. She tried again and again, to no avail.

The sidewalk blurred, and she tried to focus, tried to pay attention to where Beck was taking her, but the pain eclipsed all rational thought. She heard a car door open, and then she was thrown into a backseat. The pressure of landing on her injured shoulder shorted out her senses. Pain overrode everything, and she slipped into unconsciousness.

Lainey was jerked awake when Beck pulled her from the car. She groaned, and again tried to get her limbs to work. If she could fight him off, maybe she could escape. Despite how hard she tried, it was as if her arms and legs were no longer part of her body. She tried to think through the fog in her brain. Her shoulder was burning. Whatever kind of injury she'd sustained was still bleeding. She could feel the blood dripping down her back.

As Beck dragged her from the car, she lifted her head enough to scan her surroundings. Beck had parked the car on the side of the street. It was late enough that there weren't many people out, and the ones that were looked the opposite direction as Beck carried her into a park. Her heart froze as she realized it was the northern portion of Central Park. The same area where her sister's body had been found.

"No. Please, don't do this." Her words slurred together, as if she had been drinking all night. She renewed her fighting, which only aggravated the wound on her shoulder.

Beck jostled her, causing her to hiss from the pain. "Stop fighting. You won't win."

He carried her through the park, and Lainey frantically searched for someone to help. She tried to scream, but her voice was too hoarse and her mind too sluggish. This was it. She was going to die. The same way Emma had. The same horrible, terrifying ending. Would it hurt? Or would it be quick? She hoped quick, and not just for her sake. She didn't want to think about how Emma had suffered.

Beck's steps slowed as he approached a massive tree in the wooded area of the park. The trunk was wide, the branches rising tall overhead and spreading far out from the trunk. Orange leaves clung to the branches, shivering in the wind trying to rip them free. A few floated down, lazily twirling until they joined their brethren on the ground.

Beck dropped Lainey at the base of the tree, and she momentarily blacked out. She had never experienced this kind of physical pain before. When she opened her eyes, Beck was kneeling in front of her. A knife rested on his knee, and Lainey swallowed. Beck pulled something from his pocket and sprinkled it on the ground around Lainey before hauling her to a sitting position by her hair.

The pain barely registered on her scalp. Her shoulder hurt so badly, she almost welcomed her impending death.

"Thank you for your sacrifice," Beck said quietly. He almost sounded sincere.

Lainey watched, frozen, as Beck lifted the knife and placed it against her throat. She felt the sting as the blade reopened the initial slice he had given her. Instinct took over, and she tried to jerk back, but he held her hair too tightly. He pushed harder, and the sting increased. Warmth spread down her neck, and Lainey gasped.

Beck let her go. She collapsed to the ground, hands going to her throat. She couldn't feel much, just the blood pulsing from the slice across her neck. She tried to hold the blood in, her hands slipping in the warm liquid. At least she still didn't feel any pain. Her limbs grew heavier; her vision darkened. She fought to remain awake, fought for every last breath she forced into her lungs.

It was cold, so cold. Like it had gone from autumn to winter in seconds. She vaguely felt her hands fall from her throat, felt her legs twitching in the leaves on the ground. She could see nothing; her eyes had gone dark. Not the branches overhead or the moon hidden behind the clouds. She wished she could see the stars one last time, not that they would be very visible in the city.

A feeling of immense peace settled over her. The darkness was welcoming, beckoning her away from her mortal life. A stray thought filtered through, something telling her to keep fighting, but it passed almost instantly. Lainey let herself relax as her thoughts turned to her mom and sister. Would she see them again? She reached out to the darkness, waiting for its sweet embrace.

Through the silence around her, inside her, she heard distant sounds. Crunching leaves, men grunting, shouting. She barely felt a feather-soft caress on her forehead, and she could have sworn she heard Phoenix's voice begging her to stay with him as the final darkness swept in and claimed her.

"What the hell were you thinking, Nix?"

Lainey woke to the sound of hushed male voices. Anger was thick in the air. She could feel it prickling against her skin. If this was death, it didn't seem very enjoyable. Where were the peaceful feelings? The weightlessness and relief she'd expected? She sank deeper into the mattress in an attempt to escape the uncomfortable feelings in the air surrounding her.

Her breath hitched in her chest. She was lying on a mattress. She could feel her body. Was she not dead?

"I couldn't let her die, Ash. I had to do something."

"There were other things to try before giving her more of your blood."

She froze, her whole body stopped—her heart, her breathing, even the blood in her veins ceased flowing—at Ash's words. Phoenix gave her more of his blood? Fear spiraled through her body.

"Do you even know what will happen now? Have you ever given someone blood twice?"

"No." Phoenix's whispered reply was uncertain.

"No, you don't know what will happen? Or no, you have never given someone blood twice?"

"No to both," Phoenix snapped. "Don't lecture me, Ash. I'm

not in the mood to hear it, and it won't change anything. I did it. It's over. Done. There is nothing to be done about it now."

Lainey heard Ash's muttered cursing as he stalked out of the room. She opened her eyes, squinting at the bright sun shining through the windows. Phoenix was sitting in a chair he'd brought in from the living room. His elbows rested on his knees, and he cradled his face in his hands, rubbing his eyes.

"You gave me more of your blood?" she whispered.

Lainey watched him take a deep breath before he lowered his hands and looked at her. She stifled a gasp. His eyes looked haunted, as if he had seen something he could never erase.

"How are you feeling?" he asked after a tense beat of silence.

"Don't avoid my question. You gave me more of your blood." She didn't phrase it as a question this time.

Phoenix briefly closed his eyes. "Yes. I did."

Lainey didn't know what to do or say. She wasn't sure what it meant or how it would affect her. She wasn't sure how to feel about him doing that again without her permission. Her hand drifted to her throat, expecting to feel a scar from Beck's knife. Her fingers met smooth, unblemished skin. She swallowed and felt no pain.

Lainey struggled to sit up in the bed, and this time, Phoenix just watched her with a wary expression.

Deciding to deal with the blood thing later, she asked, "What happened?"

He stood and walked to the window, peering out over the city below them. "Beck almost killed you." His words were quiet but harsh. His back was tense, the muscles straining through his gray tee. "I don't know how we made it to you in time. I have never run so fast in my life. You were lying on the ground in a pool of blood, your throat split open." Phoenix shuddered and turned from the window. The haunted look in his eyes remained.

"But I wasn't dead yet? I mean, you can't bring someone back from the dead, can you?" With his abilities, and being born of a banshee, who knew what he was capable of?

"You weren't dead yet, but you were close. Even after giving you my blood, I wasn't sure you would make it."

Lainey shivered and swallowed. She wasn't sure how to handle this information. She asked the next question to pop in her head—anything to change the topic of her almost-death. "What about Beck?"

The haunted look disappeared from his eyes, replaced with a feral kind of anger that made his eyes burn. "Ash took him on while I was healing you. As soon as I finished, he fled. We got the amulet back, but Beck is still out there." His hands clenched into fists at his sides, and his arms trembled with restrained rage.

Fear trickled through her. The man who almost killed her was still alive. He was still out there hunting her. She felt her lungs constrict and she couldn't seem to get enough oxygen. The room tilted first one way, then the other. She grasped the sheets tightly in her fists. Before she had almost died, it hadn't seemed real. The threat hadn't really scared her. Now, it was completely different. She had felt her life ebb away. She had welcomed the darkness. That wasn't something she would ever forget.

Phoenix must have noticed the change in her breathing, because one moment he was fuming by the window, and the next he was sitting on the edge of the bed with his hand on her back, rubbing gentle circles.

"Breathe, Lainey," he said quietly. "I won't let him get his hands on you. That won't happen again. I promise you that."

"How can you promise that?" she gasped.

Determination flared in his eyes. "I'll have to be dead before he comes near you again."

His words distracted her from her panic. The seriousness with which he said them made her pause. She couldn't tear her gaze away from his face. She traced the sharp angles of his cheekbones with her eyes, and then the softer lines of his lips. Why did it matter to him so much? She watched him swallow and look away. He stood from the bed and put distance between them, easing the pull the blood bond put on her.

"What will happen now? With the blood bond."

He seemed to deflate before her very eyes. Then he walked back to the chair and sank into it. "Honestly, I don't know."

She swallowed. "Okay. So, I take it you have never done this before?"

He shook his head and wouldn't meet her eyes. "I've never given anyone blood twice."

"But you have done it before. Given blood once, I mean." For some reason, the idea caused her heart to ache. It had to be the bond making her feel that.

He eyed her warily. "Yes, I have. And I swore I would never do it again."

"But you did. Twice, now."

"Yeah. I did."

Her gaze roved over him. He was tense but cautious. He looked like he was about to bolt, and she couldn't blame him. In their experience together after the blood bond, she was more than likely to jump him where he sat, and he clearly didn't want that.

"Why did you do it?" She had to know. She needed to know his reasons for saving her twice.

He exhaled roughly and looked away. "You were going to die. Both times. I couldn't let that happen. You were forced into this world against your will, and it didn't seem right for you to lose so much because of it."

Something in her fractured a little at his response. It wasn't what she'd wanted to hear. He was right. She had been forced into this world, and part of that was his fault. She would never have been injured either time if she hadn't been with Phoenix. She also probably would have been dead at Beck's hands, but that was another thing entirely.

Now she was bonded with this fae who she really didn't want to be bonded to. She was forced to lust after him, to crave his touch and his body. Her choices were being ripped away from her, and it should have made her angry. Instead, she was disappointed he hadn't saved her because he wanted her the same way she wanted him.

But that was the thing. She didn't want him. The bond wanted him. It had been hard enough fighting the pull toward him. Now she was scared it would be even harder. She was scared the desire would be overwhelming and impossible to control. Fuck. This was not how she'd ever imagined her life going.

"I'm tired," she said quietly. Lainey avoided his gaze as she settled back onto the bed. She just wanted to lay down and never get up again.

A heaviness settled in her, and she found it hard to fight. Oh, how easy it would be to just give up. The thought of seeing her sister again, even her mom, was a temptation calling to her. The darkness she had surrendered to when she almost died had been peaceful. A small part of her was angry Phoenix had pulled her away from it. It would've been the coward's way out, but what did it matter? There was no one left in this world who would mourn her. As her thoughts drifted deeper and darker, her eyes grew heavier until she fell into a restless sleep.

Chapter Twelve

"Where is Phoenix?" Lainey had woken up groggy and pissy. She'd made herself shower and leave her room. She found Ash sitting at his computers, his brows drawn in concentration.

"Not here," he replied absently. He leaned closer to his monitors, as if that would clarify whatever it was he was studying.

"Super helpful," she muttered as she plopped onto the couch and pulled a blanket over her lap. She was sore, her shoulder ached, and her head hurt, but considering how soon after the incident it was, and how little pain she felt, she had to admit Phoenix's blood was a pretty awesome healing power. Aftereffects notwithstanding.

Ash grunted in response. Apparently, he was just as pissy as she was.

"What exactly happened to me? I don't even know what my injuries were, besides the slit throat." She shuddered and rolled her shoulder, feeling the dull ache in her muscles.

He barely glanced up from his screens, but at least he answered her. "Knife wound in the back. Turned out it was poisoned."

Lainey widened her eyes. Poisoned? Holy shit. That explained why her muscles had refused to work properly. "But everything is fine now? No more poison?"

Another grunt that Lainey took to mean everything was fine.

She stared at him. His face was lit from the screens, and his green eyes moved back and forth as he scanned the monitors. His jaw was tense, a muscle ticking every so often as he ground his teeth together.

"I'm sorry," she whispered. "I didn't ask him to do it."

Ash finally looked at her, and his eyes roved over her features, as if he was trying to see inside of her. He shook his head and bent back to the computers.

She sighed. Apparently, whatever friendship had been building between them was gone now. The thought stung a bit. She could have used a friend. Sadness welled up within her so quickly, she wasn't able to keep it at bay. Before she knew it, her magic was stirring in her veins, reacting to her emotions. Her hair fluttered, the strands lifting from her shoulders and floating around her head in the wind that was now building in the room.

Ash's head popped up, and his eyes widened at whatever he saw on her face. The curtains billowed in the magical wind, and even Ash's hair was ruffling on his head. He walked over to where she sat and wrapped an arm around her, tugging her close.

She felt his magic in the air. The scent of nature—of grass and rain—surrounded her, caressed her. She let his magic soothe her, and soon her own magic subsided.

"I'm sorry," she said again.

His big hand gently stroked up and down her back, and she relaxed further into him. She didn't realize she was crying until he wiped away a tear.

"Nothing is your fault, Lainey," he said gently. "I just worry about him, and we have no idea what will happen now that he's given you blood for a second time. I know it's not your fault, and I don't want to see you injured or killed either. It was a lose-lose situation. He did the only thing he could think of. Unfortunately, it may have unforeseen consequences we'll have to figure out as we go."

They sat in silence for a time, and Lainey gratefully soaked up his calming presence. She hadn't realized how much she enjoyed his company until it seemed he was taking it away from her. She'd never really had any friends. As soon as she was old enough, she'd started working to help Emma support them. The stigma of having a mom who had gone crazy and killed herself also didn't help in the friendship department. Having Ash as a friend would be nice.

"What happens next?" she asked after a comfortable silence.

Ash's chest expanded as he took a breath. "We'll meet back up with Madam Elvie and give her what she asked for. Hopefully, she'll be able to open a door to Faerie."

"What happens then?" She didn't want to admit her fear of them leaving her here. She didn't want them to toss her aside after she was no longer useful to them.

Before he could reply, the apartment door opened. Her back was to the door, but it could only have been Phoenix. His footsteps halted abruptly, and she turned around to look at him. The expression on his face was unreadable as he stared at her and Ash cuddled together on the couch. She quickly put some distance between them, but Phoenix didn't say anything. Ash, on the other hand, snorted.

She scooted to the other end of the couch and kicked him with her foot. He grabbed it and settled it in his lap as he dug his thumbs into the base of her heel. She groaned in ecstasy as he continued the massage, and she placed her other foot on his lap too, demanding the same attention be given to it. He smirked but obliged.

Phoenix sat in the chair opposite them, his face carefully blank. Lainey gathered herself and prepared to look at him. They needed to test what would happen now that she had been given his blood two times. Having Ash as a chaperone was probably a good idea.

She shifted her gaze to Phoenix and found his burning stare already on her. Immediately, she felt the flames of his magic surround her, licking up her body in undulating waves. She gasped and looked down at herself, expecting to see her body covered in fire. There was nothing there, but the sensation was all encompassing.

Her gaze returned to his, and the flames traveled higher over her body, gently caressing every curve. His eyes burned, the molten copper swirling violently, and she couldn't look away. She felt her magic stirring again, this time in arousal. She let her wind brush against him in a searching caress, and they both jumped. She could feel him, as if it were her hands touching him instead of her magic.

His eyes flared brighter, and the heat surrounding her soared again. She closed her eyes and let her head fall back, the sensual touch turning her to butter. She barely bit back a groan of pleasure as the flames licked over breasts. She squeezed her legs together, trying to ease the ache that was building between them.

A sharp poke on her foot and a throat clearing dragged her from the cloud of ecstasy. Both she and Phoenix snapped their attention to Ash, who was staring at them, bemused.

"Please keep your hormones in check," he drawled.

Lainey looked down to her lap, afraid to risk another glance at Phoenix, but she couldn't shake the sensation of his flames touching her. It didn't help that she could still feel his gaze burning into her.

She cleared her throat and pointedly looked at Ash. "So, when do we go back to Madam Elvie's?" She was proud of how calm and collected she sounded despite the desire still roaring through her blood.

Instead of answering, Ash looked to Phoenix.

"Tonight," Phoenix said, his voice deeper than usual. "We go back tonight."

That night, Lainey found herself once again seated on a plush, colorful cushion. Ash sat to her left, Phoenix to her right. She was studiously ignoring the latter. Difficult, considering he was so close she could feel the heat of his body across her skin, reminding her of the way his flames had felt earlier that day.

She couldn't stop the thought popping into her head. She wondered what it would feel like to have his skin against hers, his flames heating them both, driving them further into a frenzy.

As if he could sense the direction her thoughts had wandered, Phoenix's head snapped in her direction, his eyes slightly wild. Before anything else could happen, Madam Elvie swept into the room, the beaded curtain clacking behind her. Lainey swore she heard Ash mutter a prayer of thanks.

"So they return," Madam Elvie said as her gaze roved over the three of them. Her eyes widened and passed between Lainey and Phoenix a few times before she wiped all expression from her face. Sitting on the cushion on the other side of the table, Madam Elvie situated her flowing robes with precise attention.

"We have the three items you requested." Phoenix shifted on his cushion, dragging his bag to him and placing the objects on the table.

Madam Elvie grinned widely at the display. "So you do." Her gaze lingered on the amulet, lighting with something Lainey couldn't name, but it set her on edge.

Madam Elvie took the jar of essence and swirled it, the shimmery golden liquid shining like a glittery oil spill. She picked up the feather next and twirled it between her fingers. Lainey couldn't help but notice she didn't touch the amulet.

Madam Elvie stood and motioned to the items on the table. "Bring those and follow me."

Phoenix placed the items back in the bag, and they all followed her out of the room. She led them down a narrow hallway and through a sturdy wooden door. On the other side was the most antiquated kitchen Lainey had ever seen.

It was something out of a fairytale, reminding her of the cabin in Snow White. There were no modern-day appliances. A large wooden table sat in the middle of the room, with four mismatched wooden chairs around it. A fire burned in a large hearth, and a black cauldron hung over the flames. Lainey had to hold in a snort at the witch-like atmosphere. There was even a black cat grooming itself on the rug before the hearth.

"Sit," Madam Elvie commanded.

Once seated, Phoenix took the three items out of the bag again, while Madam Elvie shuffled around the kitchen, pulling containers and jars off of shelves and out of cabinets. She added a few things to the cauldron, stirring occasionally. Finally, she took the jar of wisp essence and removed the lid. She snatched up the feather and stirred it in the essence, coating the soft white fluff in shimmery goo. Then she dropped the feather into the cauldron.

A burst of purple smoke puffed up from the cauldron, and Madam Elvie smiled. She returned to the table and cocked her head, staring at Lainey and Phoenix. She looked like a bird of prey with her head canted to the side.

"Why are you staring at us like that?" Lainey asked.

Madam Elvie pursed her lips. "There is magic here that has never been seen before." She closed her eyes and inhaled through her mouth as if she were tasting the air. When her eyes opened, they landed on Phoenix. "The blood of the banshee is an interesting element, is it not?" Her eyes moved to Lainey. "You." A finger pointed at her heart. "You are not banshee, yet the blood of one flows through your veins."

"Um, yeah." Lainey glanced at Phoenix. "He used his blood to heal me. Twice."

Understanding dawned on Madam Elvie's face. "That would explain it."

"Explain what?" Phoenix demanded.

"The bond flowing between you. I thought at first ... but no. The blood bond makes more sense." She nodded as if she had just concluded an argument with herself.

"What do you know of the blood bond? Is there a way to

break it?" Lainey was hopeful. Maybe there was a way to end this thing. Phoenix's head swiveled in her direction. She could have sworn hurt flashed through his eyes, but that couldn't be right.

"A blood bond cannot be broken. Only strengthened."

Ash groaned, and Lainey kicked him under the table.

Madam Elvie studied her and Phoenix before chuckling. "I can tell you how to ease the urges you feel."

Lainey sat up straighter in the chair. "Yes, please."

"Follow through on them."

She stared at the elf, thinking she had to have misunderstood.

"The only way to calm the urges is to give into them. Enjoy a good romp in the sheets." She cackled delightedly at the flush that spread over Lainey's cheeks.

"Mother of god save us," Ash mumbled as he placed his head in his hands.

It took all of Lainey's willpower to refrain from looking at Phoenix. There was no way she could handle seeing his reaction. Either he would look disgusted at the prospect of having sex with her, or he would look like it was something he would greatly enjoy. The former would break her beyond repair; the latter would have her jumping him where they sat.

"So nothing can be done about it?"

Madam Elvie turned her attention to the amulet but still answered her question. "Nothing. I would avoid any more situations that would require him giving you more blood. If you don't plan on acting on the bond, it will tear you apart if you keep strengthening it."

She silenced further questions by hovering her hand over the amulet, and the black stone began to glow from within. She whispered a few words in a language Lainey didn't understand. Judging from the frowns on the guys' faces, they didn't either.

As quick as an adder, her hand crashed down on the amulet. All three of them jumped at the outburst and the loud crack of thunder that followed. Lainey stared in dismay as the elf removed her hand, displaying the shattered remains of the amulet.

Lainey gasped, "What did you do?"

Phoenix's brows pulled down in anger, and he growled so low the table vibrated under her hands. Ash's brows were also drawn down, but rather than being angry, he looked like he was trying to fit the pieces of a puzzle together in his head and failing.

Not saying a word, Madam Elvie scooped up the three pieces of the tourmaline, leaving the broken casing on the table, and took them to a side table by the fire. Phoenix stood as if he were going to stop her from doing something, although with the amulet broken, it seemed as if he were too late.

"Sit." Madam Elvie's command whipped through the room, and Phoenix promptly sat back down in his chair. He glared daggers at her back, though.

"I was there many years ago when this necklace was infused with Princess Azura's magic. In fact, I was the one to help her infuse it. She was a good friend of mine. Before she could use it to remove her sister from the throne, the necklace was stolen, and Azura met a fate worse than death." Madam Elvie's eyes dimmed briefly, and sadness crossed her face. "Magic still lives in the necklace. It is powerful. It is cunning. It is a beacon to those more powerful."

She turned from the smaller table, three necklaces now dangling from her hand. She placed one in front of each of them. "You will need the strength from the amulet to succeed in your task. And to survive what is coming for you. Each of you must wear a piece of the amulet. Broken in three, its power is diminished but still more than capable of doing what needs done." She stared each of them in the eye in turn, lingering a second longer on Lainey. "Broken in three, it will be harder to detect its presence. You must not reunite the pieces until the right time."

Madam Elvie turned and grabbed a jar off the mantle. She ladled out the mixture from the cauldron into the jar, careful to avoid spilling a single drop. Then she placed the lid on it and set the jar on the table.

No one said anything. Lainey wasn't sure any of them were breathing. She glanced at Phoenix, who was staring at the elf with wide eyes, like he didn't know what to do or say either. It was Ash who finally broke the silence.

"What the fuck are you talking about?"

The smile Madam Elvie leveled at Ash sent chills racing down Lainey's spine. "You're a smart boy. I'm sure you'll figure it out." She gestured to the jar, the mixture a purple so dark it was almost black. "Dribble this around the large oak tree in Central Park. It must be done at midnight on the night of the new moon. The door to Faerie will unlock temporarily. It will not remain open long, so do not dawdle." She smiled at them, nothing pleasant in her features. "Safe travels."

With her final words, Madam Elvie disappeared in a whoosh of blue smoke.

No one moved. No one said a word. They all stared at the jar and the three pieces of the amulet, thoughts spinning and sifting through Madam Elvie's words.

"Well," Phoenix said, clearing his throat. "No point in sitting here. We should get back to the apartment."

Lainey and Ash mumbled their agreement and stood, following Phoenix out of the building.

Chapter Thirteen

"Ash ..." Phoenix began as soon as the apartment door closed behind them.

"I'm on it." Ash sat behind his computer and began doing his thing.

"What are you having him look up?" Lainey grabbed a bottle of water from the fridge and sat at the bar.

"Whatever that nonsense Madam Elvie was spouting sounded like some sort of prophecy or foretelling." He pulled one piece of the broken amulet out of his bag and placed it on the counter. He stared at it like he was daring it to come to life and tell him what the elf had meant. "We each need a piece of the amulet for its power to complete a task? We need it to survive what's coming? And we are not to reunite the pieces until the right time? There is more there than she told us, of course. I'm hoping Ash can find something."

"On the internet?" Lainey asked incredulously.

"There are websites out there that so-called fanatics have created with all kinds of information on Faerie," Ash said as he powered up his computer. "Those fanatics are actually fae who have been locked out of Faerie and are trying to record our history. The websites come off as fanfic or conspiracy theories to humans. It's always seemed like a risk to me, but it could come in handy now."

Lainey hummed an acknowledgment before standing and heading to the windows. She opened the door hidden amongst the glass and stepped outside onto the balcony, letting the chilly autumn air clear her head. She leaned against the railing and looked down at the dizzying drop below. The brisk temperature helped to clear her head and she inhaled deep, cleansing breaths.

Cars drove past despite the late hour, the taillights blurring into red streamers as they drove down the street. The apartment was high enough up that the sounds of the city didn't reach her. Only an occasional siren would drift by on the wind. It was peaceful this high up. Lainey turned her attention to the sky above her. She wished she could see the stars. The city was always too bright, the light pollution dimming the constellations above.

She noticed the moon was only a crescent. Whether it was waxing or waning, she had no idea. They would need the new moon to break the curse. Then what? They would go to Faerie? Madam Elvie seemed to think her part in all of this wasn't over yet. It shouldn't have made her feel better, but it did. She wasn't ready to be discarded. She enjoyed being part of something that was bigger than her.

Lainey had never had that in her life. Her only purpose had been to bring home enough money to help Emma. Sure, she could have done without the blood bond, but despite Phoenix's gruff demeanor, he wasn't too bad.

Lainey didn't know how long she stood on the balcony in the chilly night. She didn't notice her skin cooling or her fingers and toes going numb. She was lost in thoughts she hadn't let herself think about. When she'd found out about Emma's death, she hadn't been able to stop herself from wondering what the point was, going on when she had nothing to live for. Her only goal had been to help provide for her and Emma. She had never thought about college or what her future would look like. She had survived day to day.

With Emma gone, what was the point? She was alone, and that thought had terrified her more than anything. She hadn't been sure she *wanted* to go on. Then, she almost died. She still hadn't processed everything from that incident, but she remembered the feeling of waking up and realizing she was still alive. It hadn't been with an overwhelming sense of joy. Instead, she had been disappointed.

She couldn't believe she could even entertain the idea. Having lived through losing someone to suicide, the thought almost made her sick. She was stronger than that—not that only weak people committed suicide. But Lainey knew she was a fighter. She had been fighting every day of her life. She wasn't willing to give up so easily, no matter how bad it got.

The sound of the balcony door opening behind her dragged her out of her thoughts. She turned around, expecting to see Ash, but was surprised to find Phoenix instead, a blanket in his hand. A glance behind Phoenix into the living room showed that Ash's corner of technology was empty. He wasn't around to keep a watchful eye on them like a mother hen.

Despite her determination to not look at him, her gaze drifted to Phoenix as he moved closer. The air warmed the closer he got. His eyes never left hers as he placed the blanket around her shoulders and drew the edges together in front of her. He let his hands linger there.

The warmth that surrounded her was not from the blanket. She licked her lips and opened her mouth to tell him this was a bad idea, but when his gaze dropped to her lips and his eyes began to glow, she couldn't make herself speak the words.

This was wrong. She knew she really didn't want his touch, but the damn blood bond couldn't be ignored. It screamed at her, pushed her closer to Phoenix until her chest brushed against his. She looked into his glowing eyes and knew hers were also glowing by the awe on his face as he stared at her.

He slowly lifted his hand, giving her time to pull away. She didn't. She couldn't. As the bond took over, her fight left her. She craved his touch, and she was tired of fighting it. His fingers brushed down her cheek, the warmth of his skin a pleasant burn that shot straight to her core.

He gently tilted her head up and slowly, so slowly, brought his mouth to hers. Their lips barely brushed, the softest caress, but the spark between them at that brief touch was undeniable. His hand slid to the back of her neck; the other found its way inside the blanket. He gripped her waist and drew her closer.

When he brought his lips to hers again, it was better than she'd imagined. His lips were so soft, but his kiss was demanding. The air warmed further, and Phoenix licked at her bottom lip. Lainey was powerless. She couldn't stop her mouth from opening, inviting him in.

His tongue swept in, brushed against hers, and fire ignited inside her. This is what she had been craving. The taste of him was divine, his scent and magic surrounding her almost too much to bear. The blanket dropped from her shoulders, and her hands slid into his hair. She grabbed onto the silken strands and pulled him even closer. He pushed her against the balcony, the railing digging into her lower back as he continued his leisurely exploration of her mouth.

The slow, sensual kisses were making her burn, or maybe that was his magic. He felt like an inferno against her, never hurting, only driving her higher and higher. The clothes between them needed to go. She needed to feel his skin against hers. She needed his fire burning through her in all possible ways.

She skimmed her hands down his back, feeling the hard muscles tense and shift under her fingers. When she reached his waist, she slid her hands under his shirt, and—*oh my god*—if she thought his body had been burning before, his skin was pure flame. She drew her hands up his back again, his burning flesh searing her skin. He growled deep in his chest and pushed his hips against hers.

She gasped at the feel of his hard length. There was no denying he wanted this as much as she did. Phoenix's hands cupped her ass, and he lifted her up so she could wrap her legs around him. He held her tightly to him and deepened the kiss further. No more slow-burning kisses. He devoured her mouth, tongues clashing and warring with each other. And it still wasn't enough.

She was aflame. She was burning from the inside out. She moaned against his mouth, and that seemed to drive him wild. His hands slid under her shirt, and his fingers trailed over her belly and around her waist. She wanted more.

The sound of the balcony door flying open broke them apart. They were both breathing heavily. Lainey looked over Phoenix's shoulder to see Ash standing in the doorway, thunderclouds in his eyes. She quickly tried to unwrap her legs from Phoenix's waist, but he held her there. She tried to pull back to see his face, but he dropped his head to her neck.

He began dropping biting kisses down her throat, and she couldn't help it—her head fell back, silently asking for more. She tried telling herself to pull away, that Ash was standing there pissed at the world, and they needed to stop. It was useless. Phoenix's tongue snaking out to lick her throat wiped away all coherent thought.

Ash cleared his throat, and Phoenix stopped his maddening kissing long enough to growl menacingly. The sound was pure possession. Had Lainey not been completely intoxicated by his touch, she would have slapped him for the insinuation. She didn't belong to anyone.

Phoenix gently set her on her feet, but he kept her pulled tight to his body. She could feel his heart pounding in his chest. Ash uttered a filthy curse before grabbing Phoenix by the shoulder and pulling him away. Before Lainey could blink, Phoenix slammed Ash against the glass door. Cracks spiderwebbed outward from the force. It took Lainey a moment to process the dagger pressed against Ash's throat. A menacing growl sliced through the air as he pressed the dagger harder against Ash's skin. The sight of blood dripping down his throat was a bucket of cold water on her arousal.

"Oh fuck," she gasped. Her breathing was ragged and uneven, her muscles limp and shaky. She was fighting the urge to go to Phoenix and pull him back against her. What the hell had just happened?

Her voice was what finally broke through whatever spell Phoenix was under. He jerked back with wide eyes. His breathing was as ragged as hers. He said nothing, just stared at the blood on Ash's neck in horror.

"Go inside, Nix." Ash's voice was quiet and understanding.

Phoenix stared at his friend for a second longer before hurrying inside, taking his heat with him. In the sudden chill, Lainey wrapped her arms around herself. Her shaking wasn't from the cold, though. Phoenix's reaction to the interruption chilled her to her bones. The possession, the violence, the sheer dominance. Lainey was absolutely terrified.

Ash slowly approached her and bent down to retrieve the fallen blanket. Before wrapping the blanket and his arms around her, he glanced back through the door, ensuring Phoenix was nowhere in sight. Lainey collapsed against him, his familiar earthy scent calming her nerves.

"What the hell just happened?" she whispered.

She felt him shake his head. "Both of you are in way over your heads."

"I'm so sorry. I didn't mean for any of that to happen. I know I need to stay away, but he came out here, and I was powerless to stop it."

"Shhh." His hand wrapped around the back of her head, pressing it against his chest. "I know. You don't have to apologize for anything. That was all Nix's fault. He knew better than to come out here. He knew exactly what would happen, but he did it anyway."

"Why would he do that?"

"I don't think you'll like that answer."

She pulled away to look at his face. His eyes were guarded, and his jaw was tense. He didn't like the answer either.

"You should go to bed, Lainey."

He pulled her through the balcony doors and gave her a push toward her room. She turned back around to protest, but his no-nonsense expression had her swallowing her words. He was not going to explain any further tonight.

"Goodnight, Ash."

"Lock your door, Lainey."

And with that parting remark, Lainey was sure she wouldn't get any sleep that night. She wasn't sure if she wanted to hear a knock on her door or not.

Chapter Fourteen

The temperature was dropping. Lainey pulled her hat down farther over her ears and stamped her booted feet. She stood with her two companions in front of the massive oak tree in Central Park. The one Madam Elvie said was the doorway to Faerie. The one Lainey had almost died under. The one Emma had died under.

She tried not to think about the horrors this tree had witnessed, but it was impossible. She glanced at the ground. Of course, the evidence was gone, but she still felt like she should be able to see all the blood that had been spilled under the branches. Lainey swallowed and wrapped her arms around her middle in an attempt to dispel the chill that wasn't caused by the cold.

Tonight was the new moon, and they were about to blow open the doors to Faerie. Hopefully. With Beck still hunting for her, she had no choice but to follow through with the plan to break the curse from the other side.

It had been three nights since that epic disaster on the balcony with Phoenix. He hadn't come to her room that night, and Lainey was loath to admit she was disappointed. The feeling confused her. In the past, she'd only felt the pull to Phoenix when they were in close proximity to each other.

Since that night, she had been drawn to him even when they weren't in the same building, and that had been a lot. They had avoided each other since that night, both trying to find a semblance of autonomy in the pull of the blood bond.

"What happens after we unlock the door?" she asked. Ash stood between her and Phoenix, a buffer between the bond.

"The door will hopefully remain open long enough that we can walk through," Phoenix muttered.

"What happens once we're through?"

Neither of them answered her question, which increased her unease at what was to come. And the realization that neither of them had been to Faerie before only exacerbated her worry.

All three of them were heavily armed. Lainey had two guns—both loaded with silver bullets—as well as two daggers she had no idea how to use. Ash and Phoenix were walking armories, with guns, daggers, and even throwing stars strapped to all available parts of their body. Each of them was also wearing their piece of the amulet around their neck, tucked against their skin under their clothing.

Phoenix checked his watch and took a bracing breath. His exhale fogged the air in front of him. He approached the tree and unscrewed the lid to the mixture Madam Elvie had made. With one last glance back at her and Ash, Phoenix dumped the liquid, walking in a slow circle around the tree. Once the jar was empty, he rejoined them, and all three watched and waited.

The mixture on the ground began to glow. A golden purple light flared, the base of the tree illuminated in the darkness. A humming began in Lainey's chest, slowly spreading to the rest of her body. She rubbed her arms and legs, glancing at the boys and finding them similarly affected.

Before she could ask what was going on, a flash of light flared through the darkness, blinding them. Lainey raised her arm to shield her eyes and was thrown backward in a blast of wind. Her breath left her in a whoosh as she landed on her back. She lay there for a minute as the light faded and her breathing regulated.

She heard scrambling, then Phoenix's face came into focus above her, his eyes scanning worriedly.

"Are you all right?" He gently grasped her shoulders and helped her to her feet.

She looked around and saw Ash slowly standing as well. "Yeah, I'm okay." She avoided his eyes, even though his hands on her shoulders were starting to heat her blood. He seemed to sense it and let go, stepping back and putting space between them.

Lainey gasped. Behind Phoenix was the glowing outline of a door in the trunk of the oak. Phoenix spun around, hand going to his dagger. He relaxed when he saw the door.

"Holy shit," he breathed. "It worked."

He slowly approached and ran his hands down the rough bark of the tree. With a push, the door swung open, revealing a curving staircase lit with torches sporting golden flames. He pulled a dagger from the sheath across his chest and glanced back at Lainey and Ash.

"We stay together. No one is to go off alone," Phoenix said sternly.

He gave Ash a look, and Ash nodded solemnly as he moved to stand behind Lainey. Realization flared. He'd asked Ash to keep an eye on Lainey. While she was irritated that they felt the need to protect her, she was also glad. They were stronger than she was and knew more about this world. Having them watching over her was probably a good idea.

The three of them began their descent down the gold-lit staircase, Phoenix leading with Ash guarding their backs. Lainey's fear of the unknown was so strong, it was overpowering the urge to go to Phoenix. Her heart pounded in her chest, and despite the cold, her hands were sweating. What if this had been a horrible idea?

The stairs spiraled on for what felt like forever. The silence was heavy, pressing on them the farther down they went. The only sounds were their boots on the steps and their breathing.

Just when Lainey was beginning to wonder if the steps were leading to hell, they came to a small landing.

They all crowded around another door. This one also appeared to have been carved from the trunk of a tree. Phoenix once again pushed open the door and stepped through. Lainey hesitated a second before following.

She had to squint at the sudden brightness, but once her eyes adjusted, she gasped. She couldn't look around fast enough. Her fear evaporated as wonder filled her. The door opened onto a small patch of grass so green it looked like it had been spray-painted. Directly in front of them was a stone bridge arching over a river that appeared to encircle the little island they occupied.

Lainey spun in a circle to take in the surroundings more. The tree they had exited was massive. The roots sprung up from the base like claws digging through the earth. A large arch was set in the middle of the trunk over the door they'd exited from. She craned her head back, and her gaze traveled up and up and up. The branches reached high into the sky and spread out wide, hanging over the river. The leaves cast dappled sunlight on the ground around them.

She spun back around and gazed across the river. The landscape as far as she could see was bright and colorful. Green grasses and waving wildflowers of every imaginable color spread in all directions. She could see forests and mountains off in the distance, a tiny speck on the horizon. Everything looked sharper and more colorful to her eyes than it did in the human realm. The temperature was pleasantly warm, with a cool breeze that carried the scent of wildflowers.

She glanced at her companions and found them staring in awe as well. She smiled at their reactions. Their first time stepping foot in their own world. She wondered what it must feel like to them, to finally be able to come home.

She narrowed her eyes as she looked at them. They looked different—not a lot, but just enough that she could tell they weren't human. It was as if their glamor had disappeared. Their features appeared sharper, like a mist had lifted from around them. She could see their magic swirling in their eyes as they took in the faerie world.

Not only that, but she saw pointed ears peeking out from Ash's blond hair, and Phoenix's pointed canines were on display as he gave Ash a rare smile. They were beautiful and otherworldly in their own environment.

She wondered how she was affected by being in this magical world. She felt her teeth with her tongue and touched the tips of her ears. All normal. She wondered if her eyes were also glowing. She felt deep inside herself, to that secret place of magic at her core. It felt easier to access now, like it was ready to explore the world where it had originated.

Lainey adjusted her bag on her shoulders and approached the bridge spanning the river. Before she could put one foot on the stone, Phoenix grabbed her arm and pulled her back.

"Careful," he warned. "We have no clue what to expect here."

She stared at him with her mouth hanging open. The pull she felt toward him in the human world was diminished here. She still felt it, but it wasn't as strong. It was easier to combat.

Phoenix looked down at himself, making sure everything was in place, then ran his hands through his hair. "What? Why are you staring at me like that?"

"The bond. It's not as strong here."

He frowned and cocked his head to the side. "Must have something to do with the magic." He let his gaze hover on her a moment longer before turning to Ash. "You have the map?"

To answer, Ash whipped a folded piece of paper out of his back pocket. "Right here." He squatted and unfolded the map on the ground. "I really wish I had a GPS, though," he muttered.

Lainey and Phoenix hovered behind, looking at the piece of paper. Ash had drawn up a map to the best of his ability. He had researched the realm using those websites he had mentioned and talked to his mom to get an idea of the layout.

He pointed to a spot on the map depicting a large tree

surrounded by a river. "We are here, in the Seelie Court." He drew his finger to the west, to a city on the coast. "This is the capital city of Seelie Court. This"—he drew his finger farther down to another city on the coast—"is the capital city of the Unseelie Court. Obviously, I would suggest staying in the Seelie Court. However, I'm not sure how welcoming either court will be to us." His look at Phoenix spoke volumes.

"I think we should avoid the courts as much as possible," Phoenix answered, his eyes continually scanning their surroundings. "We need to find Elvie's sister. If she created the curse, she knows the way to break it. Without Lainey's death."

"That would be ideal," Lainey said dryly and rubbed her neck where Beck had cut her.

Ash spoke up as he folded the map and placed it back in his pocket. "There is a town on the other side of the forest. We'll start there. We will have to skirt the forest, I'm not about to traipse through there without more information of what's lurking in the darkness."

"Good deal," Phoenix replied. He looked at Lainey again, his eyes smoldering before he got his magic under control. "You stay between me and Ash. Let one of us always go first. If you see, feel, or hear anything that doesn't seem right, tell us immediately."

She nodded her agreement and fell into step behind him, with Ash behind her. Together, they set off over the bridge and into Faerie.

✦ ✦ ✦ ✦ ✦

Lainey couldn't conceal her curiosity at the faerie world. Everything was the same yet different. Colors were more vibrant, objects appeared sharper, and there seemed to be an almost imperceptible shimmer about the very atmosphere. She wished her fae companions knew more about this world. Questions were flooding her brain, and she was dying for answers.

Unfortunately, they appeared to be in just as much awe as she was. She frequently glanced toward Phoenix. His usual fierce expression had melted a bit, and the small smile playing about his lips was enticing. She was thoroughly enjoying not having to constantly war with the bond. The muted temptation was easy to combat, and she was taking the opportunity to really study Phoenix.

He looked like he belonged in this world. Some of the tension he usually carried had disappeared, and he seemed more confident and at ease. His broad shoulders were more relaxed and his movements were fluid and graceful. The red in his hair shimmered in the sunlight as it fell about his shoulders, hiding the shaved sides of his head. His smooth gait was almost a prowl as his long legs ate up the distance. He looked like a wild animal in its natural habitat, and it totally turned her on. Maybe the bond wasn't as muted as she'd thought.

They traveled mostly in silence, only speaking when Ash gave them a direction to keep them on track. They planned to go around the forest, between it and the mountains, then follow the tree line to the village. Based on the information Ash's mom had provided, it would take about three days to reach the village.

They stopped long enough for a quick lunch and supper, but traveled well into the night, using the light of the full moon to guide them.

"How is the moon full here when it was a new moon in the human world?" Lainey asked when they finally stopped. She and Ash waited at the edge of the forest while Phoenix scouted for a good place to camp for the night.

She saw Ash shrug, the moonlight glinting off his leather jacket. "Time flows differently here. The twenty-three years that passed in the human world since the curse may have been a hundred here, or only a couple of days."

Lainey swallowed. She hadn't thought about that. When they finished their mission and broke the curse, would she return to the human world to find hundreds of years had passed? A trickle of fear spread through her.

Phoenix reappeared a short time later. "I found a good spot for the night."

He led them to a grouping of boulders curved into an arc. It would provide shelter on three sides and be easily defendable from the front. Ash set out to gather wood for a fire while Phoenix cleared an area for the firewood. Lainey pulled a blanket out of her pack and laid it on the ground.

"What if she can't break the curse?" she quietly asked Phoenix. She glanced up at him through her lashes.

He kept clearing the area and didn't answer for a second. When he looked at her, there was emotion swirling in his eyes she couldn't read. "We'll keep searching until we find a way. No one will hurt you because of this curse."

Lainey bit her lip and studied her hands in her lap. She picked at a thread on her blanket while working through her thoughts. There was one way to solve the problem of using her for the curse. All she had to do was have sex. If she wasn't a virgin, this wouldn't be a problem. Her gaze lifted to Phoenix. It would be so easy to make that happen.

Because of the bond, her body wanted him. She could let herself get lost in the cravings, ignore the parts of her that resented him and the bond. He seemed to know where her thoughts had traveled. His breathing hitched, and his gaze wandered over her face, searching for an answer to a question only he knew.

His eyes shuttered at whatever he saw. He turned away, his answer plain as day. He wouldn't follow through with that solution. An ache formed in her chest, one she didn't understand. Why should she be upset that he didn't want to sleep with her? Was it just because it left her vulnerable—a pawn to be used, a backup to break the curse? Or was it something more?

Hating those thoughts, Lainey turned to her bag and dug out her pack of food. She sat quietly and ate her protein bar, studiously ignoring Phoenix as he set up his own blanket across from her. By the time Ash returned, an awkward tension filled the air. Unsaid words drifted between Lainey and Phoenix, begging to be spoken.

Lainey watched in fascination as Phoenix used his magic to light the fire. It was so easy for him, it made her envious. She wished she'd had her whole life to learn and practice. Reaching into herself, she pulled up her magic, drawing forth the torrent of wind that blew through her veins. It felt easier in the faerie realm, her magic seeming to want to join with the magic floating in the air.

She lifted her hand and felt the wind stirring between her fingers. She felt it meander around the campsite, playfully exploring the surroundings. She sent a current toward Ash, ruffling the blanket he was trying to straighten. His head shot up, and he glared at her.

"Don't start with me, little half-breed. You won't win this war."

She grinned at him in response, and her next blast of air sent his blanket tumbling away. She couldn't stop laughing as she watched him chase it around the camp. Her laughter died when her gaze landed on Phoenix. He was smiling while he watched their antics, and it almost took her breath away.

With a mind of its own, her magic whirled around the fire, dancing between the flames Phoenix had created. They responded, burning brighter and hotter. She wasn't sure if that was the fire's natural reaction or if Phoenix was making them do it. Either way, she sucked in a breath and pulled her wind back to her, feeling it settle contentedly inside herself.

Ash grumbled as he finally got his blanket settled, his stare promising revenge for her little stunt. She fought back another chuckle and dug into her food again.

The tension had lessened with her magic practice, and they ate their protein bars in a comfortable silence, the popping and crackling of the fire a peaceful backdrop.

"How do you two know how to do all of this?" Lainey asked after she finished her dinner.

"Do what?" Ash asked.

"This." She gestured with her hand, indicating the camp they had made. "Scouting, camping, following a map."

Ash grinned. "Boy Scouts." He held up his right hand in the three-finger scout salute, then bounced his head side to side. "And a little bit of fae instinct."

Phoenix took the first watch, while Ash settled down for the night. Lainey was nowhere near tired. She sat on her blanket with her arms around her knees and stared into the dancing flames.

She was so lost in her thoughts, she didn't notice Phoenix had walked around the fire to sit next to her.

"How are you?"

She jumped and placed her hand on her heart, feeling it beat madly against her chest. "Holy shit, don't sneak up on me like that."

He chuckled, the sound slithering over her skin. "Sorry, I wasn't trying to sneak. I was just wondering how you were holding up. A lot has happened since your sister's death. You haven't had a lot of time to process."

Lainey sighed. He was right, she hadn't been able to process everything. She thought about all she had learned and how she felt. She thought about everything that had happened to her since she met Phoenix. Despite the fear and confusion, despite the heartache at losing her sister, she was surprised to find a semblance of peace.

"I don't know how to explain it, but I feel like I've found myself." She shrugged one shoulder, continuing to stare into the flames. "I never really fit in at school or work. I always assumed it was the stigma that came with having a parent who went crazy and being an orphan. And maybe that was part of it, but I wonder if there was more to it. I wonder if I felt deep down that I wasn't like them—that I was ... other."

"I understand that feeling of being other," Phoenix replied quietly. "I've been different from everyone my whole life. Not just humans but other fae as well. Being the reason for the curse has made me an easy target for other fae to take their anger out on. Having Ash as a friend has been the only thing to save me."

Surprised he was sharing information about his personal life and wanting more, Lainey kept her gaze on the fire and asked her next question carefully. "Ash has mentioned ..." She trailed off, scared to get shut down again. "Um, he mentioned something about not letting you fall off another ledge ..." She kept it at that. Letting Phoenix decide if he would expand on her statement or not.

He cleared his throat and leaned back on his hands. "Yeah. I have gone through some rough times in my life. I've frequently beaten myself up for the curse, and some fae have been more than willing to let me take the blame." He took a deep breath before continuing, "But what he was talking about was something else entirely."

Lainey knew she shouldn't ask, but her curiosity and his openness had the question bubbling up before she could stop it. "Does it have something to do with another blood bond?"

Lainey saw him stiffen from the corner of her eye and she immediately regretted the question. For multiple reasons. One was the irrational despair she felt at the thought of someone else sharing a bond with him. The other was that she didn't want him to quit talking. Without the pull on the bond, she was able to sit with him without wanting to fight him or fuck him. It was kind of nice. Once again, to her surprise, he answered her.

"Yeah, it does."

His words were so quiet, she could barely hear him over the crackle of the fire. A chill settled around her heart. She simultaneously wanted him to stop talking and continue his story.

"She was a friend of ours. Another fae who grew up in the human world. Since there were so few of us, it was only natural for us to be friends. We were in an accident coming back from a concert. A drunk driver crossed the double yellow. I swerved to avoid a head on collision that would have killed all three of us."

He paused, struggling to find the words. Lainey glanced at him and found her heart breaking for him. His eyes were haunted, wide and unseeing, as he relived the horror. She wanted to comfort him but refrained. She knew by now he wasn't the type to accept comfort from others.

"When I swerved, I hit a tree. A branch came through the window and pierced her stomach. She was dying, and I did the only thing I could think of."

"You gave her your blood." Just like he had done for Lainey.

He swallowed thickly. "It saved her, of course. But the bond was too much for her. She tried to fight it, but in the end, she couldn't. She couldn't handle any separation between us. She became paranoid that I was with someone else when she wasn't with me. It was driving her to madness."

A weighted pause had Lainey holding her breath and wishing he wouldn't say what she knew was coming.

"She took her own life rather than live with the effects of the bond." He rubbed his face with his hands. "I killed her," he whispered.

God, Lainey hated the anguish in his voice. She knew his pain all too well. She hadn't been enough to keep her mom from doing the same thing. She had agonized over that for years. Even though she hadn't done anything to directly cause her mom's death, she understood where he was coming from. However, he was wrong.

"You didn't kill her, Phoenix. She made the decision to end her life, not you."

"But she wouldn't have had to if I hadn't given her my blood."

"She would have died then anyway. You can't blame yourself for someone else's actions."

"My actions are the reason she felt the need to do it in the first place."

Lainey shook her head. "You did the only thing you could have in the moment. Your intentions were good. The effect may not have been the outcome you had hoped for, but you did nothing wrong."

His gaze was bleak as he stared at her. "I did the same thing to you," he whispered. "I did the exact same thing, knowing what happened the first time."

She hid her shiver at his words. She could have ended up like his friend. Hell, she may still end up like her. But she hoped she was strong enough to fight that pull. "I'm glad you did," she whispered back.

His eyes widened. He had clearly not been expecting her to say that.

"I would have died," she clarified. "While I may not have much to live for anymore, I still don't want to die. The bond may be a complication I don't want to have to deal with, but if it's the choice between that or death, I'd choose the bond any day."

Phoenix looked like she had grown a second head. The shock and relief at her words left him speechless. Without thinking about what she was doing, she scooted closer to him and laid her head on his shoulder. He stiffened under her before exhaling and letting his body relax. A heartbeat later, his arm wrapped around her waist, tucking her in close.

His warmth spread across her skin, soothing tired muscles from a day full of walking through the wilderness. She ignored all the places their bodies touched and the way sparks danced across her skin at those places. She wanted to offer him comfort, nothing else. They shared a common pain only losing someone to suicide could cause; in that, they were the same.

His warmth and comforting touch relaxed her muscles and slowed her breathing. It didn't take long for her eyes to get heavy. Before she succumbed to sleep, she could have sworn she felt him press a kiss to the top of her head.

CHAPTER FIFTEEN

THE FIRST THOUGHT LAINEY HAD AS SHE ROSE TO consciousness was how amazingly warm she felt. She was cocooned in a blanket of fire that didn't burn. She snuggled into it and sighed in content as it wrapped itself tighter around her. A steady *thump thump thump* under her ear tempted her back to sleep. Through the fog of sleep, though, reality crept back in.

The warmth, the thumping, the blanket wrapped around her —it wasn't a blanket at all. She was cuddled up with Phoenix. Her head was on his chest, her body pressed against his. His arms were wrapped around her, holding her tightly to him. She stiffened, realizing they must have fallen asleep last night after their talk.

Heart racing, she lay there for a moment as she tried to find a way to slip out of his arms without waking him. She desperately wanted to avoid that awkward encounter. She started to wiggle away and froze almost immediately when Phoenix rolled onto his side, arms tightening. He buried his face in her neck and released a sigh of contentment that did funny things to her stomach. His hips pressed against her, and heat flooded Lainey as she felt his arousal against her hip.

"Oh, for shit's sake," Ash exclaimed.

His voice startled both her and Phoenix, and they quickly sat up. Phoenix looked around confused before realizing the position he had been in with her. His cheeks burned scarlet, and he quickly stood and put distance between them.

"Guess I'm keeping watch from here on out." Ash huffed around the fire, poking it until the flames burned brightly again.

Neither Lainey nor Phoenix responded, both too busy packing up their blankets and eating their small breakfast. This was exactly the situation Lainey had wanted to avoid. Ash continued to grumble about babysitting a bunch of horny teenagers, and Lainey became increasingly angry.

"Oh, shut up already, Ash!" she eventually snapped.

Both Ash and Phoenix looked at her with surprise. A small smile pulled at the corners of Phoenix's mouth. Ash narrowed his eyes and shook a finger at her.

"Are you hangry or something? You tend to get snippy when you're hungry. I'll skip my breakfast and give it to you if that's the case."

Lainey's mouth dropped open, then quickly shut with a snap. Deciding it wasn't worth her while to get into it with him, she turned on her heel and stalked out of their little campsite. She found a rock nearby and lowered herself onto it, muttering angrily as she quickly braided her hair over her shoulder. "Maybe I'll hang Ash with it."

She knew she was lashing out at Ash because she was angry with herself. She'd let her guard down last night and ended up cuddled with Phoenix. She was confused because the bond between them wasn't pulling her toward him, but she wanted to go back in time so she could wake up next to him again.

They passed the day much the same as the day before. Ash kept a wary eye on Lainey, as well as a healthy distance. Phoenix seemed more relaxed than Lainey had ever seen him. He didn't seem bothered by the position they'd found themselves in that morning. If anything, Lainey got the impression he also wanted it to happen again. His gaze kept landing on her throughout the day. The heated fire in that gaze spoke volumes. It also caused her blood to steadily heat as the day wore on.

It was evening when they finally decided to camp for the night. Phoenix chose a spot where two rivers converged. While Ash and Phoenix set to work on the fire, Lainey walked the short distance to the river. She had never felt so grungy before in her life.

She knelt before the blue-green waters, watching the current ripple along the river stones. Like everything else in Faerie, it was beautiful and shimmery. She reached her hand in and found the water pleasantly cool and slick against her skin. She cupped her hands and splashed her face and neck, then removed her jacket and rolled up her sleeves, rinsing her arms as well.

She left her hand dangling in the water, debating removing her boots to stick her feet in. A shadow rippled along the bottom of the river. Before she could react, a creature breached the surface, its large mouth open and filled with row upon row of flesh-shredding teeth. A scream ripped from her throat as the teeth closed around her forearm.

With one sharp yank, the creature pulled her into the water. She tumbled in with a splash, her scream cut off as water filled her mouth and throat. She tried to pull her arm back, but the creature only clamped its jaw tighter, teeth digging farther into skin and muscle. As her blood mixed with the blue-green water, it turned brown and swirled around her.

Her lungs burned as the creature pulled her farther into the depths. She fought with all her strength, only managing to tear her skin more. Belatedly, she realized she had weapons on her. She fumbled at her waist, pulling a dagger out of the sheath. Blindly, she slashed toward the creature, hoping to feel the blade hit home. She slashed over and over again, until black blood began mingling with hers, but still the creature held her under.

Her lungs ached, her vision began flickering, her slashing slowing and weakening. The need for oxygen was too great. Her body automatically responded, and she gasped, swallowing blood and water into her lungs. She coughed and choked, inhaling even more water.

This was it. This was how she died. Pulled into a magical river by a monster fish.

Lainey barely registered when the creature released her, or when arms banded around her middle. Her head breached the surface, and she was thrown to the riverbank. Heavy pressure on her chest, again and again, until she vomited up all the water she had swallowed.

She rolled over, gasping and heaving. A heavy hand made soothing circles on her back as she emptied her stomach of the river. When she was finished, she collapsed on the ground, all of the strength draining out of her. Her head swam as she was swung up into someone's arms. She knew who it was immediately, his heat warming her through her soaking clothes.

"It's okay," he said quietly. "You're okay. I've got you."

She began shaking as reality sunk in. She clung to him, desperately trying to hold herself together. She had almost died ... again. She walked off, away from the boys, and stuck her hand in a river filled with unknown creatures. She couldn't have acted more recklessly.

"I'm s-s-so—" She couldn't get her apology out through her chattering teeth.

"Shh. Just relax." Phoenix sat her by the fire and wrapped his blanket around her. He sat next to her and pulled her against him, his magic swirling around them.

The heat was exactly what she needed. She leaned into him, letting the warmth thaw her and dry her clothes. Ash stomped back to the camp dripping wet and with a bloody dagger.

"It's dead." He nodded at Lainey's arm, still bleeding from the creature's teeth. "Take care of that or it will draw more attention to us. I'm going to circle the camp for a bit, make sure nothing else has been drawn by the blood."

He left their camp and disappeared into the wilderness. Lainey sat in Phoenix's arms, shaking and shivering. Before long, her clothing was dry, and her trembling began to ease. She didn't move, though. His comfort was the only thing holding her together.

"What was that?" she eventually asked.

"A cetius. A river monster."

"I'm sorry," she whispered as she stared at the dancing flames. "I shouldn't have wandered away."

"Don't apologize. We should have warned you better. I don't think we stressed enough what manner of creatures can be found here."

They lapsed into silence again. As the sky grew darker, Lainey watched the moon rise and stars appear in the blackness above them. It was such a beautiful world. Beautiful and deadly. Like the fae holding her in his arms. She noticed when his soothing strokes on her back turned leisurely, as the comfort he was offering turned sensual.

He took her injured arm in his hand and examined it in the firelight. He lifted it to his lips, his eyes never leaving hers, as he extended his tongue and licked her wounds. Lainey shivered at the touch, at the intimacy of the gesture. Then she watched in amazement as her skin began to knit back together. Soon, there was nothing left of the attack but a pale pink ring of teeth marks.

She placed her hand on his chest, feeling his heart beneath her palm. It stuttered at her touch, and she smiled. Feeling brave, or maybe reckless, she leaned into him. The firelight played across his features, casting him in light and shadows. The flames reflected in his copper-swirled eyes, and she felt herself fall away, shedding propriety and any cares she may have had. She almost died tonight. Now she wanted to live.

His head dipped down, and he pressed his lips to hers. Fire erupted in her veins. It wasn't magic, it was just her body's reaction to him. He nipped at her bottom lip with those sharp canines, and she opened for him, letting his tongue sweep in and claim her. She wrapped her arms around his neck and let herself get lost in him.

He gently pushed her to the ground, all the while continuing with his slow, drugging kisses. Her head was spinning, and she was burning, so brightly. His hand slid to her waist and under her shirt. His touch was like a brand as his skin grazed hers, fingers trailing up over her rib cage, leaving literal sparks in their wake.

She arched into his touch, and his hand traveled to the small of her back. He pressed her tight against him, and she could feel how hard he was against her thigh. She gasped and dug her fingers into his hair.

"Phoenix," she begged. "Please ..."

"Please what?" His growl almost undid her. She felt wetness pool between her legs, and she whimpered.

"I need more."

He dropped his lips to her neck, and she angled her head to give him better access. His tongue rasped up the side of her throat, followed by his sharp canines. She moaned in pleasure, arching again into his touch.

His fingers trailed along the waistband of her leggings, teasing and taunting her. His wicked grin at the slow torture heated her blood even more. The points of his canines were sharp and enticing. She wanted to know what they would feel like buried in her skin.

More teasing, more trailing of his fingers back and forth across her abdomen. Lainey had had enough. She grabbed his hand and tried to push it lower.

He resisted and nipped at her ear, growling, "Patience, little halfling."

Her whimper made him grin again, and finally his hand slipped under her leggings. He dragged one finger through her center, his eyes lighting at the wetness he found. He did it again, and Lainey's eyes closed, her focus narrowing on Phoenix's finger and the pleasure it was giving her.

He brought his mouth back to hers and slipped his tongue inside at the same time his finger entered her. She gasped at the pleasant stretch and tried to arch more into the touch, chasing the pleasure. Phoenix stopped her with a look, and she reluctantly laid back and let him explore her. Her body was heating up, his magic surrounding her and the pleasure ramping higher and higher. When he slipped a second finger inside and crooked his fingers, her magic exploded outward, a torrent of wind whipping around the campsite, causing the fire to flicker and splutter.

He drew her to the edge before retreating over and over. She couldn't bear it. She begged him for more, pleaded with him to give her everything. Finally, when she couldn't take anymore, his thumb pressed on the bundle of nerves at the apex of her thighs. Her vision fractured, and release barreled through her. She cried out, and Phoenix captured the sound with his mouth. He wrung every last bit of pleasure from her.

When she was nothing but a panting mess of limp muscles, Phoenix retracted his fingers and brought them to his mouth. His eyes flared as he tasted her and, just like that, she was ready for more. She reached her hand out to the prominent bulge in his pants, but he grabbed her wrist. He placed gentle kisses along her jaw and neck.

"Ash is coming back," he whispered in her ear. He leaned on one elbow and brushed a strand of hair away from her sweaty forehead. With a last lingering kiss and a roguish wink, Phoenix stood and crossed to the other side of the fire.

Lainey lay there with her eyes closed and reeled herself back in. As the cloud of passion faded and realization set in, she sat up and wrapped the blanket tightly around her. Suddenly chilled, she couldn't believe what had just happened. With a hollow, sinking feeling, she realized exactly what Phoenix had done.

He gave her something to appease the blood bond. He was trying to keep the desire at bay. Phoenix had gotten no pleasure from what happened between them, and he'd stopped her before she could touch him. Nausea rolled through her at the thought. She had never felt more like a burden in her life, and that was saying something.

Lainey laid down and curled onto her side, her back to the fire and Phoenix. She tucked her legs in tight and squeezed her eyes shut. This was a low point for her. A sexual burden Phoenix felt he had to deal with to keep her away from him. She bit back the sob that was rising in her throat. She would be stronger. Next time, she wouldn't let him touch her. She would defeat this bond. She would own it and not let it lead her life.

Even with her newfound determination, silent tears escaped her tightly shut eyes.

Chapter Sixteen

They reached the village the next day. Lainey's spirits had remained low while they journeyed across Faerie. Thankfully, the guys kept their thoughts to themselves, although Phoenix frequently watched her like he was trying to figure out what was wrong. The thought almost made her laugh. Almost.

As they walked down the little dirt road that widened into the village, Lainey forgot about her woe-is-me attitude. Seeing a real fae village in the flesh was something amazing. Little white stone houses with roofs of every color were clustered along the dirt path. The farther they got into the town, the bigger the buildings became until Lainey began noticing shops, inns, healers, and bakeries. Flowers grew in every open space, some she recognized and others that were so fantastical she thought they had to be fake.

The inhabitants of the town were just as mesmerizing. She noticed so many different kinds of fae. Some appeared human, while others were a mix of human and other things—animals, insects, and things she didn't have a name for. Most were dressed in loose flowing clothing, the women in dresses and the men in pants and shirts. She also saw a few without any clothes at all. Those tended to be feathered, furred, or scaled.

The fae that caught her attention the most were the ones with wings. They looked human but for the pair of gossamer wings sprouting from their backs. There were wings of all colors, shapes, and sizes. A child with a pair of pale green wings swept past, one wing brushing against her hand. It felt like silk, smooth and cool to the touch.

She couldn't help the smile from spreading across her face. These carefree fae were a light she desperately needed at the moment. At least until she took a closer look at them. The children were all smiling curiosity, but the adults studied the three newcomers with open weariness and even hostility. One small child approached with a flower. Before she could take it, the child's mother snatched her away with a glare at Lainey. Lainey's smile quickly faded.

She took a closer look at the town. It seemed her first impression may not have been correct. This wasn't a peaceful, happy little village. The buildings displayed a great deal of wear, the stones chipping and falling away. Roofs were sagging, and windows were cracked and dirty. Weeds sprouted, mixed in with the many flowers.

The villagers' clothing was not just billowy, but baggy— hanging off of slim frames that looked as if they could use a few decent meals. While the children were smiling and carefree, the adults' eyes held weary fatigue and even despair.

Phoenix shifted closer to Lainey, his and Ash's gazes sweeping the town relentlessly. She was relieved when he led them to an inn. The sign above the door, depicting a cluster of mushrooms, swung lazily in the breeze. Phoenix shouldered his way inside with Lainey and Ash following closely behind.

The inn was empty save the fae behind the bar. The floor was swept and clean, but the shabby feeling couldn't be erased by a clean floor. The tables and chairs were one patron away from collapsing. Cracks in the windows let the breeze in, and the empty hearth was more dust than ash.

"Can I help you?" The innkeeper's long hair was tied back,

but the strands falling free of the bindings were tangled. His baggy shirt hung loose on his shoulders, and lines bracketed his eyes and mouth. He studied the newcomers warily.

"Yes. We would like a room, please." Phoenix pulled a bag of coins out of his pack that his dad and Ash's mom had supplied.

The innkeeper's eyes greedily dropped to the bag. "That will be five gold pieces."

Ash jerked next to her. He was opening his mouth to speak, but Phoenix stopped him with a look.

"Thank you." He fished through the bag, digging out five golden coins.

"I'm Erich," the innkeeper said as he pocketed the coins. "I run this place. I'll show you to your room."

They followed him to the back of the inn, down a hallway lined with wooden doors. He stopped at one and gave Phoenix a key.

"We have little food, but I'm sure we could find something for you to eat should you wish it."

"We're good. Thank you, though."

Inside, the room was quite large. It looked like it had once been a pleasant space. The large bed took up most of the room, the canopy frayed and moth-eaten. A dresser stood against the wall, a couple of drawers missing knobs. A small bathroom was attached to the room, and one look made Lainey decide she was avoiding using it at all possible costs, despite the modern amenities.

"What the hell is going on here?" Ash voiced as soon as the door closed behind them.

"So, I take it this is not normal?" Lainey asked.

"Not according to our parents." Ash looked at Phoenix, his eyes creased with concern. "I'm not sure it's a good idea to stay here."

"It's too late now," Phoenix replied. "We already paid—"

"And from what my mom said, that was an outrageous amount, by the way."

Phoenix continued as if Ash hadn't spoken. "And half the village has already seen us. We might as well continue on with our plan."

"Which is?" Lainey asked, tentatively sitting on the edge of the bed.

"Ask around until we find someone who knows where Madam Elvie's sister is and pray she isn't at court."

"Phoenix, that guy over there looks like he is going to murder us." Lainey kept her eye on said fae while scooting closer to Phoenix.

They had wandered over to a tavern and had been sitting there for thirty minutes. They didn't take any food—the villagers looked as if they needed every bit left in the town—but they did get drinks. In the short time they were there, the tavern had filled with suspicious villagers. They all pretended to be eating or talking, but they clearly were keeping their eyes on Lainey and her companions.

"I see him," Phoenix muttered.

"This is all wrong," Ash added. "Faerie is supposed to be prosperous. Full of beauty and light and friendly faces. Something is going on."

Phoenix grunted in agreement. "Let's get our information and get back to the inn. I don't like being out in the open here."

They waited until a barmaid approached their table with refills.

"Can I get you anything else?" She eyed Ash, her gaze traveling over his body. It was the first friendly look they had received, and of course it was someone flirting with Ash.

"Actually, there is something." Ash leaned forward and lowered his voice. His gaze darkened and dropped to the barmaid's lips.

Lainey watched in amusement as Ash pushed his chair back and the barmaid settled onto his lap. He nuzzled her neck and whispered in her ear. The barmaid jerked back, eyes going wide with surprise. Her gaze roved over Ash, then Lainey, finally settling on Phoenix. She stood, and her eyes narrowed suspiciously. Her gaze was icy when it returned to Ash.

"The forest. Follow the birch trees." With one more glance at Phoenix, she returned to her work.

"Smooth," Lainey commented.

"Like you could have done better."

"I guarantee I could have."

Ash whipped his head in Lainey's direction. "Now that I would like to see."

"Keep dreaming, cupcake. Did we get what we needed? All these stares are skeeving me out."

Ash snorted. "Skeeving? Are you, like, eighty or something?"

Lainey stood, and as she walked past him, she smacked the back of his head. She didn't go far before waiting for Phoenix to catch up. No way was she walking around here by herself. It didn't matter. Even though she was walking behind Phoenix and in front of Ash, the guy who had been staring at them reached out and grabbed Lainey's arm.

He yanked her to a stop and pulled her closer. She yelped in shock, and Phoenix whirled around. His eyes darkened in anger as he saw the guy's hand on Lainey's upper arm. Ash was there immediately, grabbing the guy's wrist and squeezing until his grip loosened. As Lainey pulled her arm away, Phoenix shoved the guy back against the wall with his forearm at his throat.

"Don't fucking touch her," he growled.

"You're not ... welcome here," the guy choked out. "Strangers are never ... a good thing these days."

The guy's eyes were bulging out of his head, and his face was turning purple. Lainey couldn't tell if it was due to anger or lack of oxygen. Perhaps a combination of both.

Phoenix pressed in closer, increasing the pressure on the guy's neck. "I don't care what you think. But if anyone lays a hand on her again, they lose that hand. Am I clear?"

The guy glared as best he could while suffocating. "Yes," he ground out between his teeth.

Phoenix waited a couple more seconds before stepping back. The guy doubled over and grabbed at his neck. He wheezed and coughed as air flowed back into his starving lungs.

Ash placed a hand on Lainey's back and prodded her forward. "We should get back to the inn before anyone else gets any ideas."

They hurried back to the inn and made it without further incident. Once locked in the room, Lainey sat on the edge of the bed and rubbed her arm. She had a red mark where the guy had grabbed her. Phoenix noticed her actions and knelt in front of her, gently taking her arm in his hand.

"Are you okay?"

She nodded. "Yeah. It doesn't really hurt. It just startled me."

Phoenix growled and surged to his feet. He started pacing, and the air in the room grew hotter. Ash watched him cautiously from his position, leaning against the locked door. Lainey caught his eye and raised a questioning brow in Phoenix's direction. Ash shrugged and smiled wryly.

Deciding she needed to lighten the mood, Lainey said, "I call dibs on the bed tonight."

"I call second dibs." Ash flashed a grin at her.

"Don't even think about it. You get the floor."

Ash placed his hand on his chest in mock hurt. "You would choose Nix over me?"

Yes. "You're both sleeping on the floor."

Phoenix ignored their banter, but he stopped pacing, and the temperature in the room returned to normal.

Lainey risked a question. "Do you think all of Faerie is like this?"

Phoenix and Ash exchanged a glance before Phoenix sighed in resignation. "My gut says yes, and I have no idea what it means."

"Maybe having the gates locked for so long has done something negative to the realm," she offered.

"That's entirely possible. Whatever the cause, we need to be even more careful. Don't trust anyone. None of us are to ever be alone. We stick together."

Ash and Lainey nodded in agreement.

"I'll take the first watch tonight," Ash said as he settled onto the floor against the door.

Phoenix spread his blanket over the floor and laid down. He didn't look at Lainey as she settled into the bed, but she felt his magic reach out and warm the sheets. She smiled as she settled in for another restless night.

It was like an entire other world inside the forest. The trees were so dense, no sunlight filtered through. The air was thick with the scent of earth and living things. Everything was green and brown, and the air was heavy with magic. It was eerily quiet, as if sound didn't dare intrude upon this place. Ash was in his element, completely at home among the ancient trees and unseen wildlife.

They trekked through the forest, following a line of birch trees that stood out among the browns and greens, their white trunks a beacon. There was no path to walk on, so Lainey kept her eyes glued to the ground to avoid tripping over roots and rocks. They walked for the better part of two hours in the oppressive silence. By the time they reached a clearing, Lainey felt the absence of sound pressing down on her like a cloak.

"That's it," Ash said unnecessarily.

In the clearing stood a small stone house with a thatched roof. Lights glowed in the windows, pooling on the ground outside. Smoke puffed happily from a chimney at the back of the house. A well stood in the yard with a bucket perched on the lip, and a pile of wood stacked neatly next to it.

"Whoa," Lainey breathed. "I'm getting major *Hansel and Gretel* vibes here."

Phoenix snorted and began walking across the clearing. He

looked calm, but his tense muscles and his hand on the dagger at his hip told her otherwise.

"Good thing you're not a child, then," Ash whispered in her ear and poked her in the side. "But I wouldn't eat anything she offers you. Unless you enjoy eating children."

"Eww, Ash. That is so wrong."

He chuckled and jogged to catch up to Phoenix. Lainey looked around one more time before joining them.

Phoenix knocked on the red-painted wooden door, and they all stood together, holding their breath, as footsteps sounded inside. The door swung open, and Lainey's jaw dropped. Essie was an exact replica of Elvie. The only difference was her eyes. While Elvie had pale blue eyes, Essie's were pale green.

"I wondered when you would grace my doorstep." She moved to the side and gestured them in.

They filed past her into a living room where a fire burned merrily in the hearth. Despite the creepy vibe Lainey had felt outside, inside was cozy and calm. A couch and chairs surrounded the fireplace, pillows and blankets taking up most of the space on the cushions. A low table held a vase of freshly cut flowers, ones Lainey had never seen before.

"Come in, come in, and take a seat. Would you like anything to eat or drink? I just made biscuits."

"No, thank you," Lainey said quickly.

Ash laughed under his breath. "I would love some biscuits."

Essie nodded and disappeared into the kitchen. Lainey glared at Ash.

They sat on the couch, moving the pile of blankets out of the way first. When Essie returned, she carried a tray with a plate full of biscuits, a steaming pot of tea, and four cups.

Ash greedily grabbed a biscuit and took a bite. "This is delicious. What's in it?" His eyes crinkled as he looked at Lainey with delight.

"Oh, this and that. I gather my ingredients from nature. But enough about biscuits. I sense you have more pressing matters to discuss."

While she looked just like her twin, Essie was warm and inviting, unlike Elvie. Her smile lit up the room and made Lainey feel at ease. Her voice was calm and soothing, with no magic-induced otherworldliness.

"What has happened here?" Ash asked, turning serious. "This is not the Faerie my mom told me about."

Essie smiled sadly. "Indeed, it is not." She settled into a chair, preparing to begin a tale. "Twenty-three years ago, the queens requested my assistance. They wanted a way to lock the gates to Faerie. The only way to do this was to create a curse. I warned them the curse would not only affect their intended targets." She nodded to Phoenix as she said this. "But would curse Faerie as well. They did not listen. Esmeray's anger and fear blinded her. She was able to get Queen Orabelle under her spell, and I couldn't persuade her to change her mind. I did as they asked. I created a curse to lock the gates.

"Just as I warned them, curses have unforeseen consequences. The result has been the slow death of Faerie." She took a sip of her tea before continuing, her eyes shining with sadness. "Crops began failing within days. Livestock came down with incurable sickness. Even the fae of the realm began to show effects of the curse—neighbors accused neighbors of foul deeds, families were broken apart by infidelity. The queens' anger and fear were a seed that, once planted, grew and festered in every living aspect of Faerie."

Lainey kept her gaze trained on Phoenix. She knew he blamed himself for the curse. Hearing all that had befallen Faerie because of it could not have been easy on him. Indeed, shadows swirled in his eyes, and he had withdrawn into himself, lost in the guilt he felt.

"What can be done about it? How can we break the curse?" Lainey asked.

Essie's gaze settled on Lainey, piercing through her to her very essence. "I believe you already know the answer to that."

Ash spoke up. "Another way. There has to be another way that doesn't involve Lainey's death."

"There is always another way. The thing with curses," Essie explained, "is that they require great sacrifice. Death, change, loss. The other way will not be easier. In many ways, it will be harder."

"What is it?" Lainey sat forward, desperate to hear the alternative.

"That answer requires further lessons in history. You see, elves have the ability to see the threads of fate. Past, present, and future held in the palms of our hands." She cupped her hands, and a swirling purple mist formed, a faintly pulsing light emanating from the center. "When Esmeray assumed the throne, her desires for the realm were dark and wicked. Her sister attempted to thwart the queen's plans. You three now each wear a piece of her amulet, as I'm sure my sister has informed you." Her gaze dropped to Lainey's chest, where the amulet lay under her shirt.

Ash's brows were scrunched in thought. Lainey could practically see the wheels turning in his brain. "This other way to break the curse ... We have to take Esmeray off the throne, don't we?"

Essie didn't answer. Instead, she continued her story. "Azura could not stop her sister. Through the years, Esmeray's power grew, and so did her influence over the Unseelie Court. She is the reason the Unseelie Court is considered evil. Throughout her reign, many attempts have been made to remove her from the throne. All were discovered, and the conspirators were removed from the picture. Until one plan was brought to her attention." Essie looked at Phoenix.

Something began worming its way into Lainey's brain, realization slowly clearing the way for the puzzle pieces to click together. She'd never thought the reason for the curse made sense. Dread formed like a lead ball in her stomach.

"Queen Orabelle of the Seelie Court was questioning some of Esmeray's choices, and in an attempt to draw suspicion away, Esmeray offered to marry Orabelle's brother. Your father." Her gaze landed on Phoenix, pale eyes shining brightly. "He married Esmeray, despite already having a mate in the Seelie Court. Your father and Orabelle had discovered a truth that Esemray had kept secret all her life. This secret could change the course of everything. Esmeray is a banshee. A creature that is almost impossible to kill, except with the blood of another banshee. Your mother, Phoenix, is Queen Esmeray."

The blood drained from Phoenix's face. Lainey wasn't sure he was even breathing. She wanted to go to him, offer some kind of support, but something held her back.

"Your father and Queen Orabelle hoped the blood of a half-banshee would be enough to kill Esmeray. Esmeray learned of this after your birth. She planned on killing you to remove the threat. Your father fled to the human realm to keep you safe, and Esmeray used the opportunity to place her influence on the Seelie queen. She convinced her to agree to the curse. To keep you out of Faerie. You, Phoenix, are the one able to end Esmeray's reign. Or least, the only one who would be willing to do so."

Chapter Seventeen

No one made a sound as Essie's words slowly registered with each of them. Lainey stared at Phoenix, all sorts of emotions bubbling up in her. Wonder, fear, worry. Phoenix stared at Essie with wide eyes. In the time she'd known him, Lainey had never seen him so off guard. Like his walls had collapsed and every emotion he felt was playing across his face.

Not able to fight it any longer, she scooted closer to him and grabbed his hand. His head slowly turned in her direction, and they sat there in silence, looking into each other's eyes, a silent conversation passing between them. She offered him comfort, a friend to rely on. He accepted it gratefully, if a bit reluctantly.

She squeezed his hand reassuringly, and he took a deep breath before turning back to Essie.

"That is what Elvie meant," he rasped. "My task is to overthrow Esmeray, and the amulet will help with that."

"It is. Although, remember, you are not alone." Her eyes flicked to Lainey quickly before settling on Phoenix again. "You will need to accept the help given to you to succeed."

"What do we have to do?" Lainey was still reeling. She was glad there was another way to break the curse, but she didn't like the implications it had for Phoenix.

Essie didn't reply. Instead, her gaze intensified on Phoenix before her eyes clouded over. Lainey gasped, and Phoenix stiffened, his eyes widening. She wouldn't have thought it possible, but she watched as he paled further. He closed his eyes and shook his head.

"Not possible," he whispered roughly.

Essie's eyes cleared, and she looked upon Phoenix with certainty. "It is. It has been written in the stars."

Ash choked back a shocked gasp. Lainey looked between the guys, not understanding what Essie had just said. Whatever it was, it meant something to them. Something important. Ash stared at Phoenix, and Lainey could practically see the puzzle coming together for him.

"It all makes sense now," he whispered.

"What's going on? What makes sense?" she demanded.

Phoenix and Ash both refused to look at her. Essie, however, had no such qualms. Her gaze froze Lainey to the spot.

"When the time comes, you must not refuse. Acceptance is the key."

"What does that mean?" Her head swiveled back and forth, looking for answers from the guys. "Will someone please tell me what is going on?"

Ash only sat back on the couch and stared at his hands. Essie poured another cup of tea. Phoenix slowly looked at Lainey, profound sadness in his eyes. Her heart stuttered at the look.

"What?" she whispered.

He shook his head and inhaled deeply, settling his shoulders. He turned to Essie.

"Is there anything else we need to know?"

"You have all the pieces. You just have to put them together."

"Thank you for helping us."

She looked sad as she responded, "It is the only way I can fix the wrong I made by agreeing to create the curse."

Lainey blindly followed the guys out of the cottage. The clearing held a chill—or maybe it was just the uncertainty and confusion gripping her chest. She wanted to ask them what it all meant. She wanted to demand answers. But their remote expressions held her back. Lainey kept looking at Phoenix, seeing the distance he had created between them since Essie's words. Whatever she had told him mind to mind had something to do with her. She needed to know what it was.

They made their way back through the forest, following the birch tree trail in the opposite direction. It wasn't long before Lainey noticed Phoenix and Ash warily looking around. She slowed her steps and glanced through the trees, squinting to see deep into the shadows.

"Fuck!"

She heard Ash curse, and she spun around to see him fall to his knees, hands clutched to his belly. A knife protruded from between his fingers, blood seeping through and running down his abdomen. She attempted to rush to his side, but something swept her legs out from under her.

Lainey dropped to the ground, wrists barking with pain as they caught her weight. She rolled onto her back and fumbled for the gun holstered at her side. Standing above her was a massive fae male. He was wearing dark blue armor with some sort of crest displayed on the breastplate—a shield of vines with a single rose in the middle. She didn't have time to study it further. Her hand closed around the butt of her gun just as a boot landed on her forearm. The pressure caused her fingers to spasm, and she lost hold of the gun.

Distantly, she heard the sounds of metal clashing and more curses, these coming from Phoenix. She felt a burst of heat and saw red light flare in the corner of her eye as his magic swept into the fray. She refocused her attention on the fae crushing her arm.

Her other hand went to the holster at her hip again. If she could get her other gun, she could try to use it left-handed. Even if she only injured the warrior, she would have a chance at getting away. Before she could reach behind her, smoke swirled around the warrior's hand. He raised it in Lainey's direction, and she screamed as the smoke flew toward her. Blackness enveloped her, and pain exploded in her head. She fought to stay awake, but lost. Her eyes slid shut, and she knew no more.

When Lainey came to, the first thing she noticed was the cold, hard ground underneath her. She groaned and grabbed her head, prodding her skull for injuries and wincing at a particularly sore spot. Sticky blood coated her fingers when she pulled her hand away.

She rolled to her stomach and pushed herself up on all fours before taking a fortifying breath and lifting her head. Stars blinked in and out of her vision, and everything spun dizzily around her. She clamped her mouth shut and swallowed repeatedly, forcing back the wave of bile that burned up her throat.

When she was sure she wasn't going to get sick, she crawled to the wall in front of her and used it to push up into a sitting position. Her gaze was drawn to her wrist, where a metal band was clasped. It was cool against her skin, and no matter how hard she pulled at it, it remained fastened. Her stomach sank as she attempted to reach her magic. There was nothing there. No wind rushing through her veins. None of the comforting presence she had quickly gotten used to. The absence of it left her feeling empty.

She shoved her arm behind her back, as if she could forget about it if she couldn't see it, and looked around. Fear almost knocked her back down when she took in her surroundings. Rough stone walls and floors, thick iron bars, a drain in the floor stained a suspicious shade of copper. No bed, no blankets. No windows to the outside world. She was in a cell. A dungeon. Torches hung outside the cell, breaking up the darkness in flickering orange and red.

She began to shake. First her arms, then her legs. Soon her

whole body was trembling uncontrollably. She was locked in a dungeon in the faerie realm. A world she had just learned existed. She had no idea where Phoenix and Ash were. She remembered Ash on his knees, his blood spilling from a wound in his stomach. He could've been dead.

Her vision blurred, and she realized she was crying. The only sound she heard was her gasping breath as she tried to fill her lungs. Panic overtook her swiftly. What was she going to do now? She had no idea who held her captive. Was it the Seelie queen or the Unseelie queen? Surely whoever it was would kill her to keep someone from using her to break the curse.

She had to get ahold of herself. She couldn't let herself fall into panic, or she knew she would never make it out of here alive. Pressing her hands against the rough stone floor, she grounded herself and took deep, calming breaths. When she was calm enough, she crawled to the metal gate barring her exit. She tried to see past her cell, but all she could see was a rough stone corridor with flickering torches.

"Phoenix? Ash?" Lainey called into the silence. No answer. Either they weren't in here with her or they were injured and unable to answer. She pressed back her fear at that thought.

The sound of a door opening and heavy boots thudding down the hall had Lainey's heart kicking up a notch. She pressed herself against the back wall of her cell. Her heart pounded in her chest as a guard appeared.

He wore dark green clothing, and his long blond hair was pulled back to reveal his sharp features. His expression was grave, and his hand was wrapped around the pommel of a sword at his hip.

"Come forward." His no-nonsense command was spoken in a deep baritone.

Lainey couldn't move. She was too terrified. She sifted through her thoughts. Her weapons had been taken; her magic was gone. Her options were either to run when the chance arose or to follow his commands. Running would be fruitless.

She slowly approached the door, and the cell unlocked with a wave of the guard's hand. He grabbed her arm firmly, but not painfully, and led her out of the dungeon. Lainey cataloged as much as she could of her surroundings and any possible escape routes. Her reflection stared back at her from the pale marble floors veined with gold. She tried to ignore how wide eyed she appeared, like a deer in the headlights. Or how tangled and knotted her hair was.

Beautiful pieces of art hung on the walls—paintings, etchings, and sculptures—but she didn't spare a second glance at them. She looked past open doors and through windows. Her hope slowly faded the more she saw. There were guards everywhere. All well-armed and alert. It would take a miracle to make it out undetected.

She didn't understand why the only fae she saw were guards until they reached what must have been the throne room. They approached the massive golden doors carved with aspects of the elements—suns, trees, animals, streams, flowers, fire. Behind the doors, Lainey could hear the sounds of many eager voices.

Before she could prepare herself, the doors opened on a quiet wind, and the voices inside fell silent. The lack of sound was deafening. Lainey could hear her heartbeat in her ears, could hear her breath rasping in and out of her lungs. Her gaze bounced around the room, over the crowd of fae, and finally landed on the raised dais.

She barely noticed the beautiful fae sitting atop the throne. She had eyes only for the person standing next to it. Her chest squeezed painfully at the distant expression on Phoenix's face, as if he didn't even recognize her. His glance in her direction was filled with cold indifference, and it froze Lainey's heart.

What was he doing up there? Why was he looking at her like she was a stranger he couldn't wait to abandon? She struggled to contain her despair and arrange her features into the same frozen mask as his. Two could play at that game. She wouldn't give him the satisfaction of seeing her break.

When she was sure her emotions were in check, she shifted her gaze to the queen. Her beauty was indescribable. She was exactly how Lainey had pictured a faerie queen. Her long black hair fell well past her waist in loose, shiny waves. Her eyes were the most beautiful shade of purple, like chips of amethyst staring out of her dark face. She was elegant, ethereal, and calculating. Her presence demanded attention.

She smiled warmly at Lainey. "Welcome to the Seelie Court."

Lainey didn't know what to do or say. Instead, she stood tall and kept her gaze on the queen despite the pull to look at Phoenix.

The queen's smile turned vulpine. "You will kneel before me," she hissed.

Lainey's knees were kicked from behind, and she hit the floor. She bit back her shout of pain, but she couldn't stop the tears that welled in her eyes. She didn't let them fall, though.

"Queen Orabelle will be respected," her guard said.

She swallowed and looked at Queen Orabelle with her chin raised. Orabelle wasn't her queen. Lainey was part of no court in Faerie. She would have had no problem showing the queen respect, except Lainey hadn't been shown any yet. Fair was fair.

Queen Orabelle laughed pleasantly. "You have some fire in you, Elena Holloway."

Lainey couldn't keep the shock from showing on her face at the use of her full name.

"Yes, I know who you are. And you have caused quite the stir in Faerie. It seems you have the ability to break the curse." She paused dramatically. "I can't let that happen."

Lainey said nothing. She remembered what Essie had said about Orabelle being under Esmeray's thrall. There would be no talking her out of this plan.

"I have been told you have something important to Queen Esmeray, or a piece of it at least." Queen Orabelle turned her attention to Phoenix. "Thanks to my nephew, I know you are in possession of Azura's amulet. You will tell me where it is. After that, my dear, I'm afraid I cannot allow you to live, and risk someone completing the ritual."

Lainey shook her head. She wouldn't give up her piece of the amulet willingly, and she sure as hell wouldn't tell them Ash had the other piece. She didn't even know where he was. Why hadn't Phoenix told Queen Orabelle?

The queen tsked and shook her head sadly. "I was afraid you wouldn't be cooperative. How about a little incentive?"

Queen Orabelle snapped her fingers, and Lainey braced herself for some kind of magical attack. She wasn't prepared for the sharp pain of her head being yanked back by a fist in her hair. She bit her cheek to keep from crying out. Despite her attempts at not showing pain, she wasn't able to hold back a scream as green vines snaked around her body and tightened painfully.

They squeezed her like a cobra. Her lungs constricted, and she was sure her ribs were precariously close to snapping. They squeezed her abdomen, compressing all her organs. The pain was overpowering. She screamed until her throat hurt, but the pain didn't stop.

There was a commotion behind her, and even with the pain, Lainey silently prayed it was Ash coming to save her. But through watering eyes, Lainey could see the man wasn't Ash. He had shoulder-length brown hair and familiar blue eyes. He appeared older, with laugh lines around his mouth and crinkles at the corners of his eyes, like he was used to smiling. He wasn't smiling now. He looked terrified and shocked at the same time. His mouth was parted, and his blue eyes were wide as he stared at Lainey.

"Please, stop!" His voice echoed through the throne room, and he fell to his knees in front of the crowd. "Please! I beg you, my queen. Stop!"

Queen Orabelle waved her hand, and the vines disappeared. Lainey collapsed to the ground and curled herself into a ball. She gasped and heaved and cried as the echoes of pain reverberated through her body. She lifted her head enough to look at the dais, at Phoenix. His expression hadn't changed. Somehow, that hurt worse than the vines had. She turned her head to look at the man kneeling on the floor.

"What is this?" the queen demanded.

"My queen, I beg of you. Do not harm her."

"What reason do you have for your request?"

The man looked back at Lainey, bright blue eyes shining with emotion. "She is my daughter."

Chapter Eighteen

The ground slid out from under her. The word echoed through her mind. *Daughter.* Lainey couldn't comprehend it. She didn't have a dad. He left. He didn't exist. This man had to be lying. It was too much. Everything was happening too fast.

Queen Orabelle laughed, dragging Lainey's attention away from the man claiming to be her long-lost father.

"What kind of queen would I be if I didn't at least give you two time to catch up?" She snapped her fingers, and Lainey's guard once again wrapped his hand around her bicep. "Take her to a room. She might as well be comfortable before I kill her. But guard her well. We can't have her escaping. The fate of Faerie lies in her death."

Lainey was almost through the door when Queen Orabelle called out, "Oh, and Lainey? Think very hard about whether you want to keep the location of the amulet to yourself. This was just a taste of what you will endure if you do not cooperate."

Lainey slid her gaze to Phoenix. He turned away to face the queen. She smiled up at him again, and he smiled back. Lainey's breath hitched in her throat.

She was numb as the guard escorted her through the palace

halls. Too many feelings stirred inside her. Too many questions were left unanswered. She couldn't even let herself think of Phoenix. His betrayal hurt her worse than the vines had, and she couldn't understand why. She could handle the reappearance of her dad. She could even handle the threat of her impending death. But the lack of warmth in Phoenix's gaze was the dagger in her chest.

His betrayal left her aching and bleeding. She had fought that damn blood bond with everything she had, but she had still fallen under its thrall. She had come to crave his touch, his taste, his flames. She hadn't even realized how far she had fallen until he left her, like she was nothing but a pile of ashes blowing in the wind.

Lainey wished like hell she could've been happy. Wasn't this what she wanted? For him to be out of her life, or what was left of it at least? Without him, she could stand on her own two feet. She could make her own choices without the bond pulling her closer to him. Everything he had done to her had taken away her choices. At least now she could choose to stand tall and proud when her death came for her.

The guard led her to a guest room and closed the door behind her. The sound of the lock falling into place echoed through the chamber. Lainey looked around, not really seeing anything. She didn't know how long she stood there, staring at nothing and everything. Her body hurt, and her mind was spinning in a hundred different directions. A knock at the door brought her back to the present.

She turned just as her dad walked into the room. Their gazes clashed, and seeing those eyes up close caused her breath to hitch. She thought they had looked familiar. She saw those eyes every time she looked in the mirror. It was something she and Emma had shared. Apparently, they shared that with this man too.

Lainey's legs gave out, and she collapsed to the floor. She didn't know what to feel toward him. He was her dad, her blood, the reason she had magic. He was also the cause of everything bad that had happened to her. The kernel of anger that always burned in her chest at the thought of him burned hotter.

"Elena," he breathed in wonder. He slowly approached and knelt on the floor before her. He reached out his hand as if he would brush her tangled hair away from her face.

She jerked out of his reach and winced at the pain in her chest and abdomen. "No!" She stood and put distance between them. "You don't get to walk in here and act like you care." As soon as she started her tirade, she couldn't stop. Her words spilled out of her like a dam had broken. "You left us. You left us, and everything went to hell. Everything that has happened is your fault. You're the reason they're gone. You're the reason I'm alone. You're the reason I'm about to be killed for some stupid fucking curse. Fuck you! Fuck you and whatever you feel like you have to say to make everything better. You can't, so don't even try." She was crying and she didn't care. It was all just too much.

He let her rage at him. He sat on the floor and let her flay him with her words. His eyes shone with unshed tears when those words eventually ran dry. "Your mother and sister ..."

"Dead. Both of them. Because of you."

His tears spilled over, silently tracking down his cheeks. It was his expression that cooled Lainey's anger. He looked lost and heartbroken. He looked exactly like she felt. As her anger melted away, she sat on the edge of the bed, her fire spent.

Her dad looked at her with such sadness in his eyes. "What happened to them?"

Lainey exhaled before digging into the pain of her past. "Mom ended up in a psych ward. Everyone thought she was crazy. She took her own life when I was fifteen."

He closed his eyes, and the tears fell harder.

"Emma ..." Her voice broke on her sister's name. She cleared her throat before continuing. "Emma was murdered. She was used in a failed attempt at breaking the curse. An innocent half-breed sacrificed. She was killed for no reason except that she had your magic flowing through her veins."

Her dad shuddered, his shoulders shaking as he silently shed his tears. Lainey tried to feel bad for him. She tried to imagine what it must have been like to learn your wife and daughter were dead and the only living daughter left was about to be killed. She couldn't do it.

"You left us to our fates. Why?"

He shook his head. "I never meant to. I returned to Faerie to buy your mom a birthday present. The gates were locked while I was here. I had no way to return. No way to reach you. I spent all my days trying to find a way through. I never could. Now it's too late." His eyes shone with so many emotions when he looked at her. "Elena, my daughter, I never wanted to leave you. You and Emma were the shining lights in my life. Your mother was my one true love. The life we had built together, the love we had for each other and you girls. Those days were the happiest of my life."

Lainey closed her eyes. She couldn't look at him, sitting on the floor before her, pouring out his heart, saying all the words she had been dying to hear her whole life.

"My life ended the day I realized I wouldn't be able to return to you. My girls," his voice broke, and tears streamed down his face. "My three beautiful girls, who meant more to me than my own life, were ripped away from me. I can't bear the thought of the pain you went through. Oh god, Elena. I am so, so sorry."

Before she could think about what she was doing, Lainey was on the floor with him. He wrapped his arms around her, and what little control she'd held over her emotions disappeared. She became the little girl, crying alone in her room for a family she would never have, a life she would never live. She sat in her dad's strong arms as he held her, and they both cried for all they had lost, for the time that had been stolen from them.

"I'm sorry," she whispered.

His brows were drawn down when he pulled away. "Whatever are you sorry for?"

"For hating you for so long. For blaming you for everything

wrong in my life. For meeting you only so we can be separated again when the queen has me killed."

He swallowed thickly at her words. "Don't apologize for the way you felt, Elena. You had a right to all of those feelings. And, damn it, I won't let her kill you."

She barked out a humorless laugh. "How do you propose to pull that off?"

"I don't know, but I'm sure as hell going to find a way. I won't let her take my baby girl away from me again."

Lainey's vision went blurry. "I don't even know your name," she whispered.

He smiled at her and, damn, it was such a punch to the gut. It was Emma's smile.

"My name is Zephyr, but I would really like it if you just called me dad."

She sobbed, and her heart seemed to heal a little at his words. "Okay ... dad."

Not surprisingly, Lainey wasn't able to sleep that night. The bed was comfortable, but she ached all over, and her mind wouldn't turn off. She woke the next morning feeling mentally and physically exhausted. She had thought long and hard about her dad's words after he left. Lainey believed every one of them, and it crushed her to think of everything they had lost because of the curse. She wondered how many other families had been torn apart because two queens decided to play god and lock the gates to Faerie. Her anger was rekindled, this time aimed at the queens. She was more determined than ever to break the curse that had destroyed her world, her family.

Lainey spent her day wandering around the room she had been given. It was a simple room consisting of a bed, dresser, nightstand, and wash basin. She washed her hair in the basin to rinse out as much blood as she could. After, she finger-combed her hair to the best of her ability. She didn't have any clean clothes to wear, so she had to put on her dirty and torn leggings and tunic. At least they were black and hid most of the blood and dirt.

She searched the room for anything to use as a weapon and, not surprisingly, she found nothing. She also spent a good hour pulling at the bracelet on her wrist, trying to get the damn thing off. All that resulted from her attempts was a wrist rubbed raw and aching. The bracelet wouldn't budge.

Her dad didn't visit her again. Before he'd left the previous night, he'd said he had some people he needed to see. He was hopeful he could find a few who did not like the way Queen Orabelle had been ruling. He claimed that, since the curse, she had turned more violent and cruel. The queen, who loved the light and shone with it, had slowly disappeared until the fae sitting on the throne was a stranger to her people.

Lainey furiously tried to keep from thinking about a certain fire elemental. Any time he wandered into her thoughts, she pushed him out and slammed the door. She found herself doing that more and more as the time passed. With nothing else to think of besides her impending death and hopeful escape with her dad, Phoenix seemed to creep in any chance he got.

Lainey didn't know what to make of his change of heart. She remembered the conversation they'd had in New York about him technically belonging to the Unseelie Court through no fault of his own. She could understand his desire to get in the good graces of the Seelie queen, she just never would have thought he would do it the way he did.

His betrayal stung. She had thought there had been more between them than just the blood bond. She had thought they were becoming friends. They'd both opened up to each other about their past and the things that haunted them. Apparently, she'd been wrong. Maybe the bond distorted her thoughts about him. Maybe it made her want to view him in a different light than what reality was showing her.

Whatever it was, she hurt, and she hated that she was hurting because of him.

Two times throughout the day, food was delivered. The guard outside slipped it in before closing and locking the door behind him. She ate the food without really tasting it. Each second that ticked by was one second closer to her death. She paced the room anxiously, counting each of her heartbeats. Soon, they would stop, unless her dad got her out. She kept expecting the door to open and the queen to appear. The wait was agony.

That evening, after the sun had set and the moon had risen, her door opened. She didn't bother to turn around. She stared at the night sky through the small window in her room, savoring her last sight of the beauty. This was it. The time had come. Soon, she would see her mom and sister again. The thought didn't comfort her like she thought it would.

"Lainey."

Her name on Phoenix's lips was not what she'd expected to hear. She stiffened. The pull toward him begged her to turn around. She refused and kept her gaze trained on the stars outside. She didn't want to hear anything he had to say. Silently, she begged him to leave.

He didn't. Instead, she heard his footsteps come closer. The temperature slowly rose until she had to close her eyes against the familiar comfort of his magic.

His voice was strained when he said, "Lainey, please look at me."

She shook her head. She couldn't let herself do that, or she would be lost all over again.

"It's not what you think. Let me explain."

She huffed out a laugh void of any humor. "You don't need to explain anything. I get it. There is nothing here but the bond, something you regret just as much as I do. You saw an opportunity to get rid of the temptation it gives you while getting in the good graces of the Seelie queen." She finally turned to look at him.

His expression was pained. His jaw clenched tightly, a muscle ticking. He shook his head and opened his mouth to speak, but she cut him off.

"You can be part of the Seelie Court again and end the bond at the same time. You played it well, my friend. Congratulations." Tears slipped down her cheeks, and she angrily wiped them away.

Phoenix stepped closer. Lainey retreated as far as she could, until the wall pressed coldly against her back. He gently wiped a tear off her cheek, and she couldn't prevent her eyes from fluttering shut at the touch. The fucking bond, always clouding her emotions where he was involved. She hated it. She hated him. She hated that he made her feel this way.

"That's not how it works, Lainey." He rubbed his thumb back and forth across her cheek and stepped even closer. "The bond doesn't affect me."

Her eyes shot open. "What?" she whispered.

His eyes began to smolder, and the air grew warmer. "There is no pull for me. At least not from the blood bond."

She was having a hard time breathing as she let his words sink in.

"You think I don't want you? Think again, Lainey." He pressed his hips against hers, and his gaze dropped to her mouth.

She sucked in a breath. There was no denying how turned on he was, she could feel it against her thigh. Her heart was pounding at the realization.

"I want you, Lainey, and not because of a blood bond."

He took his time lowering his mouth to hers, giving her the chance to pull away. She didn't. The kiss burned through her, heating her blood and driving her to desperation. She tangled her fingers in his hair and held on tightly. He rocked his hips against hers, and she moaned at the sensation.

As his hands slipped under her shirt and left a burning trail across her skin, she managed to gather her wits. She shook her head, clearing it further of his intoxicating scent.

"No!" She pushed his shoulders, shoving him backward and

putting space between them.

"What ..." He looked dazed, lost in his desire. His hair was disheveled from her fingers. His eyes were still glowing copper. "What's wrong?"

"What's wrong? So many things are wrong, Phoenix." She took a deep breath, exhaling to ground herself. It would do no good to yell. "You may not have a bond affecting your emotions or feelings, but what about me? How do I know what I really feel for you with the bond's influence? You can make the choice to want me. I don't get to do that. I can't choose you without knowing if it's how I really feel or if it's the bond."

Phoenix closed his eyes, and his shoulders dropped. He rubbed his face with both hands. "Fuck. You're right." He looked up at her with such yearning, she almost took a step toward him. "I'm sorry. Shit, Lainey, I'm so sorry."

"And let's not forget I don't even know whose side you're on anymore," she added pointedly.

"Yours. I will always only be on your side."

She raised her eyebrows in question. "From where I was forced to kneel before the queen with my magic taken away"—she shook her wrist at him for good measure—"it certainly doesn't look that way. I was tortured in front of you, and you did nothing to stop it."

He flinched but straightened his shoulders. "They took you. They took you, and I couldn't fight them all. Ash was hurt, and you were gone. I didn't know what else to do, so I claimed to be bringing you to the Seelie queen. I was able to get an audience with Queen Orabelle. I couldn't let her kill you, so I told her you knew where the amulet was. A reason not to kill you immediately. She agreed to lock you away, which gave me time to find a way out for you. I hated seeing her torture you, Lainey, but I had no choice. I couldn't blow my cover."

She looked into his eyes, burning with sincerity and an emotion Lainey didn't want to name.

"I'm getting you out of here, Lainey."

Chapter Nineteen

His words soothed the jagged hole in her heart. She believed him. She always believed him. From early on, she'd trusted his words, even though common sense screamed at her not to. Something had always made her trust that he would keep her safe. She knew now he would do anything to get her out of the queen's hands.

She swallowed. "My dad ..." That felt so strange to say. She had to stop and regroup her thoughts.

"He's going to help us," Phoenix interrupted. "I went to him last night and explained everything. I knew he would help."

Lainey almost screamed as tears blurred her vision. She wiped at her eyes with frustration. She had never been an emotional person. Living a life filled with constant loss had hardened her. The past few days though, she had cried more than she had in her entire life. She hated it.

"How are we doing this? Wait! Is Ash okay? Where is he?"

"He's fine. He snuck off and he's waiting for us down the river."

She breathed a sigh of relief. "When do we leave?"

"Now." He grabbed her hand and started pulling her toward the door.

"Whoa, wait. Now? At least tell me you have a plan."

He turned his head to look at her, and his smirk ... fuck butterflies—an entire flock of birds took flight in her stomach.

"Where is the fun in that?"

He pulled her through the door, and Lainey saw the guard laying on the ground facedown. A puddle of blood spread across the marble floor, the red bright against the white.

"Is he ..."

"Not dead. Although he will probably wish he was when he learns you escaped." Phoenix leaned over the guard and pawed through his pockets. When he stood, he held a small, square stone in his hand. "Come here."

Lainey stepped up to Phoenix, and he grabbed the wrist with the band on it. With a wave of the stone over the band, the clasp came undone, and the band fell to the floor with the ping of metal on marble. Her magic rushed back to her, a tidal wave of wind buffeting her and filling her veins. Lainey took a moment to soak in the feeling.

"Let's go." Phoenix's shoulders were tense as he glanced down the hall in both directions.

Lainey swiftly bent down and grabbed the band from the floor, stuffing it in her pocket before she let him lead her through the palace. They had to duck behind closed doors and statues when they heard someone approaching more times than she was comfortable with. She was jumpy and on edge, which would account for her screaming when they opened the door to a servant's stairwell and found a woman standing there.

Phoenix slapped a hand over Lainey's mouth and dragged her through the door, quickly closing it behind him. "For shit's sake, Lainey. Do you want people to know you're escaping?"

She pushed his hand away and glared at him. "In case you didn't notice, there is someone standing on the stairs with us," she hissed.

"Yeah, she's helping us."

"You always leave out important details. Maybe you should have told me that before we left my room."

"Um, guys, I think we should keep moving. Your dad has organized a diversion to distract the guards." The servant gave Lainey a tentative smile. She was a beautiful younger fae with bright blue eyes and blond hair. She started walking down the stairs but turned her head back to continue talking. "I'm Nin. I'm your cousin, Lainey."

Lainey missed the next step and would have tumbled down the stairs if Phoenix hadn't caught her. "My cousin?"

"Yes. My mom is your dad's sister." She smiled, and Lainey immediately saw the resemblance. It was the eyes, the bright blue and slightly upturned corners.

"I have more family?" she whispered, once again blinking back tears.

"Oh, yes. Quite a few, actually. Grandma had seven kids. There are twenty of us cousins." Nin laughed quietly at Lainey's shocked expression.

"I had no idea."

"One day you'll be able to meet them. I promise we'll make that happen."

They reached the bottom of the servant's stairs and Nin popped her head out to make sure the coast was clear. She waved them forward, and they followed her down narrow hallways and past closed doors. They paused at every intersection, waiting and listening for pursuit. Lainey held her breath, muscles tense, waiting for the shout of alarm. It never came.

Nin motioned to a door at the end of the hallway. "That will take you to the delivery yard. Straight across is a gate. You'll have to climb it; it's warded to alert the queen when it's opened. Once you're on the other side, head for the village. Glaze and Honey is about a five-minute walk due south. My mom will meet you there."

Before Lainey could blink, Nin had wrapped her arms around her and squeezed tightly.

"Thank you," Lainey whispered.

After a final squeeze, Phoenix and Lainey were out the door and crossing the delivery yard. They kept to the shadows, and Lainey was thankful for the scattered clouds that had rolled in. When they reached the gate, Phoenix placed his hands on her waist, and the heat of him at her back caused her to lean back against his chest, desperate to soak it all in.

He leaned down, and his breath fanned across her cheek as he whispered, "Ready?"

She nodded, and he lifted her until she could reach the top of the gate. Using her arms, she hoisted herself up and swung her legs over, proud of herself for being able to do so. She landed in a crouch and looked up just in time to see Phoenix swing over. When he landed, he grabbed her hand and quickly led her away from the palace.

She couldn't believe how easy it had been to escape. She kept looking behind them, expecting to see guards chasing after them, or an angry queen wreathed in magic. So far, it was quiet, not a soul to be seen. She hoped her dad wasn't part of the distraction. She didn't want him to risk himself for her any more than he already had.

Phoenix changed their direction so they were heading south. Nin's directions were spot-on. It wasn't long before Lainey saw the sign above a striped awning: Glaze and Honey. A figure stood in the alley next to the building. When she saw them, she beckoned them forward and disappeared into the shadows.

They followed, and she led them in through a backdoor. Dim light illuminated a back room filled with boxes and crates of ingredients. The lady smiled at Lainey, and she knew immediately this was her aunt. She had the same blue eyes and blond hair as Nin. This night was just too surreal.

"Elena," her aunt said, "I am so glad to finally meet you."

"Um, you can call me Lainey." She looked hesitantly at Phoenix. She didn't know how to act around this woman, her aunt. Her only family had been her mom and sister her whole life.

"Lainey, then. I'm your Aunt Maie, your father's little sister. I can't begin to tell you how happy we are to know you're safe." Her aunt clasped her hands and gave a gentle squeeze.

"Well, I'm not safe yet."

"No, but you will be. Your father will be here any minute."

Sure enough, the sound of wooden wheels clacking on the cobbled street drew their attention.

"That's him." Aunt Maie pulled Lainey in for a hug. "I'll hopefully see you soon. We have a lot of catching up to do."

Lainey's throat closed up, and she couldn't speak. Instead, she gave a wavering smile and nodded. Maie seemed to understand. She quickly wiped under her eyes, brushing away her own tears.

"Wait here." Phoenix opened the back door and slipped outside. He returned a second later. "It's clear. Let's go."

In the alley, her dad sat on the bench of a wooden cart drawn by an ancient-looking horse. He spared her a warm smile before motioning them toward the back. Phoenix pulled away a rough blanket and hopped up, then bent and ran his hands along the bed of the wagon.

"Ha. Found it." He pulled up a hidden door and beckoned for Lainey to climb up.

She scrambled into the wagon and looked dubiously at the small hidden compartment. "You can't be serious."

"As a heart attack. Get in."

She sighed and slid in. The space was so small, she had to lay on her side with her legs curled up to her chest to fit. She jerked when Phoenix climbed in with her. She hadn't been aware he'd be joining her.

"It won't take them long to realize we are both missing and connect the dots. They can't see me either." He pulled the hidden door shut and curled up behind Lainey, his chest pressed against her back.

He banged on the side of the wagon, and Lainey felt every bump as the horse pulled its load down the street. It was dark in the compartment. She couldn't even see her hand directly in front of her face. When she reached out her arm, she immediately felt the rough wooden wall. When she reached up, she felt the ceiling. So close. The walls and ceiling were too close. She closed her eyes and took a deep breath. It didn't help.

She'd never realized she had an aversion to tight spaces. In her defense, she had never been locked inside a small space like this before. She tried to control her panic at the thought of being locked in there forever. Her heart beat frantically in her chest, and her breath left her lungs in heaving gasps.

"Hey," Phoenix whispered. His breath ruffled the hair at the nape of her neck. His hand landed on her shoulder and slid down her arm until it rested on her stomach. "Breathe, Lainey."

She shivered at his whispered words in her ear. Her focus narrowed on his hand splayed across her stomach. The temperature was rising, his magic surging. Hers tried to respond, but she kept a tight lock on it. The last thing they needed was a blast of wind blowing the cart apart.

Phoenix seemed to notice her breathing change, her frantic gasps of fear becoming gasps of arousal. His hand slid under her shirt, and his skin blazed a path up her rib cage, his calluses gently scraping.

She knew he was doing this to keep her mind off the fact she was locked in a tight space with no light. She knew he was playing to the bond, and she let him. This was better than the fear. She arched her neck, giving him access to the sensitive spot there.

He accepted the invitation. His lips brushed lightly before his tongue snaked out and licked up the column of her throat. She felt as if she would combust right there as she imagined what that tongue would feel like someplace else.

He removed his mouth, and Lainey almost whimpered at the loss of sensation until she felt his teeth scraping against her pulse point. She felt the sharpened points of his canines gently press into her skin. The nip was a promise of what could happen. He pressed harder, the whisper of pain eclipsed by her desire. Just a little harder and he would break skin. She did whimper then.

Phoenix stiffened behind her and froze. He quickly pulled away from her throat and cursed roughly. She felt him shake himself and put as much distance between them as he could in the tight space.

"I'm sorry," he said roughly.

She swallowed, disappointed he had stopped. Disappointed that she was disappointed. Why couldn't she get a grip on her emotions around him? She didn't respond to his apology. She didn't think she could speak. And even if she could have, she feared what she might say. She was scared she would beg him to continue.

Instead, she closed her eyes and counted her breaths, focused on the air entering and leaving her lungs. She lost herself in the rhythmic pattern, and before long, the horse slowed, and the cart came to a stop.

Phoenix opened the hidden door and jumped out before she could even move. He didn't wait to help her up. He was off the cart and in the woods before she was even out of the hidden compartment. She sighed in relief when she saw Ash standing at the back of the cart, arms open to help her down.

"You're okay!" She jumped down and wrapped herself around him. His earthy scent cleared her nose of Phoenix's bonfire.

"It will take more than a dagger to the stomach to kill me, little half-breed."

She chuckled and pulled away. "I'm glad you're back to your normal sarcastic self."

"Why did Nix run off like his pants were on fire?" Ash peered into the woods, but Phoenix was nowhere to be found.

Lainey turned her head away to hide the blood that rushed to her face. Her dad approached them, and she took that opportunity to change subjects.

"Ash, this is my dad, Zephyr. Dad, this is Ash. He's the other one who helped me in the human realm."

Ash's eyes widened. "Your dad? Whoa. That's quite a

surprise." He turned to her dad and stuck out his hand. "It's nice to meet you."

Her dad clasped Ash's hand and shook it. "Thank you for helping my daughter. I will forever be in your debt."

"Oh, no. Not necessary. It's been my pleasure playing babysitter."

At her dad's confused expression, Lainey glared at Ash and elbowed him in the side. "What happens now? I'm sure they won't stop looking for me. Or Phoenix, for that matter."

"As soon as the Unseelie queen learns Phoenix is here, she will start hunting him, for sure," Ash said. "As for what happens next, we need to find a place to hide and plan. Then we need to get to the Unseelie queen and take her out."

Lainey looked at her dad expectantly. "Are you going to come with us?"

He smiled sadly at her. "I wish I could. I need to return and make sure none of our family gets in any trouble for helping you escape."

Our family. Those words sent a lick of warmth to her heart. She had a family now. And she had put them in danger. "I'm so sorry. I never wanted any of them to get hurt."

Her dad pulled her in for a hug. "Never apologize for that, Elena. That's what family is for." He pulled back but kept his hands on her shoulders. "I will see you again. I will give you any help you may need in the coming days. Just send word to Maie's bakery."

She nodded and blinked away her tears. It felt so wrong to be saying goodbye when she had just found him. What if something happened? What if she never saw him again? She had so many questions. Questions about her mom and their life together. What the first year of her life had been like with the whole family. She needed to know him. She needed her dad in her life, finally.

"Don't cry, Elena."

He hugged her again, and she held on tightly, not wanting to let go. She breathed in his scent of fresh air, pulling it deep into her lungs and committing it to memory. When he finally pulled away, he placed a kiss on her forehead.

"I love you, Elena. Be careful." He gave Ash a look that promised pain should anything happen to her.

"I'll protect her with my life." Ash placed a hand on his heart and bowed his head.

Lainey watched her dad climb back onto the cart and drive away. When he was just a speck in the distance, Ash draped his arm over her shoulders and turned her toward the forest.

"Come on, little half-breed. Let's go find a place to hide for a bit."

"What about Phoenix?" She looked around, seeing no sign of him

"He'll pop up when he's ready. What did you do to send him running?"

"Where are we going to stay? I'm assuming a town is out of the question."

"Most definitely out of the question. And way to avoid my question, by the way." He grinned and squeezed her shoulders but thankfully let it drop. "I'm thinking we'll head back to Essie's place. See if she'll let us stay with her for a few days while we figure things out."

Lainey nodded. That sounded like a solid enough plan. "How did the Seelie queen find out about us in the first place?"

"I'm sure it was one of the townsfolk, probably the guy who Phoenix threatened. He most likely alerted the queen for some coin. People are desperate enough at this point to do anything."

"It's so sad. I pictured Faerie and the fae to be such a beautiful thing. Wild and carefree. This shadow of what it used to be is devastating."

Ash hummed his agreement. "Yeah. This is definitely not how my mom portrayed it. Hopefully, we can bring it back to its glory by breaking the curse and removing the Unseelie queen."

They lapsed into silence while they trekked through the woods. Ash kept a constant watchful eye on their surroundings.

Both of them kept a dagger in hand. Lainey wasn't about to be taken again.

Phoenix joined them as Essie's cottage came into view. He said nothing. He didn't even look at her. She wondered what exactly had happened in the compartment.

They stopped at the edge of the clearing and surveyed the cottage. The windows were dark, and no smoke puffed from the chimney.

"Where did she go?" Lainey asked quietly, afraid to broach the silence.

"I have no clue, but I'm sure she won't mind if we crash here for a bit. Let me scout it out first."

Lainey watched Ash disappear inside the cottage. Phoenix's presence next to her was a distraction. She wanted to ask what had happened in the cart. Back in the palace, he'd stated that his feelings for her were all his own and not because of the blood bond. But the way he'd acted in the cart made her question everything again. She had just gathered the courage to turn and ask him when Ash popped his head out the door.

"All clear," he called.

Phoenix took off across the clearing as if he couldn't get away from Lainey fast enough. Taking a deep breath, she followed him into the cottage, determination faltering once again.

Chapter Twenty

Essie's cottage lacked warmth with its owner gone, and not just because the fire was out. The colors appeared duller and the lighting more dim. The quiet that followed them inside held a sinister air.

Phoenix headed straight to the hearth and started a fire. The flames crackled to life and lit the living room in an orange glow. Ash headed to the kitchen to see what he could scrounge up for food. Lainey sat on the couch and pulled a blanket over her lap, watching the flames dance in the fireplace. Phoenix said nothing. He stood with an arm resting on the mantle while he also stared into the flames.

When Ash returned with an armful of random food, he sighed at the sight of them clearly trying to ignore the other's presence. "Will one of you please tell me what happened in the palace?"

Phoenix's shoulders tensed, and his hand fisted on the mantle.

"Well, they put me in a cell before dragging me to the lovely Queen Orabelle, who tortured me and decided I had to die. My long-lost father appeared, and the queen decided to play nice and give us time to reconnect. While waiting for my ultimate death, Phoenix enlisted the help of my entire family, and we escaped."

She smiled sweetly at Ash, daring him to say anything further regarding her and Phoenix.

Ash rolled his eyes and set the hoard of food on the table before the fireplace. "Okay, well then. What are we going to do about taking down Queen Esmeray?"

"We're not," Phoenix replied without looking at either of them.

"What do you mean 'we're not'?" Ash shot back.

Phoenix turned from the fire and looked Ash square in the eye. The fire burning in his gaze made Lainey recoil. "You know what has to happen to do that successfully."

"And your point?"

"That's not going to happen. Ever. So, we do nothing."

"You can't be serious." Ash stared incredulously at Phoenix.

Phoenix didn't respond, just held Ash's gaze intently.

Finally, having enough of their back and forth, Lainey spoke up. "Um, excuse me?" She raised her hand like she was in class.

Ash snorted. "Yes, Lainey?"

"What the hell are you guys talking about?"

"Nothing," Phoenix spoke up so quickly it made Lainey's brows raise.

"Doesn't seem like nothing."

"Well, it is, so don't push it," he snapped at her.

"Whoa. Back up, dude." She crossed her arms over her chest and glared at him. "I'll push it if I want. Besides, something tells me this has to do with me, in which case, I deserve to know. And going along with that, what happened with Essie the other day? That had to deal with me too, didn't it?"

Phoenix didn't answer, but his eyes shuttered, confirming Laney's suspicions.

"She's right, Nix. She has a right to know."

"God dammit," he growled and began pacing in front of the fireplace.

Lainey settled back against the cushions, trying to keep her anxiety in check.

Phoenix took a deep breath and rubbed his hands down his face. He didn't look at her, but he began to explain. "The fae have a special relationship with the stars. They tell us important things such as our history, our future, our births and deaths." He paused, and finally his gaze sought her out. "Our mates."

Lainey stopped breathing.

"Certain fae, usually elves, can read the stars. Apparently, it's been written that you and I ..."

"No," she whispered when he trailed off.

"We're mates, Lainey. Elvie sensed it, but when she found out about the blood bond, she assumed that was what she'd sensed. Half-breeds rarely find mates. And for us to have been in the human realm, it is even more unexpected."

She stared at him but didn't see him. Her mind had retreated. Her heart beat only because it was an automatic reaction. Same with her breathing. What control did she really have over her life? What choices did she really get to make? Her mate had been determined for her. The blood bond made her lust for him. None of it was her choice. She felt herself disconnecting. Her emotions were no longer in her control. Her magic soon followed, and her hair lifted from her shoulders, blowing about her face.

"Hey," Ash said quietly and stepped toward her.

"No." She couldn't take it. She couldn't deal with any of this right now.

Lainey stood and ran for the door, tearing it open and flying out into the night. The trees were dark sentinels—she weaved around them, their leafy branches blocking the light of the moon above. Blocking the damned stars that dictated her life and who she should love. Fuck that.

She was heaving, her lungs aching, when she finally slowed and stopped. She placed a hand on the trunk of a tree and bowed over. Gasping for breath, she felt wetness on her face. She reached up to find tears streaming down her cheeks. Again. She laughed mirthlessly.

She tilted her head back to the stars overhead that she couldn't see and screamed, "Fuck you!"

Lainey slid down the trunk and sat on the loamy surface of the forest floor. She had no clue what to do. All she'd ever wanted was to live a quiet life, to make enough money to support herself. To be able to buy coffee and books. Maybe find someone she could love, someone she could trust, who wouldn't leave her like everyone else did. Nothing had gone the way it was meant to.

The sound of a cracking branch brought her head around. Shit. Once again, she had run off into an unknown magical place. She peered into the darkness and saw a small, golden-furred fox approaching. She held her breath. The fox sniffed the air and glanced in her direction. Its tail swished once from side to side before it picked its way across the forest to her.

Lainey's eyes grew wider and wider the closer it got. When it was only a few feet away, she tentatively held out a hand. The fox snuffled against her palm, then rubbed its head against her hand. She felt a smile spread across her face and she scratched the fox behind its ears. It closed its eyes and leaned into the scratches. When she stopped, the fox walked closer and curled up in her lap.

She sat in amazement while the fox settled in and looked at her with bright green eyes, begging for more scratches. Lainey complied. She sat against the tree for what felt like an hour, petting the fox, enjoying the feel of its silken fur against her hand. Her body and mind relaxed more with each pass of her hand against the fur.

The fox shifted, and Lainey looked down. Suddenly, a bright light pierced the darkness, and a subtle pop sounded through the quiet. Lainey blinked, then blinked again. She screamed when she saw Ash's head in her lap, grinning at her.

She jumped up, dislodging him, and he cursed as his head hit the ground.

"What ... you ... I ..." she stuttered, breathing madly and rubbing her eyes.

He stood and rubbed the back of his head. "Ow."

She pointed at him. "But ... you ..."

"A fox, yes. Some earth elementals can shift into animal forms. I have never been able to until I came here to Faerie."

"You're naked!" she screeched and covered her eyes.

She could hear the smirk in his voice as he answered her. "Well, foxes don't wear clothing, so ... Gives a new meaning to foxy, eh?"

"Oh my god!"

He chuckled. "Okay, you can look now."

She peeked between her fingers to find him sitting behind a fallen tree, the trunk hiding the bits Lainey had no desire to see. She lowered her hands and glared at him.

"What the hell are you doing here? And, oh my god! I was petting you."

"Felt great, by the way. Nothing like a good rubdown."

"So gross, Ash." She shivered dramatically.

He suddenly turned serious in the only way Ash could. "You can't honestly believe we would let you run around out here by yourself? I followed you."

She sighed heavily and sat on the opposite side of the tree, their backs to each other. "I just needed some time."

"I get it. It's a lot to take in." When she didn't respond, he quietly asked, "Is it that horrible to have him as a mate?"

She broke a twig in half. "It's not that. It's the fact I have no say in anything in my life. The mate thing, the blood bond. Everything is driving me to him, and I didn't choose that. How am I supposed to know if he is what I really want when everything else is telling me this is how it's going to be?"

"Some fae forget that while the stars determine their mates, they don't force anything. Their job is to tell you this would be a good match, but it's up to you to decide. Yes, Nix may be your destined mate, but you don't have to choose him. He doesn't have to choose you. Your relationship doesn't have to be one of love or even lust. The stars don't make you feel anything for him. What you feel, that is all you."

"And the blood bond," she said bitterly.

"Think back to when you first met him. After you got to know him a bit, before the blood bond. How did you feel about him? I know you guys drove each other crazy. I know you claim to hate him. But what I've seen is the opposite. And I'm not talking about the lust or the draw of the bond."

"What are you talking about, then? Because from where I'm standing, the bond has done more than enough."

"There is a difference between love and lust, Lainey. The bond causes you to desire him physically. Take the lust out of the picture. How do you feel about him?"

She didn't answer. She didn't *have* an answer. His question threw her off guard. Taking away the desire, she wasn't sure how she felt. He drove her mad with his constant need for control and his overbearing personality and his constant commands. However, he also protected her. She felt safe around him, and she knew she could trust him. She had a feeling he would do anything for her. But was that love?

A sharp breeze blew through the forest, and Lainey shivered.

"We should head back," Ash said.

"I am not walking through the forest with you buck-ass naked."

She blinked, and the golden fox appeared in front of her with its head cocked to the side. Staring at those green eyes and the golden fur the exact same shade as his hair, she was amazed she hadn't connected the dots before.

"Let's go." She gave the fox a pat on the head and headed for the cottage.

When Lainey woke the next morning, the fire in the hearth had died down and left a chill in the air. She wrapped a blanket around her shoulders and headed into the kitchen. She stopped when she saw Ash at the table, his face carefully blank. He hadn't been quick enough to hide his features from her, though.

"What's wrong?" Her stomach dropped, and she feared what he was going to say.

Ash said nothing. He ground his teeth together and looked away, closing his eyes.

"What has he done?" she whispered. "What did Phoenix do?"

Ash met her eyes. "He left."

The blanket fell from her shoulders. "What do you mean, left? Where did he go?"

He looked away again and shook his head.

"Answer me, damn it! Where is he?" She stepped into the kitchen and got right in Ash's face, forcing him to look at her. "Tell me right now, or so help me god ..."

"Fuck." He slid back the chair and stood, running his hands through his hair. "Do you remember what Essie told you?"

Lainey thought back to that night and the many things Essie had said that made little sense at the time. Now, knowing about the mate thing, the pieces clicked into place. "She said, 'When the time comes, you must not refuse. Acceptance is key.'"

"In order for Phoenix to defeat Queen Esmeray, you need to accept him as your mate. He knew you would never do that on your own. He knew as soon as you realized he needed that acceptance you would do it just so he could successfully take on Esmeray. Phoenix didn't want the choice to be taken from you."

"Where did he go?" she asked quietly.

"To try to remove Esmeray from the throne alone. And die in the process, in all likelihood."

The world dropped out from beneath Lainey, and the room tilted. Only Ash's hand on her arm kept her from falling. The stupid bastard was going to get himself killed. She fought back tears as realization dawned. Phoenix had taken it into his own hands so she didn't feel forced to make a choice not her own. He knew he had already taken some of her choices away with the blood bond and was trying to keep that from happening again.

Phoenix was going against Queen Esmeray. He wouldn't survive. She was going to lose him, and that thought spurred her into action. She had already lost too many people she loved. Lainey would not lose another one, especially because he hadn't known she loved him. Fuck, she loved him. She really did. And the realization came too late.

She pulled her arm from Ash's grasp and headed for the door.

"Whoa, hold up! Where are you going?"

"I'm going to find him. I'm not letting him do this alone." She turned to face Ash. "Either you're coming with me or not. But you're not stopping me."

Whatever he saw in her face had him hurrying through the cottage, packing bags and preparing for another adventure through Faerie.

Lainey waited impatiently, practically bouncing on her toes while Ash gathered supplies. She couldn't keep her fear in check. How far could he have gotten? He only had one night ahead of them. If they pushed hard, would they be able to catch him?

Finally, after what felt like hours, Ash was ready. He handed her a bag, and they set off through the woods toward the Unseelie Court. Ash set an unforgiving pace. He appeared just as worried as she was. Phoenix was, after all, his best friend.

The day passed in a blur. Lainey didn't take notice of her surroundings, leaving their safety in Ash's capable hands. She was too focused on the recent discovery of her feelings. Now that she had a name to place with them, she was terrified of losing it. She had lost too many people she loved. Her track record wasn't good, and it seemed only fitting she would lose Phoenix to the curse as well.

As the sun set, Ash found a place for them to camp. Without Phoenix's magic, they had to resort to using a lighter Ash had brought with him from the human realm. Lainey sat near the flames and could have sworn they were different from Phoenix's —less bright, less warm, less welcoming.

"How long do you think it will take to get there?"

Ash glanced at the map he had pulled out to study. "About five days. We should pass into the Unseelie Court late tomorrow or early the next day."

"How far ahead of us could he possibly be? Is there a chance we could catch up to him?"

"Probably not. He's traveling alone and he will push himself to the point of exhaustion. We need to make sure we are rested and strong when we arrive, or there will be no way to get him out of there. If he's even still alive."

She looked up sharply at his words. Nausea rose in her stomach, and she pressed a hand there in an attempt to keep it at bay. The thought of Phoenix already being dead was overwhelming.

Ash noticed her dismay and sighed. "We need to be realistic, Lainey. Why would Queen Esmeray keep him alive? She would be smart to kill him on sight."

Lainey shook her head, trying to shove his words out of her ears. If she let herself fall down that rabbit hole, she would never escape. She needed to believe he was still alive until she had proof he wasn't. There was no other option. Besides, wouldn't she know if something happened to him? If they really were mates, shouldn't the bond have told her something like that? And if the Unseelie queen killed him ... Well, Phoenix's fire would pale in comparison to what Lainey would rain down on her.

Ash studied her. "What changed?"

She tried to pinpoint what exactly had changed. It was more of a *when* than a *what*. "I thought about what you said. I took a closer look at my feelings. When I realized he was gone, that he was in danger, it just hit me—the sudden realization that I can't stand the thought of him hurt or dying. That I can't lose him."

"So it's more than just you accepting the bond to keep him from getting hurt?"

"Yes," she whispered. "When we were in the palace, he told me the blood bond didn't affect him. He told me his feelings were real, not a product of the bond. The mate thing wouldn't cause that either, would it?"

"No. The mating doesn't make anyone feel any one way. What he feels, it's all him. And I've seen him with other women. I knew there was something else going on with him."

"What about your friend? The one who couldn't deal with the blood bond?"

Ash looked at her in surprise. "He told you about her?"

She nodded and looked expectantly at him. She didn't know why, but it mattered what he said.

"He never talks about that. I'm surprised he told you." He shook his head. "No, he never had any feelings for her besides friendship. The bond was hard on him. He hated seeing her like that."

In the quiet darkness, another question popped into her head. "What exactly does a mate bond entail?"

"A fae with a mate is ten times more powerful than one without. The mate bond increases your strength, both physically and magically. I'm assuming Phoenix will need that extra strength to defeat Esmeray." Ash handed Lainey a few biscuits he'd stolen from Essie. "It's pretty special to find your mate. Not all of us do."

They lapsed into silence, and Lainey nibbled on the biscuit. She stared into the flames, wishing desperately it was Phoenix's fire. When Ash settled down for the night, she asked another question that had been bouncing around her head.

"Do fae bite each other?"

Ash jerked upright and looked at her with wide eyes. He opened his mouth to answer, then shut it. He shook his head and closed his eyes. "Did he bite you?"

"Almost. In the cart, when we escaped. He stopped himself. That's why he ran off so fast."

He rubbed the back of his head before answering. "Most fae don't bite like that. Playful nips, but that's it. Nix is half banshee, though. Banshees bite and drain the blood of their prey."

Lainey's blood froze at his words. Was that what Phoenix was tempted to do? Did he have to fight that half of himself?

"I don't think Nix has any kind of blood lust like a banshee, but I don't know what a bite would do. Banshees are the vampires of the fae. Maybe the taste of your blood would send him into a frenzy. Who knows?"

She thought back to after she was attacked by the river. "He's tasted my blood before and didn't react like that."

"What the hell?" Ash muttered.

"He licked my wrist after the Cetrius bit me. It healed the wound."

Ash looked sharply at her. "Well, that was certainly risky."

"It's not like I knew! No one told me to watch out for that."

He sighed. "You're right. Nix should have known better." Ash was quiet for a moment before he sighed again. "Look, the way fae accept a mate bond is by a blood exchange. Since he has already given you his, I would avoid giving Phoenix any more of your blood unless you want to cement the bond. I doubt the little amount he already had did anything."

She tucked that tidbit of knowledge away to examine later, and they fell into silence again. Lainey curled up on her side and watched the flames dance until her eyes were too heavy to stay open. Tomorrow they would continue their quest, and she needed to be ready. She would fight with everything she had to get Phoenix back.

Chapter Twenty-One

"I THINK WE NEED TO SEND WORD TO YOUR DAD." THEY had been walking for half a day when Ash spoke up.

"About what?"

"I've been trying to think of a plan for when we get there. Unfortunately, it's going to depend on what we find out about Phoenix. Where he is being held. If he's injured. How guarded he is. I think we are going to need some backup. This is too big to take on ourselves."

"I don't know. The fewer people involved, the better, right? Won't it be easier to just get two of us in undetected?"

"Yeah, but the Unseelie queen has unimaginable magic. She is incredibly powerful. I'm afraid we are going to need all the help we can get. Also, your dad has been in Faerie longer than we have."

The idea of putting her newfound family in more danger didn't sit well with her. She didn't know if any of her family had already been hurt or captured while helping her escape. Lainey chewed on her lip, thinking of their options.

"We need to get the three pieces of the amulet together. Madam Elvie said not to unite the pieces until the last possible second. What will happen when we do unite them?"

"I wish I knew. There isn't much information on the amulet or how it was to be used. Only princess Azura knew that."

"Well, that's super helpful," she grumbled. "I don't like the idea of getting my family involved. Not when I just found them again."

"Let's compromise. Let's get your dad here, at least. He has been in Faerie this whole time. He might know what may or may not be happening at the Unseelie Court. His information could be invaluable."

"How long will it take him to get there? I don't want to wait. Every second we sit here is another second Phoenix could be hurting. Or worse."

"He can take a boat down the coast. With his wind, he'll make great time. It will only delay us a day or two. A delay that may end up saving Phoenix. We can't just rush in without more information."

Damn it. He had a point. Without knowing more, they were just as likely to get caught themselves, which would do Phoenix no good.

"How are we going to get word to him?"

Ash grinned at her and held out his hand. A small yellow bird landed in his palm and chirped at him. He ran a finger down the bird's head and whispered to it. A second later, the bird took off, heading toward the Seelie Court.

"You're a Disney princess in disguise, aren't you?"

He grinned at her. "Damn, my cover is blown."

The sun had started its descent by the time they came to the edge of the grassy plain they had been traversing. On the other side were large boulders and rocks, scattered like giants had thrown them every which way. Ash stopped and pursed his lips as he scanned the rocky ground ahead.

"The divide between Seelie and Unseelie lies in the middle of that. I would really like to get through it before we stop for the evening. Just be careful. Something doesn't quite feel right."

Lainey agreed. She had a bad feeling, like her instincts knew something was about to happen. Something cold and foreign brushed against her skin, causing the hairs on her arms to rise. Rubbing her hands up and down her arms, she squinted into the distance, looking for the cause.

"What is that?" she breathed.

"I have no idea, but we're going to cross anyway. Stay silent and alert. Weapons and magic at the ready."

Her magic surged forth as if it had heard Ash and was following his directions. She wrangled it back to herself but kept it at the ready. She also palmed her gun and clicked off the safety. After nodding to Ash, they set off toward the boulders.

Lainey had to crane her neck back to look to the top of most of the rocks. They were massive gray stones, pitted and cracked. A few of them almost looked like someone had carved something into them, like a face or a hand, but it was too weathered to make out. She wondered if they had been statues at some point.

The shadows cast by the boulders were so dark, she had to keep her eyes on Ash's blond hair, the only beacon she could see in the darkness. The sky appeared impossibly further away than it had outside of the boulder field, the moon and stars so small they barely provided any light. Only the sounds of their breathing and the occasional pebble shifting under their boots broke the heavy silence.

At least until a sound behind them, like something brushing against a rock, made Lainey spin around. She saw nothing out of the ordinary. When she turned back around, she had to stifle a gasp. Ash was gone. She looked around frantically but didn't see him. She rushed forward, staying as quiet as she could, hoping to catch up with him.

Again, the sound behind her drew her up short. She slowly turned around with her gun raised and—holy mother of god. Fear shot through her, so strong it almost knocked her off her feet. Standing not ten feet from her was the most terrifying creature she had ever seen. More terrifying than the mountain troll that had gutted and almost killed her.

This thing had three eyes, each so white there was no way it could see. Its snout was wet and dripping, and its mouth was very large. Large enough to grab her entire leg and rip it off. It had many rows of sharp teeth, but the two tusks protruding from its upper lip were what her focus narrowed on. They were pale white, and the little light provided by the moon glinted off them, illuminating reddish brown stains. It didn't have fur or feathers—it was scaled and sinewy. Powerful muscles shifted in its legs as it took a step toward her, hooved feet pawing at the dirt.

She would have screamed if she could've drawn breath into her lungs. As it was, her lungs had seized, no air in or out, and her panic rose even higher. She could feel her pulse in every part of her body as her heart thundered away. Where was Ash? She didn't know what to do. The mountain troll had only gotten pissed off when she shot at it. Would this thing be the same?

Unbidden, her magic swirled through her fiercely, a reminder that it was there and she could use it. Without understanding what she was doing or why, Lainey pulled her magic forth and wrapped it around the creature, imagining it holding the creature in place. She didn't blink as it stiffened and she felt the thing attempt to thrash against the bonds of her magic.

"Okay," she breathed, "so now what?"

She wasn't sure she knew how to use her magic as a weapon yet. She had never tried, and now didn't seem like the time to attempt something like that. With surprisingly steady arms, she raised her gun and aimed at the middle eye. Releasing a breath, she pulled the trigger. The shot rang loud in the silence. Its echo bounced around the boulders, reverberating so it sounded like a hundred shots had been fired.

The bullet streaked forward and hit the creature in the middle eye, right where she had aimed. As soon as it struck, her magic binding evaporated, the silver bullet negating the effect of the magic.

"Oh, fuck." She hadn't thought of that.

The creature reared back and let out an unearthly scream. She dropped her gun and covered her ears as the shriek made her vision blur. The ground shook as the creature charged, its muscled legs eating up the distance. Knowing it was futile to run, she stood her ground. If she was going down, she wouldn't do so like a coward, despite the fear that left her shaking where she stood.

As the creature pounced, its sharp claws punctured her shoulders and pushed her down. Her head hit the ground hard, and her vision went white. When it cleared, she could have sworn she saw something almost spirit-like streaking through the darkness toward her.

It melted into the amulet around her neck, and the warmth of it spread out through her chest and arms. She stared in awe and horror as her arms moved of their own accord. Her hand closed on the hilt of the dagger at her waist and pulled it from the sheath. Before she could blink, her arm had slashed out and sliced deep into the throat of the creature.

Thick, warm blood spilled forth, splashing her chest and face, landing in her open mouth and eyes. Lainey's scream was muffled as the creature collapsed heavily against her, unmoving. She barely noticed the flare of bright light leaving her necklace amid her struggles to move the carcass from atop her.

"Lainey!"

The sounds of rushing boots and Ash's voice drained whatever fight she had left. She stopped struggling against the dead weight of the creature and waited for Ash to help her.

"What the fuck happened?"

The pressure on her chest eased, and then the body was thrown to the side, hitting the ground with a dull thud. Lainey rolled over and spit out the foul blood. The feel of it coating her tongue made her gag, and she vomited on Ash's boots. She tried to wipe the blood from her eyes, but all she succeeded in doing was smearing it even more. She whimpered and rubbed harder, desperate to get it off.

"Here." Ash took off his shirt and helped her clean the blood from her face.

Another wave of gagging made her lean over, and this time, Ash jumped back to avoid getting more vomit on his boots. When her stomach finally felt settled, she grabbed the bottle Ash held out for her and swished the cool water around before spitting it onto the ground.

"What was that?" she rasped.

"Come on, let's get out of here before this draws the attention of something else. I'll explain later."

He gently helped her stand, wincing at the puncture marks on her shoulders. It only took five minutes before the boulders cleared and open grasslands greeted them.

"Here, sit down." Ash gathered firewood and had a fire burning within minutes.

Lainey gingerly removed her jacket, grimacing at the pain the movement caused. Ash knelt in front of her, the light from the fire playing across his bare chest. He moved her shirt aside and prodded at her injuries.

"They aren't too deep, and there was no poison on its claws, or you would be dead already." He dug around in his bag and pulled out a first aid kit.

She didn't even have the energy to care about the words he had just spoken. She felt like her life force had been sucked out of her. Ash cleaned her wounds gently and placed bandages on them. Then he laid out blankets and helped her lay down.

"Sleep, Lainey. I'll keep you safe."

She was gone the moment his words reached her ears.

"You doing okay?" Ash asked for the hundredth time.

"Yeah, just tired. You're sure there was no poison?" She had never felt this exhausted in her life. The extent of her injuries and the exhaustion weighing her down didn't line up.

"Positive." He cast a worried glance in her direction that did nothing to make her feel better.

"How much longer?"

"Thirty minutes. Forty-five at the most."

She wanted to cry. They had been traveling for over two hours and were almost to the spot on the edge of the Dead Forest where they would wait for her dad to meet up with them. She wasn't sure she could make it another step. Her legs felt like they were filled with lead, and each step felt as if she were dragging them through waist-deep mud.

She managed ten more steps before she couldn't take another. Her legs gave out, and she collapsed in a heap on the ground. Ash was by her side instantly, offering her water and helping her lift her head to drink.

"I think I'm dying," she mumbled.

"You're not dying. Quit being dramatic." He quirked a half grin at her, but it didn't mask the concern in his gaze.

"Pretty sure that's not dramatic," she replied. Or at least she tried to reply. She wasn't sure that was the way her slurred words actually came out.

"All right princess. Guess I'm carrying you the rest of the way."

She tried to protest but couldn't get her mouth to move. Ash scooped her up in his arms, and her head fell against his shoulder. She fought with every ounce of strength she had to remain awake. Her eyes closed, but she could hear Ash mumbling to himself. She felt him set her on the ground and cover her with a blanket. No matter how hard she tried to pry her eyes open or make her mouth move, she just couldn't do it.

She must have dozed off, because the sound of voices woke her, and she forced her eyes open—they felt like sandpaper.

"Where are we?" she whispered.

"The Dead Forest."

She managed to turn her head and smile. Her dad's voice was a welcome sound in her muddled state. He brushed her hair back from her face, and she thought she would cry. How many times in her childhood had she been sick and wanted nothing more than a parent to comfort her?

"How long have I been out?" She struggled to sit up, and gratefully accepted Ash's help.

"Only a few hours, according to Ash," her dad replied. "I just got here about ten minutes ago."

Ash handed her a bowl of some kind of stew. She inhaled the steam rising from the surface, and her stomach rumbled. She ate like she hadn't eaten in years, the liquid scalding her throat on the way down.

When her stomach was finally content, she leaned against the tree. She was already feeling stronger. The fog surrounding her was lifting, and her mind was once again firing on all cylinders.

"Do we have a plan?" she asked.

"Reinforcements are on their way," her dad answered.

"Then what?" she asked.

"Then we make our move." Ash grinned maniacally, and Lainey couldn't help but grin back.

The next morning, a small boat sailed down the river that meandered through the Dead Forest. Her dad greeted the newcomers and introduced them as more of her family.

"This is your cousin, Delwyn, and uncle, Aldric. They are going to help us infiltrate the Unseelie palace."

She didn't know what to say. She was grateful for the help, nervous for one of them to get hurt, and reeling from more family introductions.

"It's nice to meet you," she managed. "And thank you for the help."

"That's what family is for," Delwyn replied warmly.

They settled around the fire, and Aldric looked at her dad. "Fill us in on the details."

"Delwyn and I will abduct a guard and get him to talk. We need to find out where they are holding Phoenix. When we get the information, Ash and Elena will infiltrate the palace with the rest of us providing cover and distraction. I'm hoping they can sneak in while encountering as few guards as possible. I want the rest of us doing the fighting."

"What about the queen?" Delwyn asked.

"We're not touching her yet. We'll need to bring Phoenix back to camp and get him healed up."

Lainey swallowed thickly at his words. It hurt too much to think of Phoenix hurting.

"Phoenix and Elena are the ones who have to deal with the queen. We will make those plans after Phoenix is safe." Her dad looked at her, barely hiding the fear in his eyes at the danger she was about to face.

"We need somewhere protected to bring him. There is no way the queen won't send out search parties when he turns up missing." Ash pursed his lips in thought.

Lainey held out her hand. "Ash, let me see the map." She spread out the map and peered at it. "What about here?" She pointed to a spot she thought would work well. "It's been unused for so long, maybe the whole 'out of sight, out of mind' thing will work in our favor."

"The gate tree in the Unseelie Court," her dad breathed. "That would work. We could hide in the tree and easily defend it if necessary." He gave her an approving look.

She felt warmth in her chest at his approval.

"Okay, when do we make our move?"

"Sunset. We move at sunset."

Chapter Twenty-Two

"Will you sit still? You're making me nervous," Ash complained as Lainey made yet another pass around the room.

They were hiding in an abandoned building her uncle had scouted earlier. Her dad and cousin had left an hour ago to find a guard to bring back to interrogate. The waiting was driving her mad. She couldn't sit still. She had to move or she would go crazy. She was so close to getting Phoenix back, and it was taking all her self-control to not bust out of this building and charge into the palace.

Her uncle Aldric was standing in the shadows near the window, peering out into the streets, waiting for his son and brother's return. "They're coming."

He held the door open, and her dad and Delwyn muscled a large fae inside, shoving him into a lone chair in the center of the room. He had a patch on his shoulder and two golden stripes around his bicep that Lainey assumed meant some kind of higher position with the guards.

His wrists were bound in front of him, and Lainey could feel a shield of wind being packed tightly around him. His head lulled to the side, and a trail of blood trickled down his temple.

"Wake him up," her dad said to no one in particular.

Delwyn grabbed the bucket of cold water from the floor and dumped it over their prisoner's head. The guard's eyes popped open, and he flailed, trying to free his limbs. His magic flared, fire beating against the hard wall of air her dad had encircled him with, keeping them all safe from his magical attack.

"You don't have to watch this," Ash whispered to her. He pulled her into a corner and attempted to turn her around.

"No, I do." She shrugged out of his grasp.

Ash studied her for a moment before nodding.

Her dad knelt in front of the guard. His words were quiet and intimidating. "You will answer our questions, or you will not live through the night."

The guard sneered. "Then kill me now, because I won't say anything."

Lainey didn't even see the knife her dad pulled out until he pressed it to the guard's right hand. The scream that ripped out of the guard's throat almost made Lainey sick. She watched in horror as his finger dropped to the ground, blood spurting and hitting her dad in the face. He didn't bother to wipe it off.

"Let's try that again," he said quietly. "You will answer our questions, or you will not live through the night. And it will not be a quick death."

The guard spit at her dad. "Fuck you."

Another scream; another finger hit the ground.

"I can do this all night." The smile her dad gave the guard was chilling.

What kind of life did her dad lead that he seemed so comfortable abducting and torturing guards? Lainey shivered at the thought, and added the question to the never-ending list growing in her head.

When the guard just glared, a third finger joined the first two on the floor. Bile rose in Lainey's throat, and she leaned against the wall, pressing her fingertips to the cold stone to ground herself.

Her dad pressed the knife to the guard's pointer finger. A line of blood welled where the blade met skin.

"All right! All right!" The guard was shaking and pale. Sweat beaded on his brow and slicked his hair back from his face. "What do you want to know?"

A cruel smile from her dad. "Where is the prisoner you are keeping at the palace?"

"Which one? We have many." This time, when the guard screamed, his voice cut out, and his pointer finger dropped into the growing pool of blood with a splash.

"Don't play coy. It won't end well for you. Where is the fire elemental you took into custody a few days ago?"

An evil grin broke across the guard's face, and he laughed. "He won't be of much use to you anymore."

An icy wave of dread washed through Lainey. They couldn't be too late. She wouldn't accept it.

This time, instead of a finger, what was left of the guard's hand fell to the ground. His eyes rolled back in his head, but her dad reached out and grabbed his face, squeezing painfully.

"Don't pass out on me. We're not done, yet."

Their prisoner panted, and his eyelids flickered open and closed.

"Where. Is. He."

"In the dungeon," the guard gasped. "At least what's left of him."

"Where is the dungeon? Where are the guards posted?"

Lainey didn't hear the rest of the conversation. The guard's words echoed through her head. *What's left of him.* She squeezed her eyes shut and breathed deeply. The tang of copper in the air from the blood pooling on the ground only added to her nausea. They weren't too late. She wouldn't believe anything until she saw with her own eyes. He was still alive. He had to be. She repeated that in her head, over and over.

The sound of a sword being drawn from a scabbard drew her from her miserable recitations. She choked back a gasp as her dad swung the sword, and the guard's head rolled from his body.

"You ..." She pointed with a shaky hand. "You cut off his head!"

"Better than his balls," Delwyn muttered, wiping drops of blood from his face where it had sprayed him.

"You can't be serious?" she whispered.

"Very," Delwyn replied at the same time Ash murmured his agreement.

She shook her head at the untimely attempt at humor and forced back her emotions, reminding herself of their purpose and the very real possibility Phoenix was already dead. She took a deep breath and squared her shoulders.

"You ready?" Ash looked at her before he began checking his weapons, ensuring everything was in its place.

Lainey followed suit, checking the chamber of her gun and switching out the cartridge for a full one. The movements helped to focus her. "Let's go."

The five of them made their way to the edge of the palace gates, slinking through the shadows, quiet as mice. When they reached the first pair of guards, Ash and Delwyn quickly took them out with a quick slash of daggers across their throats, slowly lowering their bodies to the ground to avoid making noise. Once they were inside the palace gates, they headed for a side door hidden behind shrubs.

"This is it," her dad said. He readied his sword before opening the door and slinking inside.

The sound of steel against steel resonated from behind the door, and her uncle and cousin jumped into the fray. Ash grabbed her hand and pulled her inside. She didn't have time to feel nervous. He pressed her to the wall, and they snuck their way past the fighting. They rounded a corner, and he led her through the twisting maze of hallways, ducking behind statues and tapestries to avoid the patrols, until they reached a wooden door reinforced with steel bands.

"The dungeon is through here. There will be guards, so be prepared."

She nodded, and Ash lifted a finger to the lock on the door. A small vine sprouted from his fingertip and snaked inside the lock. A click sounded, and the door easily swung open.

"Another handy trick," he whispered with a wink.

A spiral staircase curved down and down. The only light came from the torches flickering in the sconces. When the stairwell opened up to a landing, they came face-to-face with three guards. Ash immediately engaged two of them, leaving Lainey to deal with the third.

She had readied her magic on the staircase, and now she flung it forward, pinning the guard's arms to his sides and his feet to the floor so he couldn't move. She rushed forward with her dagger in hand and slammed it into his throat to the hilt. Blood gushed from the hole now decorating his neck, covering her hand and making the hilt of her dagger slippery. She stared in shock as more blood bubbled up from his mouth. Her magic slipped away, and he collapsed to the ground in a heap.

Her first kill. She had never killed another person before, and she hadn't been quite prepared for it. But she didn't have time to think about it further. A shout behind her made her turn around. Ash slashed his dagger, and the last guard's guts spilled from his stomach before he fell.

"You okay?" he gasped, catching his breath.

She nodded, not trusting her voice quite yet.

"Okay, come on." He grabbed her free hand, and they made their way deeper into the dungeon.

She peered into each cell, her heart stopping every time she saw a body. They were all bloody and beaten, so much so that it was hard to see any features on their faces. She didn't see any red-tinged hair with shaved sides though.

They were almost to the last of the cells when Ash cursed. "Fucking hell."

He rushed to the cell and used his vine trick to unlock it.

Lainey pushed past him and fell to her knees next to the body. Her hands shook as she gently rolled Phoenix over. She wasn't breathing, her heart was beating wildly in her chest, and tears were streaming down her face.

"Please," she whispered. "Phoenix, please."

She cried out when she saw his face. They had brutalized him. His eyes were black and blue and swollen shut, his lips were three times their normal size, and there was dried blood everywhere. She looked lower to his bare stomach and had to close her eyes. His body was a roadmap of torture and pain. Whip marks and lacerations, bruises and burns.

She forced her eyes back to his face and gently brushed back his hair. "Phoenix," she whispered through her tears. "Please be alive."

Ash pressed two fingers to his neck, and Lainey prayed to any god who would listen.

"It's faint, but there."

Breath left her in a rush, and she leaned down to Phoenix's ear. "We're going to get you out of here. Just hang on a little longer. You're going to be okay, I promise."

Her vision was blurry when she looked back to Ash, unshed tears pooling on her lashes. "What do we do?"

He didn't answer, just bent down and lifted Phoenix as gently as he could. Even so, a moan escaped Phoenix's mouth that broke her heart. She couldn't imagine the pain he must be feeling. Lainey pushed her despair down and brought her anger back. She would need it.

Lainey led the way out of the cell and back to the stairwell. They circled up and around, and when they reached the top, Lainey almost knifed her cousin before she realized who it was.

"We have him. Let's get out of here," she said breathlessly.

They made it five steps before guards appeared around a corner, too many for Lainey to count. Her heart stopped as they fanned out, and a darkly beautiful woman sauntered around the corner, staying behind the guards. This could only have been Queen Esmeray.

A cruel smile split the queen's face. "You didn't think it would be that easy, did you?"

She was the epitome of an evil queen. Beautiful, with fair skin and hair dark as night. Her lips were painted blood red, and her dark, soulless eyes were thickly lined with kohl. Her dress was the darkest emerald green, so dark it almost looked black in the low lighting of the hall.

She stepped forward between the guards, and they reluctantly let her pass. One guard stayed close to her side. Lainey and her companions took a few steps backward. She could feel the magic in the air as everyone readied for whatever was to come.

"As soon as I heard you had entered Faerie, I knew I had to remove you from the picture. Luckily for me, my wayward son gave me the perfect opportunity to draw you into my net." Her voice was low and melodious. She would have been beautiful if it weren't for the malice leaking from her like ichor.

Lainey's dad and uncle stepped in front of her and Ash. Her eyes widened as they took a step forward, swords drawn and magic at the ready.

"No! Stop!" she yelled.

She was too late. They rushed forward at the same time they threw their magic outward. A gust of wind knocked the guards backward. The guard closest to Esermay grabbed her arm and dragged her behind the protection of her guards. Lainey's dad slammed into the nearest guards right as they closed rank around the queen.

Metal clashed as swords met. Gusts of wind blew around the hall. Fireballs streaked through the air, and vines sprouted from the ground. Lainey didn't know where to look or what to do. Ash stood next her, Phoenix limp in his arms, his eyes scanning the chaos, searching for something.

"Now!" he yelled.

Ash darted forward, and Delwyn grabbed Lainey's arm as he

rushed after Ash. Aldric and her dad had created an opening in the chaos, pushing the guards to either side of the hall. They burst through to the other side, and Lainey ground to a halt.

"What about our dads?"

"They'll be fine. Let's go!"

Delwyn pulled Lainey down the hall in Ash's wake, checking behind them every so often to make sure they hadn't been followed.

When they reached the door to the outside, two more guards stood before it. Ash slowed, and Lainey and Delwyn swept past him.

"Your magic, Lainey," Delwyn reminded her. "Use it."

Lainey pulled the same stunt she had on the guard in the dungeon, the one thing that seemed to come easy to her in the moment. She'd trapped one of the guards, but the other moved before she could expand her magic to him. He rushed Delwyn, arm outstretched. A glistening spear made of water shot toward her cousin. He quickly shielded himself with air.

A vine erupted from the ground and pierced the guard's chest, and he fell to the ground lifelessly. Delwyn rushed forward and drew his dagger across the last guard's throat. He joined his companion on the floor.

They burst through the door into the night air. As they made their way off the palace grounds and into the city, Lainey kept glancing at Phoenix in Ash's arms. Anger and pain welled inside her with every glance.

They had stolen horses before they began the mission and left them tied behind the abandoned warehouse where they had questioned the first guard. When they rounded the corner of the warehouse, and Lainey saw the five horses still tied to a fence, her steps faltered.

"What about my dad? What about your dad?"

"They will join us when they can," Delwyn replied as he took Phoenix from Ash. Lainey didn't miss the flash of uncertainty in his eyes, though.

Ash climbed into the saddle and reached down to grab Phoenix from Delwyn. He settled Phoenix in front of him and waited for Delwyn to help Lainey into the saddle. She was glad she had ridden a couple times at summer camp that one time Emma had saved enough money to send her.

Lainey's horse shuffled nervously under her, picking up on her emotions. She had no energy to spare to soothe the animal, though. She wheeled toward the south and set off, her companions following behind. She kept glancing back at Phoenix. His head lulled on Ash's shoulder and Lainey watched his chest for each ragged breath.

Delwyn kept watch behind them, searching for pursuit as well as their dads, while Ash took the lead. By the time they reached the gate tree, the sun was peeking over the horizon. Phoenix's wounds looked so much worse in the light of day.

The tree looked nothing like the one they had entered through. While just as massive, with the same far-reaching limbs, this tree was dead. No leaves or buds, just bare clacking branches. The bark was so dark, it appeared black in the reddish light of the rising sun. The air around the tree thrummed with ominous vibes.

They reached the tree, and Delwyn dismounted to help Ash get Phoenix inside. Lainey rushed forward to the door in the trunk of the tree. It opened easily, but no glowing light appeared, no stairs to the human realm, just the inside of the massive tree. She made a pile of blankets, and Ash laid Phoenix down in the middle of them. Lainey covered him up and brushed his hair back from his face again.

"We're going to help you. Just hold on a little longer. Please."

She tried not to notice how pale he was, how labored his breathing had become. She looked to Ash for instruction. He dug around in his bag, bringing out the first aid kit again. They cleaned his wounds together, wrapping them in bandages, while Delwyn started a fire.

"What else can we do?" Desperation filled her voice. She would do anything to help him.

"Nothing." He shrugged. "We wait."

They settled around the fire, and Lainey laid Phoenix's head in her lap.

Delwyn handed a cup of steaming liquid to Lainey. "See if you can get any of this in him. There are some healing plants in it that will help."

She graciously took the cup and dribbled some in his mouth, hoping it was enough. She kept her eyes on him, barely blinking, afraid that if she looked away, something would happen. Ash settled down for the night, while Delwyn took first watch outside, guarding the door and keeping an eye out for their dads. Lainey paid them no mind, her attention solely on Phoenix.

"You should try to rest, Lainey. I'll keep an eye on him," Ash offered.

She shook her head. No way would she be able to sleep. There had been no change. In fact, he seemed to be doing worse. His breathing was more shallow, and his pulse was fainter. She looked at Ash with tears in her eyes.

"It's not enough. We need to do more."

He bit his lip. "We could try something. I have no clue if it will work, but ..."

"What? Tell me what to do."

"His banshee blood should be healing him. If it's not, maybe it's because it needs to be awakened, or charged, I don't know. You could try giving him some of your blood. The banshee in him would need that to survive, but it would cement your mate bond."

Cement the mate bond? There wouldn't be a mate bond if he didn't survive. She accepted it, and if Phoenix didn't want to, they could deal with that after he woke up. She grabbed her dagger and pressed it to her wrist with a grimace. As her blood welled, she pressed her wrist to Phoenix's mouth and prayed. She waited and waited, and finally she felt the tiniest flick of his tongue against the cut. Her breath caught when it happened again, stronger. Then instinct took over, and his mouth closed around her wrist. She felt the deep pulls on her vein as he took her life force into him.

"It's working," she breathed. Her tears spilled over as she watched his color improve and the bruises begin to fade. She peeled back the blanket and watched in awe as his wounds slowly disappeared.

"Holy shit," Ash breathed. He stared, wide eyed, as his best friend healed, second by second. "I had no idea that was possible."

When Phoenix finally released her wrist, he was breathing easier, and his pulse was stronger. He was still battered and bruised, but he was healing before their very eyes. Lainey covered him again and slid underneath the blanket with him. She curled herself against him, desperate to feel his body and know he was still with her.

His warmth filled the space under the blanket, and soon Lainey was drifting off, exhaustion catching up with her. Her hand on Phoenix's chest, rising and falling with his breathing, his heartbeat strong under her palm.

Chapter Twenty-Three

"Lainey?"

Phoenix's rough voice woke her instantly. She sat up and turned to him.

"Phoenix, you're awake," she whispered. She placed a hand gently on his cheek, and he turned his head into the touch. "How are you feeling? Wait, don't answer that, that was a stupid question. Can I get you anything? That's a better question."

A smile appeared on his lips at her rambling, and her heart stuttered in her chest.

"Maybe some water?"

"Of course." Lainey jumped up and grabbed a bottle, careful not to wake anyone. She wanted this moment to stay private.

When she returned to his side, she lifted his head and helped him drink. Once his thirst was slated, he laid back down and stared at her.

"Where are we? How did you get me out?" He paused, gaze roving over her features. "*Why* did you get me out?"

"We're at the gate tree in the Unseelie Court. Ash and I got you out of the dungeon while my dad, uncle, and cousin kept guard." She didn't answer his last question. Not yet. It didn't feel like the right time. And she didn't let her mind stay on the thoughts of her dad and uncle either. She couldn't handle that right now.

"How bad?" He grunted as he tried to assess his injuries.

She pressed his shoulders back down until he relaxed. "Just lay still. Don't do anything crazy. You were really bad off. You almost didn't make it."

She refused to meet his gaze, unsure how he would react to learning she'd given him her blood, and cemented the mate bond in the process.

"What did you do?" His question was quiet, but she could hear the uncertainty in his voice.

"Well, Ash suggested it. And it worked, so don't kill me."

"You're worrying me, Lainey."

She held up her wrist, the cut scabbed over. "I gave you my blood." Her reply was barely audible.

His breath caught, and he stared at her. Emotion passed through his eyes that she couldn't make out.

"Say something," she whispered.

He took her hand and licked the scab, watching it disappear. He had to clear his throat before he answered. "Thank you."

She leaned down and very softly pressed her lips against his. When she pulled back, fire burned in his copper eyes. They stared at each other, neither moving, neither saying anything. They got lost in each other for a brief moment. Lainey's relief at him waking up was overpowering.

She finally broke the connection. "You should rest. This isn't over yet."

He nodded and stared at her a second longer before pulling her down to him and closing his eyes. She gently laid her arm across his stomach, careful of his healing injuries. She tried to fall back asleep, but her thoughts were a tangled web of fear, relief, love, and anxiety. It was a long time before her eyes closed.

Her shivering woke her up in the morning. Lainey's first thought was that the fire must have gone out. She reached out to snuggle closer to the living flame that was Phoenix, but her hand met empty air instead. She looked around. The tree was empty. Where was Phoenix? Where were Ash and her cousin?

She jumped up and rushed to the door, stepping out into the gray light of dawn. Looking around frantically, the only person she saw was her dad. Relief washed through her, and she ran to him. He wrapped his arms around her and held tightly.

"You're okay? What about Aldric?"

"I'm fine, Elena." He pulled away, and his eyes were shining with tears. He cleared his throat and looked away. "Aldric didn't make it."

Lainey's heart dropped into her stomach. Unsure how to feel, she closed her eyes and pressed her hands to her mouth. She hadn't known her uncle, but he had been family. She should've felt sad, right? She definitely felt guilt. He'd died for her. And, oh shit, what about Delwyn?

"I'm so sorry, dad," she whispered. "It's my fault."

Her dad hugged her again. "It's not your fault. Aldric made the decision to help. He knew the risks when he joined us. Please don't blame yourself for his death."

"What about Delwyn?"

"He's around somewhere, processing. He'll be okay, though."

Lainey shook her head. How could she not blame herself? Delwyn surely would. The rest of her family as well. Had she just lost all of them before she ever got to have them?

"Lainey." Her dad grasped her shoulders and drew her attention to him. "Phoenix is awake. He's around the other side of the tree with Ash."

While she could do nothing about her uncle's death, Phoenix was alive, and there was so much they had to talk about. She gave her dad one last hug and headed to the other side of the tree.

The sun was barely peeking over the horizon, making the shadows darker. Lainey tripped over roots and rocks as she rushed around the tree. Relief washed through her as she climbed over a particularly large root and found the boys leaning against the trunk, talking. Ash had given Phoenix a shirt. The white tee looked out of place on him—she was used to seeing him in only black or gray.

Ash smirked when he saw her. "Good morning, sunshine. I knew it wouldn't take you long to find him."

She rolled her eyes but didn't respond. Butterflies suddenly took flight in her stomach. Phoenix looked almost normal. Slight bruising still colored his features, but the cuts were gone, and she assumed his torso looked the same. It was time to discuss Phoenix's last question, the one she'd avoided last night.

Why did she save him?

"I'm going to check on your dad and Delwyn," Ash announced. "You two have fun." He winked and patted her shoulder as he walked past.

She stood awkwardly, staring at Phoenix, cataloging his features and the healing that had occurred because of her blood. She didn't know how to begin or what to say. It was too tempting to turn around and follow Ash. Too tempting to leave this conversation for later. For never.

Phoenix cleared his throat. "Let's walk."

The ground was rocky, and the dead grass crunched underfoot as they walked in silence away from the tree. She tried to plan what she would say, rehearsed various lines in her head. It all felt wrong. They reached a cliff and sat on the ground, shoulder-to-shoulder, watching the colors of the sunrise glint off the rolling waves of the ocean in the distance.

"Why'd you do it?" she asked. "You knew what would happen."

"It was better than the alternative."

"What alternative? What could have been worse than you dying?"

His eyes glowed copper when he looked at her. "You accepting the mating just to keep me alive. You losing the choice that you value so much. My death didn't seem quite as upsetting."

"Are you serious?" she breathed. She turned to face him, sitting on her knees. "You think I would prefer you to die?"

"I would rather have made the sacrifice instead of you."

"But you didn't let me choose. You took away my choice by making it for me."

"Lainey, so much has been forced on you lately. How could I ever force you into yet another bond?"

Looking him square in the eyes, she whispered, "Who said it would have been forced?"

Silence met her question as he stared at her. "What are you saying?" he eventually asked.

"I'm saying, I choose you. I gave you my blood knowing what it meant, and I didn't do it just because you were dying. I want it, Phoenix, I want all of it." She inched closer to him, eyes searching his face for a reaction.

He shook his head. "You don't mean that, Lainey. That's the blood bond talking."

She was close enough now to see the swirling magic in his beautiful eyes. "A wise fae once told me there is a difference between love and lust." Lainey's heart pounded in her chest; she could feel her pulse in her neck fluttering wildly. "When Ash told me you left and what you planned on doing ..." the feelings rushing up were too real and too recent, and she had to swallow before continuing. "Everything stopped. My heart, my lungs, my blood, every thought in my head. It all just ... stopped. You were too far away at this point for the blood bond to be affecting me. I knew it wasn't because of that."

As she inched even closer, Phoenix turned to face her fully. He captured a strand of her hair, wrapping it around his fingers.

Lainey closed her eyes. "There was so much fear in my heart at the thought of losing you. It made me realize there was nothing I wouldn't do to get you back. I had to. I couldn't let you die without you knowing." She opened her eyes and let every emotion she felt show on her face.

"Without me knowing what?" Phoenix didn't appear to be breathing.

The spark of hope lighting his eyes gave her the courage she needed to say, "I love you, Phoenix. I love you, and I choose you. I choose the mating, I choose the blood bond. All of it. If it means I can have you, I choose it."

He didn't say anything. He looked as if he couldn't have spoken if his life depended on it. His eyes scanned her face, searching for truth in what she'd said.

Deciding actions spoke louder than words, Lainey leaned forward and grasped his face in her hands. "Nix," she breathed before closing the distance between them and placing a featherlight kiss on his lips. When she pulled back, anxiety blossomed in her gut. What if he didn't want her? She removed her hands quickly and asked, "Did you mean what you said at the Seelie Court?"

This time, it was Phoenix grabbing her and pulling her closer. Before his lips met hers, he paused. "I meant it. I meant all of it."

He crushed his lips against hers in a rough kiss, and she wrapped her arms around his neck. Opening her mouth, she welcomed him inside, moaning with pleasure at his taste and feel. The warmth, the blessed warmth that was all Phoenix, wrapped around her, and she straddled his waist and tangled her fingers in his hair. The kiss was frenzied and frantic, both of them trying to feel and taste as much of the other as possible.

With tremendous effort, Phoenix pulled away, breathing as heavily as she was. "I just ... I just have to make sure."

He was so close she could see her reflection in his burning eyes. She could see her own eyes swirling like storm clouds as her magic raged inside her. The blood bond was a force she had to fight to keep from pushing him to the ground and having him right there. Clearing her head, she understood why he needed the reassurance.

She put distance between them to keep the bond at bay. "I'm sorry it took you almost dying to realize what was in my heart. I think I was scared to admit it because I have lost everyone I've ever loved, and I thought if I acknowledged it, I would lose you too. It was easier to blame everything on the blood bond when, in reality, I was drawn to you before then."

Tension left his face, and he smiled his half smile that she loved so much. "You called me Nix," he said quietly.

"Is that okay?"

"Yes," he breathed and lowered her to the ground, holding himself up on his elbows to keep his weight off her. He traced her lower lip with his thumb. "I love you, Lainey."

"I love you too." She pulled him down on top of her, relishing the feel of his weight on her.

This kiss was slow and languid. Drugging her into oblivion with his touch, taste, and smell. His arousal pressed against her thigh and she groaned, wanting more of him. Wanting all of him.

Somehow, she managed to stop him from sliding his hand into her leggings. "Wait," she said breathlessly. "Not here. Not now."

He exhaled roughly and rested his head on her shoulder. "You're right, damn it."

Rolling off her and pulling her up with him, they sat on the ground and stared at each other in wonder before Lainey finally brought them back to the present.

"We should probably head back," she sighed.

Phoenix groaned before standing and reaching down to help her up. They were halfway back to the tree when she stopped.

"What about the mating? Do we have to do anything else to accept it?" She paused, and looked at him through her lashes. "Do *you* want to accept it?"

"Well." He looked at her nervously, rubbing the back of his neck. "It's too late now. The blood has been exchanged. But yes, I want the bond. I want you."

She blinked, then blinked again. "Okay," she said, and awkwardly looked from him to the ground and back.

Phoenix chuckled and tugged her close. He placed a gentle kiss on her lips before draping his arm around her shoulders. The sound of his chuckle and his casual touches made her feel warm and tingly inside—a sensation she wasn't used to.

When they rounded the tree, Ash and her dad were standing outside talking quietly. Delwyn was leaning against the trunk next to the door with his arms crossed over his chest, staring at nothing. Ash was the first to see them and he grinned at the sight of Phoenix with his arm around her.

"We're glad to see you healed up," her dad said. "If you guys really plan on removing Queen Esmeray from the throne, we need to talk about what happens after. Do you have someone in mind to take her place? Because I would really suggest that you do, or else we'll have a bigger problem on our hands with succession."

Silence met his question, giving him all the answer he needed. He nodded and gestured to the door in the gate tree.

"I thought as much. Let's at least sit around the fire to discuss this."

Once seated around the fire, everyone waited for her dad to speak. Lainey sat close to Phoenix, his magic warming the side of her body that brushed against his.

"If you don't have a plan for after you remove the queen, this is a failed quest."

"There has to be someone in the Unseelie Court who would be capable of taking her spot," Ash offered.

"I wouldn't count on it. Everyone in her circle is just as awful as she is. You would remove one monster only to have another replace it."

"Then what are our options?" Phoenix asked.

Her dad leveled a stare at them. "If you take responsibility for killing the queen, you need to take responsibility for ruling the court. At least until you find someone suitable."

Lainey looked toward Phoenix. He didn't look at all surprised. "You expected this," she said quietly.

He nodded. "I did."

"Are you going to do it?" She wasn't sure how she felt about the thought of him becoming the king of the Unseelie Court.

"Esmeray is apparently my mom." He shrugged. "In all actuality, the crown would fall to me upon her death. It would give us the chance to reform the court and bring it back to its original glory."

"Are you up for that challenge?" Her dad's voice and face were grave.

Phoenix didn't answer. Instead, he looked at Lainey. "It would mean you would become queen."

Everyone but Ash jerked in surprise at his statement. Lainey just closed her eyes briefly and swallowed.

"I don't know anything about being a queen."

He smiled at her. "And I don't know anything about being a king. We could learn together. If you would still choose me."

"If I said no?"

"Then I'd walk away and let someone else try to overthrow the queen."

Her eyes burned. "You would really do that for me?"

"I would let the world burn if it meant being with you." His gaze was intense as he cupped her cheek with his hand.

"Then I suppose it's a good thing I look damn good in a crown, Your Majesty."

His answering grin was wild and dangerous. Too bad she didn't quite feel the same.

When she finally turned from Phoenix's gaze, she felt her cheeks heat as she looked at her family. Unsure what to say, she stared at her lap, pulling on a loose thread in her leggings.

"Well," her dad began, "If you're positive, Phoenix, our next step is to figure out how to get close enough to Queen Esmeray to kill her."

Phoenix gasped and put his hand to his chest. "My piece of

the amulet. It's gone. She must have taken it when she captured me."

Ash and Lainey exchanged wide-eyed glances with Phoenix. If they were missing part of the amulet, there was no way they would succeed.

"We have to get it back from her," Lainey said.

"What amulet? What are you guys talking about?"

Phoenix explained how they had found Azura's amulet, and how Madam Elvie had broken it into three pieces, giving a piece to each of them. He explained how she'd said the amulet would help them defeat Esmeray but that it must not be combined until the right time.

Her dad and Delwyn looked stunned when Phoenix was done.

"You mean you actually found Azura's amulet?" Delwyn breathed. "That would change the tide in any battle. Lainey's right. You have to get it back."

Chapter Twenty-Four

"Be careful, Elena." Her dad pulled her in for a lingering hug. "I can't lose you too."

"I'll be careful. I promise." Words she probably shouldn't have spoken. There was no way to promise something like that with what they had planned. There was a very real chance none of them were walking away from this alive.

Her dad looked at Phoenix, a long, hard stare. "That is my only surviving daughter you're taking in there."

"And I will guard her with my life. You have my word."

Having had enough of the male posturing, Lainey placed a hand on Phoenix's chest. "Let's go."

Phoenix and Lainey were going up against the Unseelie queen, while Ash and her family provided distraction and backup. No one was sure if their plan would work, but it was the best they could come up with.

Phoenix's strong hands on her waist were a welcome touch as he lifted her into the saddle. With a quick movement, he mounted behind her, one arm around her waist, the other gripping the reins.

"Ready, my queen?"

He didn't wait for an answer, just spurred the horse forward, and they were off without a backward glance. Ash and her family would follow behind at a safe distance. They would let Lainey and Phoenix get captured, then approach the palace to create a distraction.

No words were spoken between them as they rode. The crunching of the dead grass under the horse's hooves and the wind in their faces were the only conversation, a depressing medley of things to come. The landscape was dreary and not much to look at. Stunted and dead trees grew from the dusty ground where the patches of dried grass didn't grow. There was no color, only browns and grays, except for the blue of the sky.

The closer they got, the more nervous Lainey became. So much could go wrong so easily. Never in her life had she had so much to lose, and the thought was paralyzing. As devastating as it would be to lose her dad again, the possibility of losing Phoenix was too much to bear.

As if he knew the direction her thoughts had traveled, Phoenix whispered in her ear, "Don't think about it. You have to keep your focus where it should be. Don't worry about what may happen."

"It's hard. You would think it would get easier, the risk of losing people—it's all I've ever known my whole life—but it only gets harder."

His arm tightened around her middle, and his warmth settled around her as she nestled against his chest, relishing this last moment of peace between them.

"I'm going to do everything in my power to get everyone out alive," he promised. But just like her promise to her dad, there was no guarantee. It was out of their hands now. The plan would play out how it would, and they were along for the ride.

They were a couple miles away from the city surrounding the Unseelie Court palace when Lainey heard the sound of clinking armor. Up ahead, a patrol of guards blocked the road.

"Halt!" A fae wearing black armor, with the moon and stars

of the Unseelie Court crest emblazoned on the breastplate, stepped forward from the group.

Their horse came to a stop, and Phoenix sat stiffly behind her, his muscles tense to the point of shaking.

"Get off the horse and don't even think of using your magic." More armored fae stepped forward. Too many for them to fight.

"Here we go," Phoenix whispered in her ear before placing a kiss on her temple. He slid from the horse and helped her down, keeping at least one hand on her the whole time.

The fae, who must have been a commander of some sort based on the silver braided rope over his shoulder, marched forward with a sword at the ready. A heavy blanket of magic enveloped them. It felt like a shield of air, and Lainey knew she wouldn't be able to get her magic past that barrier.

"Hold out your hands."

A guard grabbed them roughly and bound their wrists in front of them, smirking when Lainey winced in pain as the rope cut into her flesh. A low growl reverberated through Phoenix, but there was nothing he could do in his own bindings.

Once satisfied they were going nowhere, the commander marched them off the road and into the forest of dead trees, heading toward the palace but keeping them out of sight of the villagers. The pace was unforgiving, and Lainey struggled to keep up with her shorter legs. Rocks and roots grabbed at her, trying to pull her down and slowing her progress further. The butt of a sword prodded her back incessantly, nudging her to keep moving. As if she wasn't trying to do just that.

Just as she was about to snap at the guard poking her, the forest cleared, and the palace came into view. Dread sluiced through Lainey at the sight. When they'd rescued Phoenix from the dungeon, it had been dark. She hadn't been able to see the threatening fortress looming above the landscape. In the light of day, it looked exactly like an evil queen's palace in a fairytale, all dark stone, sharp angles, and glowing torches with even darker shadows. It wouldn't surprised her to see a dragon rear up spewing flames.

An ancient drawbridge shuddered under their boots as they were marched to the front doors of the palace. The sound of snapping and splashing under the bridge told Lainey all she needed to know about the inhabitants of the moat below. The front door to the palace looked like a massive, twisted knot of branches twining around each other. It opened on a silent wind, the motion causing the torches inside the entry hall to flicker and hiss.

More guards were waiting inside, these wearing armor that was lighter in weight, but no less threatening in appearance. Like that of their captors, it was all black with the Unseelie Court insignia on the breastplate. A myriad of weapons were held in armored grasps—swords, spears, bows, even whips.

They were handed off to the new guards and marched forward through another set of double doors. Their breath fogged with every exhale in the frigid temperature of the throne room. The floor, black marble veined in gold, was covered in a slight frost that crept from the floor up the columns and walls to the arching ceiling high above.

Queen Esmeray sat atop a throne of twisted branches. She was wearing a deep red dress that matched her lip color. Her black hair hung loose, and a dark crown of twisted metal perched upon her head. She was smiling as they approached, but there was nothing nice in that smile.

Lainey and Phoenix stopped short of the dais. Lainey squared her shoulders and shoved her fear aside. Phoenix's reminder echoed through her skull: focus on the task at hand, nothing else.

"What do we have here?" Esmeray's voice was low and melodic and sent chills skittering over Lainey's skin.

"We found them in the woods outside the palace, Your Majesty."

Queen Esmeray inhaled, and pearly white teeth with pointed canines glinted in the torchlight of the throne room. "Everyone out. Except you, my dear." She nodded toward the guard who had spoken. "I know you won't leave."

Tension filled Lainey and Phoenix as they waited for the throne room to clear. It felt like an eternity had passed, but they couldn't have asked for a better situation. They wouldn't have made it far with so many guards in the room.

Queen Esmeray studied Phoenix with unnerving intensity. Phoenix shifted next to Lainey and the sound of his steady breathing filled the room.

"Do you even know the power your blood holds?" she asked.

"I have an idea." The words were more growl than anything.

"What a marvelous pet you could be—if you could be tamed. That silly queen in the Seelie Court had no idea what kind of weapon she had in her control. Shame she let you get away. I won't let that happen a second time."

A glint of dark stone caught Lainey's eye. With a sinking heart, she saw the amulet nestled in the queen's generous cleavage. She had hoped it had been locked somewhere for safe keeping. It would be harder to get it off the queen's body.

Those dark eyes shifted to Lainey, and the queen's smile made her shiver. "You, I'm afraid, I have no use for. I certainly can't let someone use you to break the curse. You see, once Faerie has been well and truly brought to its knees, that is when I will step in and remove the Seelie Court from the map. My influence over Orabelle only goes so far, unfortunately. With her and the rest of that dreadful court out of the way, I can then move on to the human realm."

Lainey barely had time to register Esmeray's words. Everything happened so fast. A snap of the queen's fingers, and Lainey was roughly grabbed from behind. A kick to the back of her knees sent her crashing to the floor, and her head was forced down.

Time seemed to freeze as the sharp edge of a blade was pressed into the back of her neck. Lainey ceased fighting. She turned her head a fraction and saw Phoenix frozen in place, his copper eyes wide in utter terror.

"Let her go," he demanded uselessly. The queen would never let her walk free.

Her dark laughter rippled through the room. "How precious, but no, I don't think I will."

Before the queen could motion for Lainey's head to roll, Phoenix rushed the dais. He didn't make it far. The queen blasted him with her dark power, shadows slamming him backward. He skidded across the marble floor, coming to a stop against the wall with a grunt.

His action had the intended consequences, though. The sword at Lainey's neck lifted a fraction as the guard tried to decide whether to protect his queen or continue guarding Lainey. Using that hesitation, Lainey rolled over onto her back and kicked the guard's wrist. The sword flew through the air, and she reached up to pull the dagger out of the sheath at his waist. With a surge of adrenaline, she jumped to her feet, and her blade sank into the soft skin of the guard's neck.

The scent of copper filled the air as blood gushed from the wound, coating her hands in wet warmth. More blood bubbled from his mouth, and he grabbed his throat in a useless attempt to keep his life's blood inside his body.

His choking and spluttering was loud in the silence that had fallen in the throne room. The dagger was yanked out as his body fell to the ground in a crash of armor. The shield surrounding her and Phoenix disappeared as the guard died. With shaking hands, Lainey stared at the body. The dagger fell from numb fingers as realization of what she had done settled in.

A piercing shriek filled the silence, a heartbreaking sound that brought Lainey's head around toward the queen. Pure, undiluted hatred filled the queen's face as she sent a wave of power at Lainey. The burst of magic slid her along the floor and slammed her against the wall, hard enough for her head to rebound and stars to dance in her vision. The queen rushed forward and wrapped her hands around Lainey's neck.

Breath was choked from her lungs as the queen grasped her throat. She scrabbled to pry the queen's hand off, desperate to get any bit of air into her lungs. Behind the queen, Phoenix forced himself to his feet and charged forward again. His hands were still bound, but his fire now wreathed his arms. He made it three feet before the queen reached back and let loose another blast of power. The black wave hit Phoenix in the chest, and he flew through the air until he crashed into the wall on the other side of the throne room. The sound of his head hitting the stone was sickening.

Lainey would have screamed if she could've gotten air into her lungs. The sight of Phoenix's lifeless body as it slid down the wall tore through her. The blood smeared on the black stones where his head hit was a punch to the gut. Tears sprang into her eyes at the sight—and the loss of oxygen. She fought harder, but it was no use. Muscles deprived of oxygen weakened, and her vision started going dark at the edges. This was not how it was supposed to end.

She was sure she was hallucinating when a bright white light erupted from the amulet around her neck. A glowing image appeared next to the queen, and Lainey's eyes widened in shock. An ethereal version of the queen stood there in a flowing gown, with long dark hair blowing in an invisible breeze. Princess Azura. It had to be the queen's sister, they looked so much alike.

The queen must not have been able to see it, but Lainey could, and she watched with dimming vision as the specter mouthed the words, "The bracelet." With a sudden burst of clarity, Lainey reached into her pocket and felt the cool metal of the bracelet that had blocked her powers when she was captive at the Seelie Court.

Her muscles shook, and she couldn't get them to do what she wanted. The glowing ghost reached forward, and a burst of energy shot through Lainey's body, an electrical charge that gave her the fuel she needed to grab the bracelet and pull it from her pocket. Her arm tingled and felt like it was disconnected from the rest of her body as it slowly rose and clasped the bracelet shut on the queen's wrist. Queen Esmeray reared back in horror as her magic was ripped away from her, and her grip on Lainey's throat loosened enough for Lainey to gulp down huge lungfuls of air.

The door to the throne room burst open, and a second later, a blur of blond hair rushed toward Lainey. Esmeray was forcibly removed as Ash shouldered her out of the way. The floor rushed up to meet Lainey as her legs gave way, and she sat sucking air into her deprived lungs. The queen regained her composure and unsheathed the sword at her waist, leveling it in Ash's direction.

"The amulets!" Lainey croaked, her voice rough from the queen's handling.

With a jerk, Ash pulled his amulet from his neck and tossed it to Lainey while pulling his own sword free. The queen's blurred through the air, and the sound of metal on metal rang out as Ash met her attack head-on. Clearly, both Ash and the queen had been trained in sword fighting. Their movements were a dance, filled with power and intent.

She knew she should've helped him, but her thoughts flew to Phoenix, and she scrabbled over the ground, ignoring the puddle of blood soaking into her leggings from the guard she had murdered. Phoenix still hadn't moved, and her heart was a mad drum in her chest as she knelt above him.

"Phoenix." She gently touched his face and placed her fingers at his throat, praying for a pulse. "Please be okay, please be okay, please be ..." She collapsed against his chest when she felt his pulse steadily beat against her fingers. "Oh, thank god." Sitting up, she brushed his hair away from his face and whispered to him, begging him to open his eyes.

A shout from the queen drew her attention away from Phoenix. Vines erupted from the floor at Queen Esmeray's feet, wrapping tightly around her legs, climbing higher over her waist. She hacked at them with her sword, trying to free herself, but it was no use. Ash reached out and yanked the amulet from her neck. It skittered across the floor in Lainey's direction, and she hastily crawled toward it.

Just as her hand closed around the black stone, the queen's sword arm broke free from the vines. Moving faster than Lainey could track, the queen's sword pierced Ash's chest. The sickening crunch of metal meeting bone was something she would never forget.

Ash looked down in shock at the sword protruding from his chest. He coughed wetly, blood bubbling from his mouth, and turned to look at Lainey with wide eyes.

"Ash! Oh, god, no!" Amulet forgotten, Lainey stared at her friend as his knees crashed to the floor. "No!"

Queen Esmeray smiled as she yanked the sword out of Ash's body. The vines dissolved as Ash's life force leaked out onto the floor. Queen Esmeray took one step toward Lainey, blood dripping from the blade, staining the floor crimson. Shaken from the horror of Ash's lifeless body, Lainey screamed at the queen. She raged and yelled until her voice was hoarse.

The two pieces of the amulet in her hands seemed to pulse with energy, and Lainey jumped, remembering the task at hand. She yanked off her piece of the amulet and held all three pieces together.

As soon as the black stones touched, a bright golden light erupted from the amulet, blinding Lainey as a burst of wind blew her hair back from her face. When the light cleared, princess Azura stood before her, more corporeal than before but still with shimmering edges.

"No," Queen Esmeray gasped. "It can't be."

Lainey left the sisters to their reunion and rushed to Ash's side. "Oh, god, Ash." Her hands covered the hole in his chest, attempting to stem the flow of blood. "Hold on. Just hold on. We'll get you help."

"Little ..." He coughed, cutting off his words. Blood

splattered Lainey, landing on her cheeks like tears. "Little half-breed." His smile wavered, and his eyes began to dull.

"No, Ash. Don't go." Tears mixed with the blood staining her cheeks. "Please, don't leave me." She couldn't lose him, not another person who meant so much to her.

From the corner of her eye, Lainey watched as Princess Azura waved her hand, and some kind of magic froze the queen in place. The princess's glowing form knelt next to Lainey.

"Thank you for helping me complete the task I began all those years ago." Her semi-transparent hand waved over Lainey's bound wrists and Ash's body.

The rope binding her disappeared. The blood pulsing out of Ash's chest with each slowing heartbeat stopped. Then the edges of the wound glowed and slowly knit back together. His eyes cleared, and his breathing came easier. Within moments, he was sitting up, staring at the princess in wonder with his hands pressed to his chest. No death wound, only smooth, pale skin.

Princess Azura smiled and stood. Before she turned to her sister, she said, "I'm afraid this will only buy you time. It is not over yet."

A sob escaped Lainey's throat, and she threw her arms around Ash, holding him tightly. Looking dazed and unsure what was happening, Ash squeezed her back just as tightly.

"Sister," Azura began. "It has been an age since last we met."

"How ..." Esmeray visibly paled, and her hands trembled on her sword hilt.

"Some spirits are harder to break than others, despite your attempts." Azura's slow steps backed Esmeray into a corner.

"Mercy, sister," Esmeray pleaded. "Have mercy."

Azura mused, "Mercy. What is mercy? Was it mercy you showed me when I begged and pleaded with you during those years of torture you put me through? I remember uttering that very word many times over. Did you show me any mercy?"

Esmeray's throat worked as she swallowed, and she tugged

uselessly on the bracelet around her wrist. She looked around frantically for help. She would find none.

"I didn't think so." Another step closer, and a bright, shimmering light erupted from Azura. Esmeray's sword fell from her grasp. "However, lucky for you, I have always been the more merciful of the two of us."

Relief shone briefly in Esmeray's eyes at those words, but it was quickly replaced with fear as she beheld her sister's sinister smile.

"Instead of torturing you for years as you did to me, I will give you a quick death. More than you deserve, I'm sure."

"No!" Esmeray wailed. She raised her hands, pleading with her sister.

"Oh, yes." Azura's form became smoke and shadow. It rushed forward, entering Esmeray's body through her chest.

Light spilled through her body, filling every dark place she had created. Cracks fissured over her skin as it hardened into stone. A loud crack echoed through the throne room, followed by the sound of stone hitting the floor as pieces of the queen exploded into rock and dust. When the dust cleared, nothing remained of the queen but chunks of gray stone. Azura's glowing light was nowhere to be found.

A groan behind her drew Lainey's stunned gaze away from the aftermath. Phoenix was struggling to sit up, and Lainey rushed to his side.

"Are you okay?" She gently prodded the back of his head, and he winced. "Sorry. You're bleeding. Do you need my blood to heal?"

He shook his head, then winced again at the motion. "I'll be fine." He forced his gaze to her and scanned her from head to foot. "Are you okay?"

"Yeah, I'm okay. The queen is gone. It's over." Lainey quickly cut the ropes binding his wrists.

"I believe this belongs to you now." Ash stood in the pile of debris, a black crown dangling from his fingertips. "Your Majesty."

Her lip curled in disgust. "It's so ugly."

Phoenix barked out a laugh, then a groan. "Don't make me laugh. It hurts."

Her adrenaline ebbed away, and she found herself sitting on the floor next to Phoenix. "She helped me before. Princess Azura. She helped me during that attack in the stone field. I didn't realize it until now. She used my body to stab the creature."

Ash knelt next to Phoenix and prodded at his head until Phoenix batted his hands away. "That would probably explain the extreme exhaustion you felt afterward. I'm guessing she would have had to use an extraordinary amount of your energy to pull that off." Ash's eyes narrowed on her. "I expect that will happen again this time once your adrenaline wears off."

"I feel fine," she replied.

"For now."

"Either way, how about you come here so I don't have to try to catch you when you fall? As fast as I heal from injuries, I'm not sure I wouldn't drop you." Phoenix held out his arms for a welcoming embrace.

"I'm not going to pass out." Still, she snuggled against his chest, inhaling his smoky scent.

She felt his chest rumble as he murmured something, but she didn't hear it. His warmth blanketed her, and the last of her adrenaline left her in a rush. No matter how hard she tried, she couldn't keep her eyes open.

CHAPTER TWENTY-FIVE

"How are you feeling?" Phoenix's soft words were the first thing she heard when she woke up, and she decided his voice was the best alarm clock in all the realms.

"Actually, pretty good." She stretched her arms above her head and felt her back pop. "How long was I out?"

"Not long. A few hours." He sat on the edge of the bed, one hand on her thigh, the other brushing her hair back from her face.

"What's happened while I was out?"

His head bounced side to side. "A lot, but nothing at the same time."

She leveled a dead stare at him. "That makes no sense."

His smile warmed her from the inside. "Delwyn rode to the gate tree and said the steps were there, leading to wherever that tree opens up. The curse was broken with Esmeray's death."

Lainey released a breath, feeling a weight lift. She no longer had to worry about being a sacrifice, but Princess Azura's words floated to the forefront of her mind.

"Before she took care of her sister, Princess Azura said something. She said, 'This will only buy you time. It is not over yet'. What does that mean?"

Phoenix frowned and shook his head. "I have no idea. Maybe we can ask Essie?"

"If we can find her. But, what happens now?"

"Everyone who was loyal to Queen Esmeray is fleeing. The rest of the court will have to swear an oath to us in order to remain alive in this realm.

"So this is really happening, then?"

"Only if you want it to. I stand by what I said."

This realm meant nothing to her. The only reason she could think of to agree was that it was her family's home. Phoenix's home. She closed her eyes and nodded. "Let's do it."

His smile lit up the room. "Good, because the coronation is tonight." He stood and walked to the dresser like he hadn't just dropped a bomb on her.

"Tonight?" she screeched.

"The sooner the better. We need to fill the void quickly, before anyone gets any bright ideas."

The image of the black crown dangling from Ash's fingertips reared its ugly head. "That crown is so ugly."

"It's a good thing I found a new one, then. I think it may have belonged to Princess Azura." He turned toward her with a wicked glint in his eye, holding a black velvet box. When he knelt on the floor next to the bed, his eyes were serious. "I know it's not a ring, and I promise I'll get you one of those, but maybe you'll accept this?" He opened the box, and her breath left her. "Will you, Elena Holloway, be my queen and reign by my side, as my equal in all things, for the rest of our lives?"

Black crystals, made to look like a crescent moon and stars, adorned the golden diadem nestled in the box. The facets caught the light of the fire, and the gems threw sparkles and rainbows around the room that shimmered from the faint tremor of Phoenix's hands.

"It's certainly not what I would have expected, a crown instead of a ring."

"Is that a yes?"

Tears blurred her vision, and she nodded. "Yes. It's a yes."

There was a sharp exhale of relief before he launched himself at her, tackling her onto the bed. She yelped in delighted surprise, then melted under him as his heat and magic surrounded her. The blood bond flared to life, and a need, sharp and aching, overwhelmed her. His mouth claimed hers, and she let herself surrender to his power. His hips pressed against hers, and she wrapped her legs around him, pulling him closer.

Phoenix pulled away from her mouth and trailed kisses down her neck with little nips from his teeth. She was burning, and it wasn't nearly enough.

"Phoenix," she moaned as his teeth latched on to the spot where her shoulder met her neck. Her hands fisted in his shirt and yanked it up, desperate to feel his skin.

A knock on the door, followed by a female voice, interrupted them.

"Ugh, the maid," Phoenix complained, pulling away from Lainey with a rueful grin.

"Make her go away." She tugged him back, not ready to let him go yet.

His kiss was short and sweet, but his smile promised wicked things. "Later. We probably should get ready for tonight."

Her arms unwrapped slowly from his neck, reluctant to let go. She pouted as he got off the bed and walked to the door. Realization of what was happening that night temporarily froze her. Was she really prepared to sign on for being queen of a realm she just learned existed? A realm filled with magic and rules she knew nothing of? Her gaze drifted to Phoenix, muscles shifting in his strong back. Could she do it with him by her side?

"We could just leave," she said quietly. "We don't have to take this on."

He paused by the door. "I thought about it." His eyes were thoughtful as he turned to face her. "I really did. Unfortunately, I think your dad is right. Whoever replaces Esmeray will be ten times worse, and we can't guarantee they won't set their eyes on the human realm." He approached the bed again and leaned over. "Just say the word, Lainey. We will leave this all behind."

Possibilities swirled in her mind, different paths to walk in different realms. The question was, which one did she want? She hadn't left much behind in coming to Faerie. Just a world she knew and was comfortable with. She would gain more by staying —a mate, a family, friends, a purpose. She pushed herself up and brushed a kiss over his lips. "This means a lot to you, and in the end, I just want to be where you are."

"I love you, Lainey."

"I love you too, Nix."

"You look beautiful, my lady." Cerise was a maid from the palace. She had been thoroughly interviewed and screened by Lainey's dad before being sent to her room.

"Are you sure it isn't too much?" Her reflection stared back at her, and Lainey wondered if she really looked that wide-eyed and terrified.

"Oh no, my lady. It's perfect."

She had to admit it was a gorgeous dress, it just wasn't something she would normally wear. The bodice was sleeveless, the gold tulle embellished with little silver and gold flowers that flowed onto the full black tulle skirts on twisting vines. A black cape attached to the back of the bodice flowed behind her.

The temptation to wipe her sweaty palms on the dress was hard to fight. She fidgeted nervously with the golden bracelet the maid had placed on her wrist. It matched the necklace and earrings she wore. Her hair had been arranged in loose curls with a braid around the crown of her head, set so that the real crown would sit in front of it.

"I think you're ready, my lady."

"Thank you, Cerise."

A knock on the door reminded Lainey of why she was dressed

in the beautiful black and gold dress in the first place. In a few minutes, Phoenix would place a crown on her head, declaring her queen of the Unseelie Court. It would also declare her his queen, and he would be her king.

Cerise opened the door, and Lainey's dad entered. His eyes misted over as he looked at her. "Not the wedding dress I imagined walking you down the aisle in, but it is much more fitting this way, isn't it?"

"It really is."

"You look so beautiful, Elena. I wish your mother could be here to see you."

"I'm just glad I have you. I never thought my dad would be able to walk me down the aisle."

"Are you ready?"

"I think I am. I can do this. I really can."

"Of course you can. I have every faith in you both."

Lainey took his offered arm, and he led her through the palace. Her nerves were too fired up for her to pay attention to her surroundings. An impression of black and dreary was all she got. If they were planning on living here, some much-needed remodeling would have to happen.

They stopped at the doors to the throne room. Her breathing came fast, and stars danced in her vision. This wasn't something she'd ever expected for her life, and she hadn't had any time to process everything. What if she was making a mistake? This wasn't as simple as choosing the wrong pair of shoes to wear with a dress. An entire kingdom would now be affected by her actions. The responsibility was staggering. She could barely manage her finances in the human realm; what made her think she could rule a kingdom?

"Elena." Hands cupped her cheeks and turned her head. Her dad's bright blue eyes were shining with emotion. "You are not alone in this. Your mate will be by your side through all of it. As will I, and Ash, and the rest of your family. Everything is going to work out, so take a deep breath. Good. Better?"

He was right. She wasn't alone. She was surrounded by people she loved and who loved her back. It was time for a new adventure, a new life. No more pain or heartbreak. No more loss.

With a solidified resolve, she smiled at her dad. "I'm ready."

As the doors opened, her gaze immediately landed on Phoenix standing in front of the throne. The rest of the room was empty save her family and Ash. The fluttering in her stomach disappeared. The uncertainty plaguing her disappeared. Her mate was waiting for her, and he was breathtaking.

His hair was down and swept to one side, the shining brown strands catching the torchlight, causing the red to shimmer almost magically. The black jacket had gold buttons that went from his neck to his waist, flared out at his hips, and fell to his knees, where his black pants were tucked into knee-high boots. His shoulders looked impossibly bigger. A sword hung at his waist, though the hilt encrusted with black diamonds made it purely decorative.

With her first step into the throne room, his eyes flared copper and she could feel the temperature increase from the back of the room. In response, a gentle breeze swirled around her, swishing her skirts this way and that.

Time distorted. She couldn't remember walking toward him, but suddenly, she was standing right in front of him. Phoenix bowed to her dad with a hand on his heart, then took her hands and led her up the dais.

"You look absolutely stunning," he whispered in her ear.

A little man appeared in front of the dais. He wore billowing white robes with a hood that couldn't quite conceal his untamed gray hair.

"Welcome. As this it is just us here today, we will move straight to the oaths. Phoenix of the Unseelie Court, do you swear upon your blood and magic to rule this kingdom with fairness and strength?"

"I swear." Phoenix's voice rang out strong through the room.

"Do you swear upon your blood and magic to protect this kingdom with iron and blood?"

"I swear."

"Do you swear upon your blood and magic to care for this kingdom with body and heart?"

"I swear."

The officiant approached and produced a crown from his robes. "Then I hereby pronounce you Phoenix, King of the Unseelie Court."

Phoenix bowed to allow the officiant to place the crown on his head. When he stood, he smiled at Lainey, and her heart swelled. He looked every bit a king with the black crown sitting on his head and his shoulders thrown back with pride.

"Your turn," he whispered.

She swallowed and folded her hands at her waist. After a nod, Phoenix took the golden diadem from the officiant, the one he had used to propose to her. It was Phoenix who posed the same questions to her.

"Elena Holloway, do you swear upon your blood and magic to rule this kingdom with fairness and strength?"

"I swear." Unlike Phoenix, her voice was thin, and it wavered. She cleared her throat, ready for the next.

"Do you swear upon your blood and magic to protect this kingdom with iron and blood?"

"I swear." Better. Not quite as thin as before.

"Do you swear upon your blood and magic to care for this kingdom with body and heart?"

"I swear." That was more like it.

His smile was radiant as he said, "Then I hereby pronounce you Elena, my queen, and Queen of the Unseelie Court."

The crown was surprisingly light as he placed it on her head, a feeling she was sure wouldn't last.

He surprised her by burying his hand in her hair and pulling her to him tightly, kissing her in front of their friends and family. She was breathless when he pulled away.

"Remember," he whispered, "that is just a promise of what is to come tonight."

Her toes curled in her velvet slippers, and her core heated in desire. "You keep saying that, but here I am, still waiting."

The wicked glint in his eye was something she would never tire of seeing.

Hand-in-hand, Phoenix led her out of the throne room and into the hallway. He looked around, then pulled her to a door set under the massive staircase in the entry hall. It was dark inside, but Phoenix used his fire to create a flame that hovered over the middle of the small space.

It was a cleaning closet from the looks of it. Shelves of cleaning supplies lined one wall, and brooms and mops leaned against another. Phoenix closed the door and pushed her against the empty wall. His body pressed against hers. She could feel the hard planes of his muscles through their clothing—clothing she couldn't wait to remove. The blood bond flared, and her own blood heated at the thought of what would finally happen tonight.

Phoenix narrowed his eyes at her. "What are you thinking of right now?"

She gave him a sweet smile. "You. Me. No clothes. Horizontal in bed."

Copper-heated eyes stared into hers, and the temperature raised around them. Her head tilted to the side of its own accord, and he lowered his head to her neck, his tongue trailing up the column of her throat.

"Nix," she breathed and tightened her grasp on him.

A knock on the door drew them apart. "Your Majesties." Ash bowed dramatically after opening the door without prompting.

"What, Ash?" Phoenix grumped.

"Zephyr wants you in the study. He has a few of the higher members of the court for you to meet."

Phoenix sighed and looked at Lainey. "And it begins."

Chapter Twenty-Six

Phoenix and Lainey left the study overwhelmed and exhausted.

"Whose idea was this?" Phoenix asked.

"This was all you, buddy. Better suck it up."

"I have a better idea." He tugged her in the opposite direction of the throne room. "The staff have been tirelessly preparing the king and queen's suite. I think we should check it out. Make sure it meets our standards."

Phoenix's boots and the soft swish of her skirts filled the silence as they made their way through the palace. Lainey let her gaze wander around, taking in the details of her new home.

"We need to do some remodeling. It's awfully gloomy here."

"It *is* the Unseelie Court. They aren't known for rainbows and sunshine." He looked around with a frown. "A few upgrades wouldn't hurt, though."

They stopped in front of a set of double doors. Wood so dark it appeared black nearly blended in with the black marble walls. Carvings of the phases of the moon were painted gold and stood out in the darkness.

"Is this it?" Lainey whispered, eyes roving over the carvings.

Phoenix answered by pushing the doors open and pulling her inside. She had no time to look around—Phoenix pushed her against the closed door and molded his mouth to hers. Her hands tangled in his hair, and she lost herself in the way his body felt against hers, the way his bonfire scent filled her nose. This is what she had been waiting for.

He broke away and looked at her, his eyes dark and glazed with lust. "You look so beautiful in that dress, but I want it on the floor. Now."

Goosebumps broke out on her skin as Phoenix's hands trailed over her shoulders and around to her back. His fingers made quick work of the laces on her bodice, and cool air caressed her chest as the dress puddled in a heap of tulle at her feet. Phoenix's eyes latched onto her breasts, and his gaze was hungry as her nipples hardened in the chilly air.

A gasp escaped her throat when he sucked one of her nipples into his mouth, the warmth a stark contrast to the cold. Her head fell back against the door, and her blood heated. She ran her hands over his chest and slid them under his jacket, pushing it off his shoulders and onto the floor. Phoenix switched to her other nipple while she unbuttoned his shirt. It didn't take long for it to join the pile of clothes on the floor.

His skin was warm and smooth as Lainey ran her hands over his back and down around his waist. He shifted and began raining kisses on her neck, interspersed with nips of his canines. She found his belt and unbuckled it, then unbuttoned his pants. She couldn't get his clothes off fast enough. She was desperate to see him and feel him against her skin.

Phoenix paused long enough to kick off his boots and pants, then he stood before her, naked in all of his muscled glory. His gaze traveled over her body, heating at what he saw. Lainey returned the favor, and her mouth went dry as her gaze landed on his arousal. She reached her hand out and wrapped her fingers around him, the skin warm and silky over the iron core of him.

Phoenix groaned in the back of his throat and placed both hands on the door on either side of her head. She pumped her hand up and down, watching as he slowly came undone. She enjoyed seeing him like this, flushed and sweaty, chest heaving as his breath left his lungs. He was rarely anything but composed, with a solid wall of iron erected around him to protect himself. She enjoyed the power she had over him at being the one who could tear that iron wall down to reveal the real Phoenix behind it.

He didn't let her enjoy it for long. He scooped her up and carried her to the bed. All that registered in her mind was black silk sheets and a soft mattress under her before Phoenix wiped away all coherent thought. He knelt between her legs, wearing nothing but the crown on his head, and slowly spread her thighs, baring her to him.

She had no time to be self-conscious or feel any anxiety. He lowered his mouth to her core, and the first swipe of his tongue had Lainey lifting her hips, begging for more. His chuckle reverberated through her, and he placed a hand on her stomach, holding her in place.

"Patience, my queen."

He worked his tongue and brought her to the edge, over and over. She was past the point of burning. She was flame so hot it was cold. She was going to erupt, and she couldn't wait any longer.

"Please, Nix." She was breathless, desperate, so close to falling over the edge.

The sight of him lifting his burning eyes from between her legs sent her over the edge. She fractured under him, and his tongue continued to work her higher and higher, bringing her through it until she was limp and shaking.

Phoenix's smile was all male arrogance as he slowly climbed up her body. "We're not done yet." His knee pushed her legs wide again, and he settled on top of her, propping his weight on his elbows.

Lainey leaned up and kissed him while wrapping her legs around him. His arousal brushed against her sensitive core, and she whimpered.

"Fuck," he breathed, unable to keep his hips from rolling against her.

"I want you. I want all of you. Now," she begged.

He reached down and angled himself at her entrance. "Are you sure?" His eyes were serious as he looked at her.

She nodded. "I love you, Phoenix. You are what I want."

"I love you, too, Lainey." He pressed a gentle kiss to her lips and slowly inched his way in.

She gritted her teeth at the intrusion, the stretch almost too much to handle. Phoenix rolled his hips gently, pushing in inch by inch.

"Breathe, Lainey." He paused once he was seated at the hilt, giving her body time to adjust. "Are you okay?"

She waited a few seconds before responding. When she was more comfortable, she nodded.

He pulled back before pushing in again in slow, short thrusts. The pain faded and pleasure built in her core. She lifted her hips to meet his, and Phoenix's thrusts grew quicker, rougher. He felt amazing inside her and around her. His skin against hers, their breathing growing rapid while their heartbeats quickened. Lainey was completely lost in him.

Phoenix dropped his head to her neck, and he dragged his canines up her throat, the sensation making her cry out.

"Lainey, I want to bite you."

She angled her head to give him better access. "Do it."

The sharp flare of pain as his teeth sank into her skin quickly faded, replaced by pleasure so intense it almost overwhelmed her. She pressed his head closer to her neck, urging him on. Her hips rolled in time with the sucking sensation on her throat as Phoenix pulled her blood into his body. The pleasure built and built until it left her in a crescendo. Her core tightened on Phoenix and they both cried out as release barreled through them.

When they both stilled, Phoenix licked the puncture at her neck, stemming the flow of blood. He rolled over, pulling her with him, and she draped herself over his body. They lay tangled together as their hearts slowed and their breathing returned to normal. His hand smoothed up and down her back, and she snuggled closer to him.

He lifted the crown from her head and placed it on the table next to the bed. His crown joined hers a second a later. "I want you to wear that crown every time we have sex."

She chuckled. "Why am I not surprised?"

"You are my queen. The ruler of everything I am. And that crown looks sexy as hell on you."

She kissed his chest and closed her eyes. Finally, she felt like she had found a home, a family. With this man, she was complete.

Lainey stretched and reached an arm across the bed, searching for the warm, hard body next to her. Her hand met cold sheets. She sat up and brushed her hair away from her face so she could look around the room for the first time.

The bedchamber in their suite was, like the rest of the palace, all black. The floors and walls were beautiful black marble, veined with gold. The furniture was black with accents of gold—gold thread, gold pillows, gold gilding. What caught her eye was the carving on the ceiling above the massive round bed she was lying in. The phases of the moon, similar to the door, were carved into the ceiling and painted with a shimmering gold paint. It was intricate and breathtaking, with beautiful stars and swirls.

It made her think of something Phoenix had said when they'd stolen the amulet from the Met. He had said Princess Azura's power was of the moon. Suspicion grew in her gut. She looked toward the balcony doors and saw what she was looking for.

Phoenix stood on the balcony wearing nothing but low-slung

cotton pants, his hair down and shining in the morning light. Lainey wrapped the sheet around her body and rolled out of bed.

"Was this ..." The question she was going to ask dried up on her tongue. As she approached the balcony, her eyes grew wider and wider. "Whoa."

Phoenix didn't turn toward her but reached an arm out. She ducked under it, and he pulled her in close. "It was like this when I woke up."

The dried brown grass that had been spread over the Unseelie lands had turned vibrant and lush. The trees in the dead forest in the distance now spread branches toward the sky, decorated with leaves in shimmering reds, purples, and golds. Wildflowers danced in the warm breeze, as vibrant and magical as the rest of the lands.

"It's beautiful," she breathed. "But what does it mean? It has to be a good sign, right?"

Phoenix huffed out a laugh. "I hope so. We take up the crown, break the curse, and the next morning, the lands are flourishing. It would seem like a good omen."

They stood in silence and stared out at the colorful landscape. Somewhere in the distance, the fae of the Unseelie Court who had not sworn fealty to her and Phoenix bided their time. Waiting for the right moment to take back the crown and keep the court in its dark and dismal state. There were many things that needed to be addressed, including the Seelie queen. Despite the beautiful view and peace of the morning, Lainey knew this wouldn't last.

As if he sensed the direction her thoughts had gone, Phoenix turned to face her and framed her face with his hands. "Good morning, my queen."

He kissed her deeply and slowly until her breathing was uneven and her blood was boiling. He pulled her back inside, eying the bed the whole time.

"Don't you have more important things to be doing this morning?" she asked while letting herself get tugged along.

He tilted his head from side to side and grinned at her.

"Important, yes. More important?" Another kiss. Another step closer to the bed. "Never."

END
For Now.

Acknowledgments

As always, this wouldn't have been possible without the constant support of my husband (even though he has yet to read a single word I've written). Thank you for always letting me have the time to write while you take care of the kiddo.

To my parents who instilled the love of reading in me at young age. If it weren't for that, I would never have started writing.

To my sister, who will always be my first go-to beta reader. Thanks for always encouraging me and listening to my crazy book ideas.

To my MTP fam. You guys have been absolutely amazing. Thanks for the inspiration, laughs, support, and encouragement! Because of you, I strive to be a better writer.

And finally, to Hazel at Equality Book Tours. I never thought this book would lead me to such an amazing person who is quickly becoming an amazing friend! Thank you for all of your support, encouragement, and cheerleading. It really means the world to me.

About the Author

Whitney L. Spradling is a full time Occupational Therapist and autism mama, who has had a dream to write and publish a novel since she was a little girl. She lives outside of Cincinnati with her husband, son, and two cats. When she is not writing she can be found in her craft room making custom tumblers, or curled up with a good book and a cup of coffee (or glass of wine).

ALSO BY WHITNEY L. SPRADLING

The Obsidian Artifacts

The Obsidian Sword

The Obsidian Crown

The Cursed Realms

Of Flames and Curses

Of Smoke and Betrayal (coming 11.2023)

Fates

These Dangerous Fates

These Deadly Dreams (coming 1.2024)

Standalones

Those We Couldn't Burn

New recruit Zira has one thing on her mind, and it's taking out the Changelings that slaughtered her family. She's full of vengeance, but she can't deny how difficult it is to focus in the presence of the captain.

With tensions rising in Frosteria and the mortal world, Korreth and Zira must work together, however, it will take the strongest of wills to ignore the call of a mate bond. That is, if they even wish to.

Frost Mate is a whole new, sexy, and action-packed retelling of Krampus! This novella will surely satisfy lovers of spicy monster romances, while still bringing the reader on a journey into an epic world.

***

In Flames by Nicole Northwood

When Seraphina Fox, a medical student at Kestral Medical College for the Supernatural, accidentally uses her matchmaking abilities to pair with both of her incredibly alluring dormitory neighbors, Alexi

Bonneau and Dario Accardi, she thinks that she's made a mistake that could cost her reputation.

However, in trying to decipher her attraction while denying her skills, Sera uncovers a secret through the ghost of a past student and fellow matchmaker: the ability to pair soulmates is rarer than she thought, and the college is working to study the blood that can predict the future of relationships. As Sera, Alexi, and Dario find themselves in the middle of a love affair, feigned death records, and an appalling research trial of what it means to have humanity, they must search out the truth before Sera loses everything... including maybe even her life.

www.ingramcontent.com/pod-product-compliance
Lightning Source LLC
Chambersburg PA
CBHW021147310726
48971CB00002B/529